Dimwater's Door

By

Sam Ferguson

ISBN: 9781943183593

DIMWATER'S DOOR

Other Books by Sam Ferguson:

For Anthony.
Thank you for your friendship and encouragement.
You will be missed, but never forgotten.
Until we both meet again on the other side of life, I
wish you adventure and happiness.

Table of Contents

Prologue

Njar panted for breath. Exhausted, he forced his arms to push against the muddy ground. Dirt and blood clung to his fur. A human corpse, contorted by the magic blast a moment before, lay to his right. A satyr warrior, like himself, was to his left. He blinked twice, trying to get the sharp granule of sand out of his left eye. Footsteps caught his attention, forcing his ears to twitch like a deer's might when startled by a sudden sound. Njar stood up and peered through the smoke.

Kyra was running toward a tall man with silver hair. Behind the man was a mountain of bleeding flesh that had moments before been a living, breathing dragon.

"Severin," Njar hissed. Smoke clogged the air above, swallowing the sunlight and allowing the silver-haired vampire to move freely across the battlefield. Kyra raised her staff, but the vampire was too quick. Severin's body blurred as he shot toward the young sorceress. Crimson liquid gushed from her left arm as a glinting sword took her hand. "NO!" Njar shouted. He rushed to Kyra's aid, hindered by a gash across his right thigh and a throbbing, gaping wound in his abdomen. Even as he sprinted, he knew he could never reach her in time.

Severin spun around with his sword, slicing Kyra across the back. The young woman cried out in pain and went to the ground.

At that moment, a young, dark-haired apprentice of the sword appeared through the smoke and engaged the vampire.

"Kathair, get Kyra out of here!" Njar shouted, but his words couldn't be heard over the sound of their swords crashing together.

A deft parry here and a counter there, and soon Kathair was on his knees, bleeding from several shallow cuts and gashes lining his torso.

"Pathetic, the lot of you!" Severin declared. The vampire swept his sword to the side, taking Kathair's head clean off his neck. The vampire, as if stopping to admire his work, paused at the end of his swing. Blood dripped from his blade, hitting the ground just before Kathair's lifeless body toppled to the side.

Njar ran faster, but his pains grew within him, cramping his muscles and leaking his very life force. The satyr stretched out a hand, summoning his magic to reach Severin before the vampire could finish his work of death, but Mother Terramyr did not respond to Njar's call. The earth withheld her powers, and Njar could only shout his protest while Severin reached Kyra and plunged his blade through her heart.

With her last gasp, Kyra turned her eyes to Njar. Pleading, pained eyes that lost the shine of life a moment later.

"You should never have opposed me," Severin said. The silver haired vampire turned back toward Njar. "This was always how it would end."

"No," Njar said. "Not like this." The satyr fell to the ground with a whimper. His shoulders slumped as he bent down to the dirt. "Not like this!"

In an instant, Severin was before him. The once bright blade now stained with Kyra and Kathair's blood swung in front of his eyes like a pendulum. "How else could it end?" Severin asked.

Njar, tears in his eyes, looked up at the vampire and felt pure, unadulterated hatred run through him. The satyr reached up, but even at his best he would have been too slow to catch Severin by surprise. The vampire sliced across Njar's chest and then drove his bled down through the base of Njar's neck, allowing the satyr to live just long enough to hear Severin's triumphant laugh.

Blackness overtook Njar, and he drifted to the Plane of the Dead, a place where spirits unable to cross bifrost into Volganor, the Heaven City, may find rest in the afterlife. As light returned, the satyr found himself in a green field of clover. Leatherback, Kathair, and Kyra were all waiting for him, but something wasn't right. They had their forms, but no color. Their skin, hair, and eyes were all ashen. They stared at him blankly, as if under some sort of hypnotic spell.

"What is this?" Njar whispered as he forced his spirit to focus. "Why have we not found rest?"

"Rest?" Severin's voice cut through the air like a flaming arrow. "There will never be any rest."

Chains appeared around the others and pulled them slowly into the earth. Njar reached for each of them, pulling against the chains and fighting Severin's magic, but it was no use. Kathair was the first to disappear, followed by Leatherback. Finally, Kyra sank into the ground, but not as quickly as the others. Njar almost managed to stop her descent, and that was the maddening part. Kyra cried out for help over and over, but Njar couldn't free her.

"Mother Terramyr!" Njar called out. "Give me strength!"

Severin's laughter filled the air. "There is no help for you here," the vampire taunted.

A flash of darkness swallowed Kyra the rest of the way and left Njar sitting on the squashed and torn clovers holding an empty set of chains.

"NO!" Njar screamed.

Everything went black. Had Severin pulled him under as well? Could the vampire truly imprison their spirits in some sort of abyss? The darkness around him grew colder and more solid. It became hard to breath. Was he drowning?

Water.

Njar's eyes opened and then he knew the truth of it once more.

He was still trapped here, at the bottom of the Pools of Fate. The drowning sensation was the water filling his lungs. The golden sphere glowed brightly before him, holding him prisoner in this magical hell that Severin had left him in. A sharp pain in Njar's neck reminded him of Severin's bite. He reached up and felt the two holes left by Severin's fangs. The stinging venom coursed through his body.

I will not break. My mind is my own. I will not become your thrall, Severin.

The golden sphere glowed brighter, and pulled Njar into a different, yet equally realistic, illusion. As with every other illusion, he knew he was going to be tortured with visions of Kyra's death, among others that he loved. The cycle wouldn't end until he either gave up his mind, or someone broke the vampire's spell. Even as he steeled his mind for yet another assault, the satyr knew it was pointless. No one had any idea where he was. Help would never come.

Chapter 1

Kyra grinned to herself, thinking back to the time when she would have needed a lock pick to enter the library at Caspin Manor. Not so anymore. She needed only to pic a time when she knew that Lord Caspin would be away. A night such as this one, when he was conducting trade negotiations at the annual market in Clendale. It provided the perfect opportunity for her to sneak into the house and take the rest of the items he owed her, and perhaps a few that he didn't.

She focused her mind on the library she had broken into countless times before when she lived in Caspin Manor. She could see the shelves, chairs, and even the desk in her mind's eye. She concentrated, securing an end point in the center of the room for her portal. She felt a tingling energy build up in her chest, extending down her right arm and concentrating in her hand. She spoke the words for the spell and a blue sphere jumped to life in front of her. Flashes of light sparked and pulsed silently as the sphere grew and then the center stretched until a pinhole of white light appeared. That pinhole grew to fill the entire portal, finalizing the passageway and allowing a full grown adult to walk through. She then uttered the words of a stabilizing spell to hold it open while she conducted her business in Caspin Manor, thus affording her a quick exit once she was ready rather than needing to reconjure the portal.

"No need for lockpicks now," she said, then she stepped through the portal and her sly grin grew into a wide smile at the sight of all the books. "First things first," she told herself. She turned to Lord Caspin's desk at the far end of the room. She made her way to the desk, careful to keep her footsteps soft, just in case there were any servants around. Kyra gently pulled the handle on the top drawer and found it unlocked. It slid out easily, revealing several large books. She had been in this library enough to know which one she needed. She reached down for a large, beige book with worn corners on the binding.

She carefully set it on the desk and opened the cover to reveal an ornate depiction of a family tree. Her family tree, on her mother's side of course. Now that Lord Caspin had disowned her and fully pretended she didn't exist, she was more than happy to return the sentiment. If she was completely honest with herself, his recent rejection still hurt her somewhere deep down in the recesses of her heart, but she suppressed those feelings well enough, replacing them with the contempt she felt he deserved for abandoning her after her mother's murder. Biology aside, Lord Caspin had raised her as his own for her first fourteen years until he discovered the truth about Kyra's mother. Still, Kyra could easily see that it wasn't her mother's fault. She had been charmed by a vampire after being abducted, it was hardly the same as a willful act of betrayal. In Kyra's mind, Lord Caspin was the one who betrayed the family. Shaking her rising anger, she traced her finger from the bottom, where her mother's name had been delicately written, up through the lines for several generations until she came to a Lord Alister Dimwater. She turned a few pages of written family history and found the original deed to her mother's home that had been gifted to Lord Caspin upon their wedding. "And now, the house that Alister built shall once again have a Dimwater as its owner." She smiled and closed the book before gently sliding it into her knapsack.

Without wasting a moment, she moved on to the bookshelves lining the walls. Having previously made a mental catalogue of the titles she desired, both those she thought were legitimately hers and those to be taken as punitive damages, she moved quickly through the library. Her hands nimbly selected the titles and slid the chosen books into her bag. When she finished, she made one final check to ensure she had taken anything related to

Kendualdern or to dragons in general. She doubted any of those books would discuss safe planes on Terramyr, but she hoped she might find some information about dragons that might serve to help Leatherback in his current situation.

She also took two tomes about mystic planes that she hadn't expected to see in her father's library. She had to adjust the knapsack, shouldering it with some effort until she cast a spell to make the load lighter for her to carry as she continued searching for additional books. After finding one more about continents beyond the oceans northward, she pulled the drawstring tightly around the books bulging from the top and then stepped back through her portal.

Returning to her dorm room in the top of one of Kuldiga Academy's many towers, she sighed and looked around. It was a strange place, her new home. When she had first arrived she thought it would only be a temporary residence until she graduated, but now it was the only place she could call home. She adjusted the knapsack on her shoulder and a half grin tugged at the left corner of her mouth. Perhaps she could make a home of Dimwater Manor. After all, it was hers now. What better place to conduct her research and try to figure out how to help Leatherback? She thought to examine some of the books, but decided it would be better to do so another time. She still had studies to attend to, and she had neglected her fire spells for several days now. Kyra opened a black trunk at the foot of her bed and stashed her books, then she sat cross-legged on the floor, ready for exercises.

Kyra closed her eyes, sitting silently for several moments as she let her mind clear of all other thoughts. She could feel her power coursing through her, warm and dangerous, yet soft and comforting at the same time. Extending a hand and supinating it, she summoned a small fireball. It was barely more than a spark at first, then it grew to the size of a candle's flame. She let it dance from one hand to the other, feeling its heat and its hunger. She opened her eyes and focused on a spot above the table in her dorm room. The fireball grew to the size of a melon as it rose to its new location.

As the sphere of flame spun on its axis, Kyra played with its characteristics. First she increased its heat, changing the flames to a greenish-blue. Once she had the outer flames turning white, she smiled and cooled the fireball back to its yellow color, then she experimented with its shape, stretching it into an oblong club of fire, then squashing it into a flat disc of flame above the table. She spent several minutes running through various exercises. She found it not only cleared her mind, but it also strengthened her abilities.

A knock at the door broke Kyra's concentration. The fireball she had been levitating over the table dissipated, producing a wisp of dark smoke and a slight sulfuric odor.

"Come in," Kyra said. She stood to face the door and folded her hands before her.

The door swung inward and Master Fenn stepped through. "I didn't see you at dinner," he said.

"I wasn't hungry," Kyra replied.

Master Fenn glanced to a pair of recently emptied plates, with crumbs still lining the smaller one and a large chicken bone on the other. "I see." Master Fenn didn't come further into the room. He looked to Kyra and shook his head. "I hope that one day you will come to trust me. I have nothing but the best intentions for this school, and for each of my students."

"Including Kathair?" Kyra's eyes narrowed on the man and she felt a flush of anger rising up into her chest and spreading toward her right arm, threatening to evolve into a magical expression of her feelings. It had been several weeks since Master Fenn had whisked Kathair from this very room, and as of yet she hadn't heard of his fate.

"He is not expelled," Fenn replied quickly, putting a hand up in the air. "However, I can't have him here, either. Though, I am relieved to hear your absence from dinner is because you are angry with me over Kathair's new assignment."

"What else would it be?" Kyra snapped.

Fenn shrugged. "I had thought you may not approve of my becoming the new headmaster. I would not like to have you as an enemy in any degree."

Kyra snorted. She couldn't give two frog-bubbles who led the school. "I understand what Headmaster Herion did. He had to step down in order to quiet the rumors that have swirled about."

It was Fenn's turn to narrow his eyes. "And you don't feel the least bit responsible for that?"

"Why should I?" Kyra said. "He is a grown man, capable of making his own decisions. As for what I did, perhaps if others did their jobs better, then Kathair and I wouldn't have needed to get involved."

Master Fenn bristled. "I see." He turned to the side and motioned toward the door. "In any case, I have come for another reason entirely. Now that the feast is over and my appointment as headmaster is complete, I want to resume the work Herion was involved in. It is a little premature to discuss in detail at this juncture, but I would like you to consider joining the group that operates out of the academy."

Kyra's eyebrows flicked up for a moment as the words hit her. The group Fenn spoke of was highly secretive. Authorized by the king himself to perform special duties that were either too dangerous or delicate for the normal soldiers or knights that might otherwise carry out missions for the king.

"The group is traditionally commanded by Kuldiga Academy's headmaster," Fenn said. "Which means I will be looking for people that show special talents." He produced a small parchment from his pocket and placed it on the table in front of her. "The group doesn't have a name, but these are the tenets we operate under, and this is our mark." Fenn poked a mark that looked like some sort of ancient run set against a shield. She glanced at the tenets, and then back up to Fenn. "We can discuss it in more detail later, but I wanted you to be aware of my interest in your involvement."

"Would I join after graduation?"

Fenn pursed his lower lip and made an almost imperceptible shrug. "I suppose it will depend mostly on your abilities, how quickly they develop, and how you choose to use them."

Kyra nodded, not interested enough to press for a more specific answer.

"In any case, I brought a visitor to speak with you."

Kyra looked to the doorway and saw a very large man step through. She recognized him instantly. A jagged scar rested heavily beneath deep green eyes that seemed to carry the depth of an entire forest within them.

"Hello again, Miss Dimwater," Mindaugas said. Addressing her by her chosen family name caused a smile to form upon her face.

"Hello, Master Reif," Kyra replied. Mindaugas Reif, the Keeper of Secrets, was the one person she had wanted to see tonight. Rumor had it he would be leaving Kuldiga Academy soon now that the new headmaster was in place, and she still held out hope that he might have some ideas to help her.

"I wanted to speak with you, if you have time," Mindaugas said.

Kyra nodded. "I was only practicing some minor spells," she replied. "If you have come to talk about Leatherback, I haven't seen him since the last time we spoke."

Mindaugas held up a thick hand and shook his head. "No, I haven't come to talk about your dragon."

"He isn't *my* dragon," Kyra replied. "As I said before, he is my friend, but not my pet."

"No offense meant by it," Mindaugas said with a smile. He gestured to a chair. "May I sit?"

Kyra gave a short nod and the two sat at the table.

"I will leave you both to it, then," Master Fenn said. "I have some accounts to settle regarding the school and some of the patrons."

Mindaugas cast a wave of his hand, but didn't bother turning to properly say goodbye to Headmaster Fenn.

This made Kyra smile too, though she did her best to hide her pleasure. After the tall wizard left, Mindaugas drummed his fingers on the table and looked at Kyra, studying her eyes just long enough that she began to squirm in her seat.

"Do you know much about what I do?" Mindaugas asked. "As the Keeper of Secrets, I mean."

Kyra shook her head. "Not entirely."

"To put it in the simplest terms, I am an agent of the Ancients, and that means that like you, I am a friend to dragons." Mindaugas sat back in his chair, folding his muscular arms over his bulky chest. "Though I have many duties, my main mission is to find a prophesied champion, someone talked about in some very ancient texts that will have the power to destroy Nagar's Blight, and free the dragons to return to the Middle Kingdom once more without threat."

Kyra's eyes shot wide. "Is such a thing possible?"

Mindaugas nodded. "It is."

"Leatherback could return, then, once the curse is destroyed?"

"Precisely," Mindaugas said. "As could the Ancients themselves, which, as you know, would be a wonderful event in our kingdom. We been without their guidance for far too long. King Mathias is great, don't misunderstand, but the Ancients were the glue that bound our kingdom together, and the bridge that allowed us to mingle with the dwarves in Roegudok Hall."

"Who is the champion you spoke of?" Kyra asked.

Mindaugas shrugged. "I don't know. None of us do, in fact. However, there are certain clues that will help me find the right person." Mindaugas leaned forward. "Kyra, might I have a look behind your ear?"

11

"Behind my ear?" Kyra asked.

"I am looking for a special mark, a birthmark in the shape of a crescent. Would you mind?"

Kyra shook her head and leaned in close. His big, warm fingers reached out and gently folded her ears over, first the right, and then the left. A few seconds later Mindaugas sat back and sighed. Whatever he had hoped to find was obviously not there. "You thought I might be the one?" Kyra said.

Mindaugas nodded. "I did."

"The last time we spoke, you told me of a test you would give me, was this it?"

The large man shook his head. "It was not the test itself, but it is a prerequisite. The prophesied champion will have a special mark behind the ear. Have you ever heard of the Sahale?"

Kyra shook her head.

Mindaugas made a wave of his left hand. "Well, no need to get into that now. Without the mark, you cannot be the one." The two sat in silence for a few moments before Mindaugas smiled once more and gently slapped the table. "Still, even without the mark, I should like to take you with me to Valtuu Temple. You have proven yourself a powerful ally, and I know you want to find a way to help Leatherback return."

Kyra nodded. "What would I do at the temple?" she asked. Her mind brought up images of the three priests that had meddled in her affairs over the last several months. She didn't relish the idea of constant supervision by priests who could see into her very soul with their magic.

Mindaugas said, "They have a vast library there. Given that the order serves the Ancients, they have many tomes that speak of Hammenfein, Hatmul, and many other topics that might prove useful in your search."

"Hatmul?" Kyra said.

"The ruler of hell, the god of Hammenfein. Surely you know of whom I speak?"

"Of course, but what does he have to do with Leatherback?" She hadn't told anyone of her deal with Khefir, Hatmul's brother. Had the priests discovered it? Did Master Fenn know?

"Hatmul has long been subtly warring against the Ancients. Likely, he was the one who planted the idea into Nagar the Black's mind that led to the curse's development in the first place. In any case, from what Headmaster Herion told me, Leatherback is currently residing in a plane not entirely of this world. Hatmul has made many such places, and the priests at Valtuu Temple have records detailing some of them, as well as the magic that rules them. Perhaps studying that may help with Leatherback. And…" his voice trailed off for a moment as he locked eyes with her. "They may know a way for you to find your way to Viverandon."

Kyra nodded, trying to maintain her composure. She wanted to jump up and shout at the prospect of helping her friends, but she didn't want to make the wrong impression by seeming too childish. Additionally, though Mindaugas' reputation was honorable, she wasn't sure what his angle was. Why would he want to help her find Njar and Leatherback?

"I know you haven't heard from your satyr friend in a long while, so I assumed you would want to find a way to his homeland. I can't promise anything, but if there is a way, you will find it in that library. The Ancients have long coexisted peacefully with the Natural Races created by Mother Terramyr, and since neither the priests, nor I have ever seen any evidence that this particular satyr harbors any ill intent, then I would be happy to help you."

"Why are you doing this?" Kyra said. She folded her arms across her chest and stared into those green eyes, suddenly wishing she had the priests' abilities to see into a person's soul and decipher the truth of their feelings and motivations.

"I know you have been manipulated in the past," Mindaugas said. "The wizard masquerading as Cyrus has likely made you quite wary of others, but I can assure you that I have no secret plans. Another mission I have is to find and recruit powerful allies that would be willing to fight for our cause. I hope to help you grow more powerful with your abilities, and I want you to continue to learn as much as you can about Nagar's Blight, Hammenfein, pocket-dimensions and secret planes, and anything else that might give us an edge over those that would seek to use Nagar's Blight for nefarious designs."

"Something other than torturing and destroying dragons?" Kyra asked.

Mindaugas nodded. "The magic itself is still out there. As the Keeper of Secrets, I am tasked with hiding and protecting the source of Nagar's Blight until such a time as the champion is found who can destroy it. Make no mistake, if the wrong people found the magic, they could use it to destroy everyone, consuming their minds and possessing their souls in very much the same way the magic twists a dragon's heart. You have great talent, and the potential to become one of the greatest sorceresses the Middle Kingdom has ever seen. I want you fighting on our side."

"And what about Kathair?" Kyra said. "Master Fenn whisked him away, and I haven't heard anything about him since."

Mindaugas tilted his head to the right and cocked an eyebrow. "Headmaster Fenn has ordered complete silence. No one is supposed to talk about Kathair Lepkin's current whereabouts or assignment." Kyra shook her head and was about to reply, but Mindaugas held up a hand and grinned. "However, as Keeper of Secrets, I have a certain amount of autonomy from the normal traditions and rules that govern the Middle Kingdom. So, I am not bound by Fenn's wishes."

Kyra smiled wide. "Where is he?"

"He is in Tualdern, the city of the sand elves. It has recently come to his attention that his parents were murdered, and he wants to find out why."

"Murdered?" Kyra echoed. "I thought they died of sickness during their travels from the north country."

Mindaugas frowned. "I am afraid not. As you can imagine, Kathair is anxious to learn the truth, and has gone to the home of his adoptive father to look for answers."

Kyra understood exactly how Kathair felt. "I have to go to him."

"No," Mindaugas said.

"But he helped me solve my mother's murder," she insisted.

"I am afraid this is something he must do on his own. I may not be bound by Fenn's rules for secrecy, but I do agree with him that the two of you should not work together at this point."

Kyra's cheeks flushed. "Feberik?" she guessed. His arranged betrothal to Kyra was still in play, despite her objections, and she figured he was involved somehow in this decision.

Mindaugas shook his head. "I won't presume to speak for the headmaster, but Feberik Orres doesn't figure into my reasoning. I need you to train in Valtuu Temple. Events are unfolding now that will require my attention, and by extension your own attention, as you will become a member of the secret group that operates within this very academy under the king's direction. I'm afraid I can't waste valuable training time by allowing you to hunt for leads that may not exist. For now, I need you to concentrate on helping your other friends, and studying as much as you can."

"I can't leave him alone," Kyra said.

"You must," Mindaugas replied. "Besides, he won't be alone, not entirely. Kathair is also valuable to me, and to my order. He has a hot temper, but behind that is a power that may yet blossom into a great asset, as long as the Dragon Slayers don't ruin his mind."

Kyra understood. "The longer it takes him to find the answers, the less time he will spend with the Dragon Slayers."

Mindaugas nodded. "Additionally, he will be training his own mind, becoming a capable sleuth. In the end, if his clues lead him to confrontation, then he will gain more skill with the blade as well. Telstian will not abandon his adopted son in his hour of need. I

15

am certain the elf will accompany Kathair, or at least appoint a guardian for him. Beyond that, the three of us share a mutual friend that I believe will also assist Kathair."

Kyra knitted her brow. "The three of us have a mutual friend? Who?"

"His proper name is much longer than I can accurately pronounce, but he goes by Al, and runs a smithy down in Buktah. I believe he helped the two of you not so long ago, in fact."

Kyra smiled. She remembered the dwarf quite well. "All right. If Telstian and Al will be with him, then I can hold back." She held back two words that might have displeased the large man sitting opposite from her, but internally she could only promise to hold back *for now.*

Chapter 2

Kathair pulled the bowstring back, smooth and slow, taking in a quiet breath to steady himself while keeping his eyes on the stag seventy yards away. The animal nibbled at clover on a small hillock. It raised its head, the large ears twisting this way and that while the dark eyes scanned the trees. Kathair felt the fletching against his cheek for only a moment before he released the string. The arrow zipped between the trees, dead on its mark, but just before it reached the stag, another arrow struck Kathair's missile, knocking it away.

The stag bounded off down the other side of the hillock and disappeared into the forest.

Kathair grunted. He could already guess who had foiled him, Larriel, an elf youth only a year or two older than Kathair. The tall, blonde-haired boy had taken an instant dislike to Kathair the moment he had returned from Kuldiga Academy, despite the fact that they had once been friends several years before. Kathair walked toward the hillock to find what was left of his arrow. As he came around a large redwood, he spied Larriel and two others leaning against a knotted oak trunk.

"I should thank you," Larriel said. "It is hard to find appropriate targets to practice with these days. Had it not been for your arrow, I might have failed to find anything worthy of my skills."

Kathair ignored him and searched the grasses for his arrow.

"Be a good boy and grab mine as well," Larriel added.

"Find it yourself," Kathair replied.

The two elves with Larriel snorted.

"Does he dare challenge you?" one of them asked.

"Surely the northman knows to show respect to his betters," the other said.

The way the youth spat out the word *northman* threatened to waken a fire within Kathair's chest, but he quelled the spark before it could catch.

"Perhaps he needs reminding of that fact," Larriel suggested.

Kathair shook his head, keeping his eyes focused on the ground around him, but sure to listen for Larriel's approach. Such arrogant condescension wasn't uncommon in Tualdern. Even so, it became more aggravating each time he was faced with it. Still, Kathair knew what Telstian would expect of him.

The largest of the three youths approached. "I could teach him for you, Larriel."

"Bring me his bow," Larriel said. "Losing that should help him understand."

"Why?" the large youth asked. "It's a northman bow, not nearly as good as ours."

"Exactly, I'll be doing him a favor by ridding him of it, and I'll be doing the rest of us a favor by disposing of it outside our fair city."

Kathair grit his teeth. The bow had belonged to his father.

"I'll be taking that," the large youth said.

Kathair hung the bow over a low hanging branch nearby and turned to square off with the large elf. "No."

The elf laughed. "He thinks he can stop me," he said.

"Show him, Olverin. Teach him respect," the other youth next to Larriel said.

The large elf nodded. His left foot slid across the clover until he was in a horse stance. Kathair knew the fighting style that would come with it. Telstian had taught him this very style when he was only seven. It relied heavily on blocking with the arms and striking with powerful kicks.

"Let me be," Kathair warned.

"I'm taking that bow," Olverin said. The boy launched into a flurry of kicks, but Kathair expertly blocked each one. A few seconds into the fight, Olverin shifted his weight and twisted his shoulders, telegraphing the forthcoming roundhouse a fraction of a second before the foot came up, but that was all the notice Kathair needed. He hooked the leg in the crook of his left arm and came down with two knuckles, jamming them deep into the muscle just a few inches above the knee joint. Olverin cried out and dropped his hands. Kathair raised the leg higher up and then stepped toward Olverin, throwing the tall elf to the ground with enough force to knock the wind out of him.

As Kathair knelt down to strike at Olverin's exposed stomach, the second elf came rushing forward. Kathair punched Olverin and then jumped up and to the side as the second elf dove for him. The elf realized his mistake and rolled through a somersault, regaining his feet without allowing Kathair a chance to strike. He turned and lunged for Kathair, swinging quick fists through the air. Kathair ducked the first strike and then stepped to the side, evading the next two that followed. The fourth punch came at Kathair's face, but the northman was able to snatch it with his left hand, stopping the punch several inches away from his face.

"Unhand me, Northman!"

Kathair felt the fire in his chest rise. "You should have brought weapons," he snarled. A savage blow to the elf's jaw knocked the youth unconscious and his knees collapsed under his weight as he slumped to the ground.

"That's enough," Larriel shouted.

Kathair looked up, ready to fight, but realized that Larriel had readied his bow. A mix of rage and confusion swelled within him.

Larriel shrugged. "As you said, we should use weapons."

"So much for proving elves are better than northmen," Kathair shot back.

"Because you can best us in a fist fight?" Larriel asked. "No, that only shows you have the same ferocity as a bear might, but it doesn't mean you are anything close to our equal."

"Put the bow down, and I'll show you," Kathair said.

"I think not, now move away." Larriel jerked his bow to the side, indicating where he wanted Kathair to go.

Kathair knew that if he did so, Larriel would take his father's bow. "No," Kathair said. He turned to walk back to where he had hung his bow but an arrow zipped past him, the fletching burning his cheek as it streaked by. Kathair winced and spun away from the arrow. "Are you crazy!?"

Larriel had already prepared another arrow. "I could say it was a hunting accident. You jumped between us and the stag."

The fire within Kathair's chest went out, replaced by a knot forming in his stomach. "You can't do this."

By this time, Olverin was back on his feet, rubbing the cramps out of his leg and coughing as the air returned to his lungs.

"Get the bow, Olverin," Larriel said.

"Don't do this," Kathair said.

"You have to learn to respect your betters," Larriel replied. "You northmen are all savages, like dogs in the street outside the city walls. You infest our homes with fleas if we take you in, so it's better to shew you away like the mongrels you are."

"We had been friends, Larriel," Kathair said. "Do you not remember spending summer nights with me in the fields catching fireflies?"

"I was only an infant," Larriel replied.

"We were seven," Kathair answered sharply.

"Barely more than a baby in elf terms," Larriel said. "I was too young to understand what you really were."

Olverin removed the bow from the branch.

The knot grew heavy in Kathair's stomach, threatening to pull him into the very ground below. "That's my father's! Give it back."

Kathair took a step forward, but an arrow pierced the ground just an inch in front of his foot.

"Stay still, mongrel."

Olverin smiled and walked to a large rock half-buried next to a large oak. "A northman's bow shouldn't be allowed in this forest," he said.

"I agree. They aren't good for anything more than kindling."

Olverin nodded and wedged the upper limb of the bow between the rock and tree.

"Stop!" Kathair shouted.

"Hold still!" Larriel shouted.

Olverin pulled on the bow, flexing the limb back and forth. Kathair almost hoped that the bow would survive the abuse, but within a couple of minutes Olverin managed to bend it beyond its threshold. The upper limb snapped half way down. Olverin wrenched the weapon free and finished separating the wood at the crack. Laughing, he turned and threw the weapon into the upper branches of a nearby pine.

Kathair watched silently as Olverin helped the unconscious elf back to his feet and then started walking away. Larriel was the last to leave, keeping his arrow trained on Kathair until the three of them were well ahead of him.

"Khefir drag you all down to Hammenfein!" Kathair shouted after them.

Whether in answer to his curse, or as a final warning, another arrow flew near him, whistling through the air until it sunk into a tree.

Kathair climbed the pine and retrieved his broken bow. He slung the limbs over his shoulder, wrapping them with the string so as not to come loose, then he descended and started his trek back to Tualdern. Every few steps he would reach up to touch part of the bow with his right hand, as if it were a living memory of his father that was now losing life. He ranted under his breath, cursing

21

Larriel and the others while kicking at rocks or pine cones on the forest floor. Then, after a mile or so, he thought of Telstian.

"Why didn't you just pick up Larriel's arrow?" Telstian would ask.

"Because I shouldn't have to," Kathair would answer. Then, invariably there would be a long lecture about abilities, choices, and consequences. Ultimately it would end with Telstian emphasizing that Kathair could have made a choice that ultimately would have led to a desirable outcome, instead of the consequences he suffered.

Kathair grit his teeth and shook his head. *Larriel shouldn't have knocked my arrow from the sky. They started the fight, not me! Things would have gone differently if Larriel and I had both wielded swords.* This final thought stuck with Kathair as the bow gently thumped against him with each step. He reached up and untied his broken bow, and freed the longer half of the weapon from the string. He grabbed it by one end and gave a practice swing. It was unwieldy to be sure, but it would do.

He broke into a run. If he hurried, he might catch them before they entered the city.

It had taken him over an hour to reach the forest at the foot of the mountains north of Tualdern, but he made the return trip in less than half that time. Unfortunately, Larriel and the others had already made it through the gates.

Worse than that, the three of them were leaning against a building waiting for him, and this time they had another four elven youth around them.

"Here he is now," Larriel shouted with a sweep of his arm toward Kathair. "You all should have seen the oaf. He not only missed the stag that I had so graciously allowed him to hunt, but he even tripped over his own feet and snapped his bow."

"Northman quality craftsmanship," Olverin added.

"Well, we can't compare his kind to ours, it really isn't fair," Larriel said.

The group laughed.

The fire swelled through Kathair now so that he could almost feel flames shooting from his fingers. "I remember things a bit differently," he growled.

"Oh, I don't mean to embarrass you, Kathair. None of us expect you to rise to our level, don't worry. You did fine for a northman, I'm sure," Larriel said.

Kathair strode up to the group, his eyes locked on Larriel.

Olverin and another youth moved to intercept.

"Kathair, why don't you go—"

Kathair swung his makeshift club, catching Olverin under the chin and splitting the skin open, spraying the adjacent elf with a bit of bright blood. Kathair followed this move with a front kick to Olverin's knee, snapping the joint backwards and dropping the large elf. The others in the group started shouting and moving in all at once.

The second elf reached out for the broken bow, but Kathair lunged in with a head-butt, squashing the elf's nose and knocking him back. Kathair then swung the bow back, slamming it into Larriel's right arm.

"GAH!" Larriel shouted.

Sunlight glinted off a knife as the third elf who had been in the forest lunged at Kathair. The young northman came down with his bow, snapping the elf's arm just below the wrist.

Two more elves jumped into the fight, while the remaining elf ran off down the street.

Fists and feet pummeled Kathair's sides and stomach, but he maintained his focus. Being in close meant he couldn't swing his broken bow, so he flipped it around and jabbed the jagged, broken edge at Larriel, opening a few small cuts and scrapes along the youth's chest.

A fist slammed Kathair's face. A sharp ringing filled his ears and his vision darkened around the edges, but his rage was too hot to feel any pain. Another elf ripped the broken bow from his grasp, so Kathair switched to fists, punching back twice as hard for each strike he received. Soon only he and Larriel were left standing. Kathair stepped forward, snatching Larriel by the throat with his left hand and smashing the elf's back into the building.

"You dishonorable cur," Kathair snarled, coming in close to stare into Larriel's wide eyes. "You attack me in the forest, draw your bow on me while I am unarmed, and then come here and lie to others about it so you may laugh at my expense?" Kathair pulled Larriel a couple inches away from the wall and then slammed the elf back into it. "You're right, we are not equals, not in the least, but if I am a dog, then you are something much lower than that. You are a coward, and a discredit to your people." Kathair delivered a massive punch to Larriel's gut that would have chopped the elf down had Kathair not been holding him upright. He wound up for another, but hands seized him from behind and ripped him away effortlessly.

Kathair tried to struggle, but before he could even utter his protest he found himself on his knees. Three city guards had him, and there was nothing he could do about it. That was when he looked up and saw the one elf that had run away pointing at him and talking to someone. As soon as he realized who the elf was talking to, Kathair wished the guards would haul him away right then and lock him in the dungeons. Better that, by far, than to face Telstian.

"I'll take him," Telstian told the guards.

"My lord, this one attacked the group of elves. He must not be allowed—"

Telstian held up a hand. "I would rather not remind you that disobeying a direct order from a council member comes with a strict penalty." The guards released Kathair and stepped back. "See to the others, inform their parents that I will make arrangements with them to settle the matter."

"Yes, my lord," one of the guards said.

The young elf that had run to fetch Telstian approached them both, wringing his hands and glancing back and forth between them. "Uncle Telstian, if I may…"

"You may not, Braxen. Run along home now." Telstian turned his icy blue eyes to Kathair and held out a hand. Kathair took hold of it and clambered to his feet.

"Larriel started it," Kathair said.

"Indeed," Telstian replied. "And I suppose you thought you should be the one to end it, is that it?"

Kathair grunted and looked away. "You don't understand."

"I don't need to," Telstian insisted. "Were you in immediate danger?"

Kathair folded his arms. "Not here, but in the woods—"

"Then there is little you can say that will convince me of your innocence."

"Telstian, please…"

Braxen returned at that moment, holding the broken, and bloody, piece of Kathair's bow. "Here," he said.

Kathair reached out and offered a smile of thanks.

"Braxen, I told you to run along home," Telstian said. His words drove fear into the youth and he turned and nearly ran down the street. Telstian reached out and placed a hand on Kathair's shoulder. "Come with me. I would have words with you in private." Telstian led Kathair to a nearby guard station back at the gatehouse. As they entered, the three guards inside abruptly abandoned their game of dice and exited, closing the door behind them.

"They broke my father's bow," Kathair said, setting the broken limbs on the table with the dice.

"And that gives you the right to beat them with it?"

"It is the only memory I have of him," Kathair said. "I can't remember his face, or my mother's either. All I remember is this bow."

Telstian sighed and locked the door before sitting at the table. "Kathair, you will never be able to find peace in this life if you cannot control your emotions. It is our control that separates us from the wild beasts of the forest."

"Tell that to Larriel," Kathair said.

"Kathair, I know the others give you grief because of your heritage, but that doesn't give you the right to—"

"He pulled his bow on me, and threatened to shoot me!" Kathair shouted. "I can't let him get away with that."

Telstian's brow drew into a knot. "He drew his bow in town? Were there any witnesses?"

Kathair shook his head. "Not in town, in the forest. He and two others ambushed me. Larriel shot my arrow out of the sky when I fired at a stag. Then, because I wouldn't hunt for his arrow, the other two tried to attack me."

"Tried?" Telstian prompted.

"They came at me with their hands. I tried to tell them not to, but when they attacked I had no choice but to defend myself."

"And when they lost, Larriel drew his bow on you, is that it?"

Kathair nodded. "Then the big one, Olverin, broke my father's bow as punishment."

"And then?"

"They left, but Larriel fired several arrows in my direction to make sure I knew what he would do if I tried to stop Olverin from breaking my father's bow."

Telstian nodded. "You should have come and told me."

"You may be on the council, but you are only one member. The others would have sided with Larriel. Olverin and the other one would have lied, and you know it."

Telstian nodded. "It is a possibility." Telstian sighed once more and shook his head. "Still, if you are going to live here, then you must follow our ways."

"But that's just it, I don't want to live here. I want to be out there," Kathair pointed at the wall with one hand and thumbed his chest with the other. "I want to find out what happened to my father and mother."

"And when you discover the truth, what then? Will you beat everyone responsible with the broken limb of your father's bow?"

Kathair didn't hesitate. "Yes."

Telstian leaned back in his chair and folded his arms across his chest. "Kathair, you are a proud young man, and you have reason to be so, but your temper will cause far more harm than good. For example, think about what just happened in the street. You taught Larriel a lesson he will never forget."

"One that he deserved!" Kathair interjected.

Telstian held up a hand. "Be that as it may, he is not the only one affected. The others will remember, and so will their parents, and their siblings. You have temporarily defeated a handful of enemies, but you have made many more new enemies than you originally had. If, on the other hand, you had let me handle this in a council session, that could have been avoided, and I could have created a solution that would keep Larriel away from you."

"But he still would have gotten away with what he did. He should be punished."

"Sometimes you must think farther ahead, and devise a strategy that will get you what you want without compounding grievances. What good is it if you defeat him only to have to defeat his older brothers tomorrow, then their father the day after, and who knows where it will go from there?"

Kathair shook his head and grunted. Even through his anger he understood the point Telstian was making, but that didn't mean he had to agree with it aloud. "It doesn't fix what happened."

"And beating Larriel did? Tell me, is your father's bow whole now because you beat Larriel with it? Did it erase the events of the past?"

"No, but it might make him leave me alone in the future."

Telstian sucked his teeth and gently slapped a hand to the table. "I can see this is going nowhere. Kathair, sit down."

Kathair sat at the table, but made an effort to stare at the floor. "Let's forget about Larriel for now."

"Gladly," Kathair huffed.

"You remember I told you of a northman that was in the same caravan as your father?"

Kathair nodded.

"I found him. His name is Magnus. He doesn't live far from here, actually."

"Where?" Kathair asked. All evidence of anger drained from his voice. He had been waiting for this next clue ever since he had returned to Tualdern a couple weeks prior.

"Magnus lives with his wife and daughter in Lugtoliv, a small town a couple days south of Valtuu Temple."

"Then we have to go to him," Kathair said. "If he knows my father, then he might know why he was murdered."

Telstian held up a hand. "Of course, you must go, but I cannot."

Kathair frowned. "Telstian, you promised you would help me."

Telstian nodded. "Tarthuns are coming dangerously near our border-fort in the mountains. I have been ordered to take a detachment of warriors to bolster our defenses in case of attack. I am sorry, but it is an order I cannot refuse. However, I have appointed a guardian for you. Do you remember Wendin?"

Kathair smiled. "Wendin will go with me?"

Telstian nodded. "If I cannot accompany you, then he is the only other soul I would trust. He has risen in position since you last saw him, but he remembers you well, and fondly at that. He will serve you well."

"Did you tell him everything?"

"Everything I know about your parents, he now knows. I told him that Magnus grew up with your father, and may hold some clue that we do not. In fact, Wendin was so anxious to help that he insisted on helping with the search for Magnus. It is largely thanks to his help that we located the northman."

"Does Magnus know I'm coming?"

Telstian shook his head. "We were discreet. Until we know what Magnus knows, we didn't want to risk spooking him and losing track of him."

Kathair leaned forward. "When do we leave?"

*****

Rheddis opened the letter, breaking the seal of black wax, and read its contents. He then crossed his left leg over his right as he leaned back in his wooden throne. "Are you certain of this?" he said, holding up the letter.

The human messenger before him wrung his hands and retreated half a step. "I'm not privy to the message, but my master said he was entirely sure of its accuracy."

Rheddis reached up and brushed his long, silvery hair back over his pointed ears. "And when were you sent with this message?"

"Two and a half days ago. I rode straight here, changing horses at the usual spots so as not to delay."

"And you weren't followed?" Rheddis pressed.

The messenger shook his head. "N-no, I'm sure of it."

Rheddis nodded. "Very well, then you shall receive your payment." Rheddis reached down to a small chest beside the throne and came up with a bag of silver coins. "Tell your master that I am pleased." Rheddis threw the bag to the messenger and then dismissed the man with a wave of his hand. The human bowed several times, nearly tripping over his own feet as he awkwardly shuffled toward the exit.

After the human was gone, Rheddis snapped his fingers. A pair of figures emerged from the shadows behind the support columns near the outer walls. They strode toward him confidently, and then knelt before the throne. Rheddis let his eyes fall upon the tattoos that covered the blacktongues' bodies, studying the tribal markings for a few moments while reveling in the order he was about to give.

"After more than a decade, we finally have what we need to finish what we started," Rheddis said. "You will find the one who escaped in a town called Lugtoliv. Kill him, and anyone else with him. There can be no witnesses."

The Blacktongues nodded and then jumped up to their feet. They closed their eyes and bowed their heads once more as they each held a dagger close to their hearts, then they turned and sped out from the throne room.

Rheddis smiled. He admired their silence almost as much as their efficiency. He rose from his throne and walked to a table in the back of the room. He unrolled a map and smoothed it out with his left hand as his eyes fell on Valtuu Temple. "First, the one who got away, and then the temple." A sly grin stretched his pale, gray lips across his face. "Nagar would be pleased."

Chapter 3

"What's in the bag?"

Kyra turned around to see Mindaugas approaching. "Books," she said.

"I did warn you that we were taking horses, and not a carriage, didn't I?"

Kyra frowned, and then followed Mindaugas' gaze to the other bags at her feet. "Oh…" She smiled and shook her head. "Not to worry, I found something that will be quite useful for this."

"Oh?" Mindaugas asked.

Kyra took one of the smaller sacks at her feet and picked it up, stuffing it into the bag that was already secured to the saddle. "I managed to perfect a holding spell. I already have seven bags of books in this one, and it will easily fit the others without adding any significant weight for the horse."

Mindaugas approached and peeked into the large bag. "That's a nice trick, but, if you can put all of the books into this bag, then why have them separated into other bags?"

Kyra smiled and gave a shrug. "They're categorized by subject, so I don't have to rummage through the whole bag to find one book."

"Ah," Mindaugas replied with a nod. "Perhaps you can help me enchant my saddle bags. I could always do with a bit more food. I find myself running low on jerky regardless of how long or short my travels are."

Kyra laughed. "I could help with that."

"Then it's a deal. I know a great butcher in Buktah. He makes jerky from beef, venison, elk, you name it." Mindaugas let out a playful sigh as he gazed wistfully toward the stable's ceiling.

"You're not at all like the priests," Kyra said. "They never make jokes. Honestly, I'm not even sure I have ever seen one of them smile."

Mindaugas laughed. "I know what you mean, but you know, my father always said that laughter was the spice of life. Without it, everything would be bland and dreary. You would have liked him. He loved dragons too. He always thought we got things backwards when we created the Dragon Slayers."

"Sounds like a man after my own heart," Kyra replied.

"Careful now," Mindaugas said. "He's married, and my ma is the jealous kind." He gave her a wink and then turned to check his own saddle bags.

Definitely nothing like the priests. Kyra smiled to herself and finished packing the last of the books into her bags. "And what about you, are you married?"

"Are you proposing?" Mindaugas called out over his shoulder.

"What? Me, no, I was just… you mentioned your father and…"

"Relax, I'm just teasing. I was married once."

"What happened?"

Mindaugas shrugged. "Not sure. I went to work one day, came back and she was gone. Left me a nice note and all. Something about wanting to find her true self and not being cooped up in our little cottage. Said she couldn't see herself with a carpenter for the rest of her life."

"You were a carpenter?"

Mindaugas nodded. "Until my early thirties. Joke's on her though, I guess. Seeing as I am now the Keeper of Secrets, endowed with awesome power and authority. Not to mention I sold that little cottage and have permanent living quarters at the palace just for me."

"Serves her right," Kyra said.

"Nah." Mindaugas mounted his horse. "She's better off somewhere else. When I was a carpenter she was never lonely, but she didn't have the finer things she wanted. As the Keeper of Secrets, I could give her the finer things now, but she'd always be lonely. Hopefully she found someone who can give her everything."

"You still love her," Kyra said.

Mindaugas gave a short nod. "I suppose I always will, in a way. But, I wouldn't trade my life now for the one I lost." He smiled wide. "I guess we both had to find ourselves."

Kyra nodded and let the conversation die out. She could only hope that Feberik Orres would realize he needed to find himself as well, because no matter how long he held onto the idea of their betrothal, Kyra was not going to agree to marry him. In her mind, the arrangement was dead as soon as her father had disowned her, but even without that she wouldn't have agreed to marry the oaf. Not only was he too old, but they were far too different.

The two finished their final preparations and rode out through Kuldiga Academy's main gate. The forest was alive with chirping birds above and scampering squirrels below. The occasional deer would dash through the woods at their approach, while a pair of hares stared at them, their noses twitching. The fresh breeze rustling through the trees only heightened Kyra's enjoyment. It was as if the whole world was rejoicing with her at her newfound freedom. No more living under Lord Caspin's rules and traditions. No need to follow the curriculum at Kuldiga Academy either, now that she was on an official assignment with the Keeper of Secrets. So long as he vouched for her progress, and she passed certain milestones with her magic, she would graduate with honors, and receive a full title. Then she could return to her own manor, that of her real ancestors, and create the life she wished.

Her eyes caught sight of a green lizard then, skittering up a white oak and stopping to look at her. The way his head twitched and the dark eyes looked at her reminded her a little bit of Leatherback. How she missed him. She had cared for the dragon since before he had hatched, and the two of them had shared many adventures together. She could only hope that he was safe now, off hiding in a special pocket dimension created by Khefir, the collector of the damned. She tried not to imagine Leatherback suffering in Hammenfein. Khefir had promised he wouldn't allow such a thing to happen, and Kyra had paid the god the price he required. He was bound to abide by the terms of their agreement. Besides, everything Kyra had read about Khefir noted that although he collected the evil souls of those bound for eternal punishment in the fires of Hammenfein, he himself was an honest god, unlike his brother Hatmul, who was known to double-cross whomever he could, including the very gods themselves on occasion.

Kyra tried to content herself. *Leatherback is all right for now, and it won't be long before I can find a way to help him more.*

"Kyra, where are you going?"

Snapped from her thoughts, Kyra looked up to see that Mindaugas had taken a left fork in the road, while she had allowed her horse to take the right and amble along, munching on clover and grasses that sprang up in the dirt.

"Sorry." She redirected her horse and cut through to the other road. "I was just thinking about Leatherback."

"Let's save the deep thinking for the library. Out here you need to stay focused," Mindaugas said. "I know it's hard, I want to save him as much as you do."

Kyra couldn't help but snort derisively. "You don't know him."

"I don't have to know him, Kyra," Mindaugas said. "I am the Keeper of Secrets. My whole existence revolves around bringing the dragons back to the Middle Kingdom. I mean, I protect the kingdom from the curse too, but my ultimate goal is to bring the dragons back. This kingdom was founded with the help of the Ancients, and it won't ever reach its full potential without them."

Kyra turned to look at him. "You mean that, don't you?" she asked.

"Of course," Mindaugas said. "Leatherback is the first dragon in a long time that has held out against the curse. If he can show us how to defeat Nagar's Blight, then we might finally be able to bring the dragons back. It's as simple as that."

Kyra shook her head. *Simple is not the word she would use to describe any of it.*

"That's why Headmaster Fenn wants me to talk to you about the secret group operating out of Kuldiga Academy too. He's hoping I can convince you to join so you can help us rid the kingdom of those that would seek to keep dragons out, bring necromancy back, and all sorts of other things."

"And I suppose you would be my mentor then, is that it?" Kyra guessed.

"No," Mindaugas said quickly. "I can help design a suitable training program, but I wouldn't be a good mentor for you."

Kyra raised a brow. She hadn't expected that kind of response.

"I don't actually know any spells. I'm just a really good swordsman who happens to hold a position of note with a particular order, that's all."

Kyra laughed. "True, I suppose it would be best if I was trained by someone with magic. I guess I just assumed that Fenn was trying to push you into the role so he could control me."

"He can be a bit… rigid… but don't discount him. His heart is in the right place. It would be good for you to join the group. You would make the team quite a bit stronger, and if we can keep Leatherback safe as well, then…" Mindaugas let the sentence hang unfinished. The two of them fell into silence, allowing Kyra to ponder the invitation.

The group was certainly interesting, but her primary focus now was helping Leatherback, and her understanding was that she would have to travel far beyond the Middle Kingdom to have any hope of keeping him safe. If she could also figure out what happened to Njar in the meantime, then so much the better. The only issue that made it hard for her to envision herself flying away with Leatherback was the fact that Kathair was looking for his parents' murderer. She knew he was capable enough on his own, and that he would have help, but she still wanted to be with him. It wasn't just the fact that he had been there for her either. She missed him. He was the one person she could talk to about anything in the world and not feel judged for her opinions or thoughts. Mindaugas was nice enough, but even he kept some distance between them, not to mention it didn't feel nearly as comfortable discussing closely held hopes with someone who was essentially a stranger to her.

The more she thought about it, the more she solidified her decision not to join the group. Leatherback and Kathair weren't part of the group, and she would much rather be with them than anyone else.

The two continued along the road, passing by a pair of men on horseback heading the opposite direction and a farmer in a wagon making his way to a field with a load of fresh cut hay that sent Mindaugas into a sneezing fit. They made camp for the night, eating their fill of bread and beans before setting up their beds in a copse of trees that sheltered them from the night winds. Mindaugas set a large campfire and then promptly went to his bed, assuring Kyra that his horse would wake him at the first sign of any trouble.

Kyra pretended to sleep until she heard Mindaugas snoring heavily, then she snuck off around a thick patch of bushes and went to work conjuring her portal. She had the deed to her mother's manor, but as yet she hadn't had the time to actually visit it. She focused her magic, directing her portal until she could see the front door of her new manor, then she stabilized the spell and took in a breath.

"Finally, a home for me." She stepped through and found herself standing in front of a large two-story house with sloped and rounded roofs. Ivy climbed the front wall of river rock and clung to the roof itself. A garden of iris, in desperate need of weeding out, stood off to her left, while a row of roses grew like a living wall off to the right, curving around the side of the house and disappearing. The windows were shuttered from the outside, and the door had cobwebs in the upper corners. Despite the neglect she could feel the home's inviting warmth. She reached into her pocket for the key and pulled it out, laughing as she skipped toward the door and slid the key into place. She gave it two turns to the left, her heart nearly skipping with each click of the tumblers, but when she went to grab the knob she found it would not turn.

She tried again, but was met with the same result.

"Maybe it's rusted," she surmised. Kyra turned the key the other direction to lock the door once more, and then she walked around the house, trying each of the shutters. To her dismay, none of them would open either. She sighed. If she could remember what the inside looked like, she could teleport into the building, but she hadn't been here for many years, and had only barely remembered what the front of the house looked like.

Kyra found a large outbuilding behind the main house, so she went to it, hoping to find a ladder or something she could use to try the upper story windows, but the outbuilding was locked as well.

Frustrated, she turned and sat on the ground, listening to the crickets chirping as the moon rose high above the manor.

"I have to get inside," she told herself. "Maybe there is another key. Or… maybe my mother put a spell on the place." If that was the case, then she would need to return to Caspin Manor and search her mother's old study. She recalled a lesson she had with Cyrus – or at least the wizard that impersonated Cyrus—and concentrated on a spell she knew would help her detect the presence of magic. She held out her left hand, focusing the energy on the door. Instantly, the door began to glow bright blue, as if encapsulated in a tight shell. Kyra then tried to dispel the ward. She knew several defensive spells that could dispel magic, but none of them affected the ward on the door. Each of them crashed against the shell only to fizzle out, sparking and turning to smoke once defeated by the ward on the door. Kyra sighed and shook her head. She could only hope there would be a clue in her mother's old study back at Caspin Manor. She would have to investigate another time, though. She didn't want to risk Mindaugas waking to find her gone.

Kyra hurried back through the portal and got into her bedroll. As she drifted off to sleep, her mind worked on the puzzle of her locked home, and what might be inside that would have required a magical seal.

The next morning, Mindaugas woke her a half hour before sunrise. They ate breakfast and then broke camp and continued along their way to Buktah. Shortly after midday, they emerged from the trees and saw the city walls, dark and tall with long spikes jutting out to ward off would-be invaders. Beyond the walls a few tall roofs and towers reached upward, some of the chimneys emitting thin gray smoke that drifted upward until absorbed by the sky. Soldiers walked the battlements along the walls, each carrying long spears in their hands and bows slung across their backs.

"Not very inviting," Kyra commented to herself.

"It isn't much to look at, and most of the people living there have a sense of humor similar to the priests you adore so much, but deep down they're good folk, even if a little too cautious of strangers."

Kyra turned to regard Mindaugas. He offered a wink and kept riding on.

"Perhaps that's why Al likes it there. The humans remind him of his surly kin folk."

"Not what I expected at all," Kyra said under her breath.

The two made their way toward the gatehouse while Kyra studied the towers filled with archers and the high walls with soldiers patrolling along. The simple gatehouse framed a pair of large iron doors with spikes protruding outward and a pair of guards flanking them.

One of the guards stepped forward and said, "State your name and your business."

The other guard quickstepped to the first and backhanded the man across the chest before gesturing to Mindaugas.

The first guard started to scowl, but then looked to Mindaugas and blushed. "Oh, sorry sir, I didn't recognize you."

"It's all right," Mindaugas said.

"I'll open the door right away." The first guard turned and gave a signal to someone watching from an open window in the gatehouse. Metallic clanking and creaking rang out as the doors opened and the portcullis was raised. The two guards moved to the side and offered salutes as Mindaugas led Kyra into the city.

"Does everyone treat you like that?" Kyra asked.

Mindaugas nodded. "It comes with the title." His voice was different now, more somber somehow, and his smile had faded, almost giving way to a grimace. "Sometimes they recognize my face, other times they see the insignia on my left bracer, or upon my sheath." Kyra looked as Mindaugas held up his left forearm, turning it over so she could see the back of his wrist. A small, yet distinct, dragon's head was emblazoned in gold along the back of the black leather bracer.

"I hadn't noticed that before," Kyra said.

Mindaugas nodded. "I'll admit, it's subtler than the knights who ride with flowing banners and shields painted with their family crests, but it gets the job done when necessary." He offered a quick smile and patted his sword. "Usually it's the sword they notice first."

Kyra watched as others in the street would look up and hurry to clear a path once they recognized him. "Come along, I'll take you the short way." Kyra studied the vendors as they would cease their negotiations to watch Mindaugas pass by. They didn't look upon him with fear, but there was a palpable tension in the air to be sure.

Mindaugas turned his horse onto a cobblestone road that crossed the dirt road they were on. Kyra was quick to keep pace. The two sped their horses into a light trot. The horses' hooves danced across the road with a pleasant *clippity-clop* as they rode by several buildings. Kyra noted several signs. Some were ornate with fresh paint or elaborate engravings, others were a bit more weathered. Each sign was cut in a different shape and hung above the front door of the respective inn or tavern. There was the Rosewood, the Midnight Traveler, The Spotted Owl Inn, and then there was one plain sign that simply had the word "Inn" etched lightly into its side. Mindaugas stopped in front of the inn with the plain sign and secured his horse to the hitching post.

"It's around back," Mindaugas said. He helped Kyra hitch her horse to the same post and then took her large bag of books. A grin crossed his face. "That spell really works," he said, hefting the bag up and down to test its weight. "Remember you promised to enchant my jerky bag." Mindaugas winked and then motioned for Kyra to follow him around the back. The two of them had to turn sideways as the space between the inn and the building next door was very narrow. As they came around the back of the inn Mindaugas pointed to a blacksmith shop. "That's where we're going."

Kyra followed Mindaugas into an open area where the coal for the furnace was piled higher than Kyra was tall. She could feel the heat coming from the open door of the shop and was careful not to breathe in too deeply as the air around her grew stifling. The kiln made the air heavy and somewhat difficult to breathe in, but it had an alluring quality to it as well.

"Al, you here?" Mindaugas called out.

A tall man emerged from a door in the back. "Master Sit'marihu is out for the day, I'm afraid. Is there something I can help you with?"

Mindaugas frowned. "Is he ill?"

The young man frowned. "No. Why?"

Mindaugas shrugged. "I've never seen him away from his forge."

"Oh, no, you misunderstand. He is making a delivery to the captain of the guard. He should be back soon."

"Al doesn't make personal deliveries," Mindaugas said. The Keeper of Secrets folded his arms over his large chest and glanced back to Kyra. "Al hates making deliveries," he told her before looking back at the young man. "Let me guess, you botched something, am I right?"

The young man shifted his weight onto his right leg and his cheeks reddened. "Not really… it was a… misunderstanding."

"Ha!" Mindaugas laughed and shook his head. "Don't take it too hard," he told the man. "If you're still allowed to work here after the fact, it couldn't have been all that bad."

The young man shrugged. "No, it wasn't work related, I mean, not really. I delivered the right equipment to the correct address. It's just…" the young man looked to Kyra as if she might be able to help him, but she just returned his gaze, waiting for the rest of the story. "I was delivering a sword to Mister Jonstone, and his wife is really short, see. So, when she opened the door, I asked her to get the master of the house…"

"You didn't!" Mindaugas said as he clapped his hands.

"When she looked at me puzzled, I tried to rephrase it."

"Oh no!" Mindaugas said with a widening smile. "What did you say?"

"I told her to go and get a grown-up. I didn't know who she was, honest!"

Mindaugas lost himself in a belly laugh and had to turn away. "That's golden. I love it." He turned to Kyra then and placed a hand on her shoulder. "Mister Jonstone is the quartermaster for the town guard. So, if you insult his wife…"

Kyra understood. "Then the joke becomes famous through the whole town guard," she guessed, doing her best to stifle a laugh threatening to erupt from her as well.

Mindaugas nodded and wiped a tear from his eye. "So you see, Al has to go personally to deliver the equipment now, because if this guy goes, then they'll just make fun of Mister Jonstone's wife all over again."

"I tried to apologize," the young man interrupted. "I went to her house with a special ring that I made myself, and I even brought her flowers."

Mindaugas stopped laughing and his eyes shot open wide. "What kind of flowers?"

The young man scratched the back of his head. "Well, the kinds I can gather. You know, daisies, poppies, and blue-bonnets."

Mindaugas put a hand to his mouth. After a moment he said, "But Mrs. Jonstone is allergic to daisies and poppies!"

"Well I didn't know that until after!"

Mindaugas laughed again and turned Kyra around, ushering her out of the blacksmith shop. "Come on, we should leave before he tries to give us gifts."

Kyra waved at the apprentice, hoping her gesture might soften his embarrassment.

"I didn't mean any harm!" the young man shouted after them.

Mindaugas snorted and kept walking.

"You shouldn't be so hard on him," Kyra said.

"We'll wait inside," Mindaugas said as he reached for the inn's back door. "I know the owner here. He'll have some good food ready."

"Really, I think you may have hurt his feelings," Kyra said.

Mindaugas shook his head. "Al's always hiring knuckleheads, but then that's what he gets for setting up shop in Buktah. A normal apprenticeship would last decades, but he is lucky if he can keep an apprentice for more than a year or two. It's hard to find a man who can keep up with a dwarf in any endeavor, but especially so in the forge."

"Anyone could have made the same mistake," Kyra insisted.

"Could you imagine?" Mindaugas said, ignoring her comment. "Asking Mrs. Jonstone to go and get an adult? Oh, I would have paid good money to see the look on her face!"

Despite herself, Kyra found herself incapable of keeping a straight face.

The two of them were still laughing when they reached the bar in the front room and ordered some stew to pass the time while they waited. Al came through the rear entrance less than half an hour later wearing a scowl that made him look much less approachable than the last time Kyra had seen him.

"Mindaugas, why are you messing with my apprentice?" The dwarf slapped Mindaugas along the back for emphasis. "It's hard enough to find a human with any amount of smithing skill. I don't need you chasing them off."

"If they run off on account of me, then they weren't really good enough for you anyway, Al." Mindaugas turned to look at the red-headed dwarf and raised a mug of ale. "Care for a drink?"

Al shook his head. "I have a lot of orders to fill, so if you want to chat, we need to take it back to my shop."

Mindaugas nodded and slapped a few coins on the table. He then nudged Kyra's arm. "Let's go."

She followed the two back to Al's shop while they made small talk about the weather and Al's most recent orders from various people in and around Buktah. When they reached the forge, Al barked a few orders to his apprentice, who began shoveling more coal into the furnace and prepping various slabs of metal for use.

"I just got a large order from Ten Forts. I guess the orcs have started testing the borders again," Al said.

"Serious?"

Al shook his head. "I doubt it. The orcs would have to be pretty dumb to challenge Ten Forts in a frontal assault."

"Well, they are orcs," Mindaugas replied.

Al grunted. "They may be a bit too savage for my liking, but the orcs aren't as dumb as most humans would like to believe."

Mindaugas nodded.

"My bet is it's a couple groups of young orcs out to prove themselves by saying they led raids on the humans at Ten Forts. Still, it means that I get more work out of the deal, so it will put a few extra coins in my pockets as well."

"I see," Mindaugas said with a nod. "In any case, we are passing through on our way to Valtuu Temple."

Al stopped his work and looked up at Kyra as if he only now realized she was there. "Icadion's beard, are you set to take the Test of Arophim?"

Kyra shook her head. "No, I don't have the mark."

Al grunted and shook his head. "Too bad. I know all about your battle with Severin. You would have made a great champion, if you were a Sahale that is."

"She might yet prove a powerful ally in our fight," Mindaugas cut in. "After all, her dragon has yet to succumb to Nagar's Blight."

"He isn't *my* dragon," Kyra said a little more testily than she meant.

Mindaugas shrugged. "You know what I mean."

"I wouldn't be so sure," Al commented. "It's one thing to hold out a bit longer than other dragons, but if you're saying that she had anything to do with keeping him safe I wouldn't bet on that."

Kyra frowned. "Njar helped create a grove of aspens that buffered some of the curse," she said. "And the priests never found a trace of the taint in Leatherback. So surely there must be something to it."

Al tugged on his beard. "I'm not a wizard of course, but Njar sounds like he might be onto something. I haven't heard of a spell that was effective against the blight until now. You sure it was him?"

"Yes, I watched him create the grove myself."

"Do you know the spell he used?"

Kyra shook her head.

Al shrugged. "Sounds to me like you need to find Njar."

Mindaugas sighed. "Yes, that's one of the angles we are working on."

Al arched a brow. "Meaning what, exactly?"

"Leatherback is safe for now," Kyra began. "He's hiding in a special pocket dimension for the time being. Njar, on the other hand, disappeared, and I haven't heard from him. He said he would be there to help me deal with Severin during the final battle, but he never showed. I'm afraid something might have happened to him. He always came through on his promises before."

"I see," Al said. He grabbed a long bit of iron with a pair of tongs and set it into the furnace. Sparks and waves of heat flowed out as he buried the iron in the hot embers. "So you were hoping I might have an idea to help you find him, is that it?"

"That, and any ideas about the blight you might have for us to research while at the temple," Mindaugas replied. "Up until now I thought the only way to bring the dragons back was by finding the champion, but maybe we can use something like what Njar and Kyra have been doing for Leatherback."

Al nodded and wiped a bit of sweat from his forehead. "I can't help you with Njar. Occasionally the satyrs have been friendly with my people in the past, but that was well before my time, or even my father's time for that matter. Even in the best of times none of us knew how to reach Viverandon. They always maintained a level of secrecy about the whole thing."

"Not even a rumor or legend?" Mindaugas asked.

"No," Al replied. He turned the now red-hot iron over in the furnace and held it for a few seconds before pulling it out. "Stand back," he said. The dwarf slapped the hot iron onto his anvil and proceeded to pound it out with a sturdy hammer, sending sparks several feet out from him with each strike. "Perhaps the priests will know better. Either in their books of prophecy or perhaps in some old almanac. The dragons had some amount of rapport with the Natural Races."

Mindaugas folded his arms and watched Al work for a few moments. Then he turned to Kyra. "I suppose we should get moving then."

"You may as well stay the night," Al said. "I have heard the roads have been perilous of late. An increase of highwaymen at night."

"That would explain the town guard's new orders," Mindaugas surmised.

Al gave a single nod. "New armor and weapons for the patrols. We've only lost one guard in the last few weeks, but it's still reason enough to minimize nighttime travel if possible."

"Very well, I'll go and get us a couple of rooms at the inn." Mindaugas turned and walked away.

"How is Kathair?" Al asked after Mindaugas left.

Kyra shrugged. "I haven't heard from him in a while."

"Oh? You two have a falling out? It happens sometimes with young couples."

Kyra blushed. "We aren't a couple…"

Al raised a hand and patted the air. "Sure, sure, my mistake." The dwarf then gave a wink and went back to work on the iron.

"I'm betrothed," Kyra blurted out, as if she needed a defense.

"To Feberik Orres. Yes, I heard about that too."

Kyra narrowed her eyes on him. "You seem to hear a lot about me."

Al shrugged. "You tall folk talk a lot. Rumors run through Buktah like a mighty river seeking the ocean. I hear a lot of things about a lot of people. Still, I don't need anyone else to tell me that you'll never marry Feberik. I can see that just by looking at you."

"And Kathair is the one you think I should be with?" Kyra poked back.

Al shrugged. "I'm just saying, I saw the way you two looked at each other the last time you visited me. Either way, you're both a bit young anyhow. Still… I have a knack for these kinds of things."

Kyra sighed and shook her head. "Mindaugas told me that Kathair is in Tualdern," she said after a moment. "Something about investigating his parents' murder."

Al stopped working and glanced up to her. "Well now, that is something serious."

Kyra nodded. "I don't know much about it, other than Kathair found a letter in Headmaster Herion's office discussing it."

"What did the letter say, exactly?"

"I'm not sure. Kathair said Headmaster Herion found him and destroyed the letter."

"Probably for the best," Al said.

Kyra stepped forward. "Do you know something about that as well?"

Al glanced to the inn and then back to Kyra. He lowered his voice and leaned closer. "Some secrets are best left hidden. I don't know much about the circumstances around Kathair's father's death, but I do know that he was traveling to Valtuu Temple by invitation."

"What do you mean?" Kyra asked.

Al set his hammer down and tugged on his beard. "I shouldn't tell you this, but since you're close to Kathair, I suppose it won't do much harm."

"What?"

"In the past, I have been close with the priests at the temple. Part of my family's responsibilities, I suppose. Anyway, Kathair's father was invited to the temple because one of the priests had a vision about him."

"A vision?"

Al nodded. "You have to promise to keep this to yourself, understand?"

"I will."

"Mindaugas was not the first choice to become the Keeper of Secrets. Many priests thought that Kathair's father should take on the role. That's why they sent for him."

Kyra's mouth fell open. She didn't know what to say. She glanced toward the inn when she heard the door slam closed. Mindaugas had just emerged.

"Got us a room with two beds," he called out. "Tried to get two separate rooms, but they are full up for the night."

"Not a word, Kyra, understand?"

Kyra nodded to Al.

"What are you two talking about?" Mindaugas asked as he rejoined them.

Kyra shrugged. "Al was trying to convince me that I should marry Kathair."

Mindaugas laughed. "Well, at least he is closer to your age than Feberik," he said.

Kyra forced a laugh, hoping it was enough to keep Mindaugas from prying further. Al took his flattened piece of iron and went back to the furnace with it.

"I don't wish to be an inhospitable host, but I have much work to do," the dwarf said.

"No worries," Mindaugas said with a wave of his hand. "We can head up to our room. The sun will be setting soon and Kyra has a lot of books she brought to read."

"Actually, I wanted to ask Al something," Kyra said.

"Oh, well go on then," Mindaugas replied.

Kyra bit her lip and glanced between the two of them.

"Oh…" Mindaugas gave a nod when he finally caught on. "Something private is it? All right. I'll go get the room situated and see you in a few minutes."

After he was back inside the inn, Al turned back to the anvil and began working the metal again. "What's on your mind?"

"Al, can I ask…" she paused, considering how best to phrase what she wanted to say.

"Spit it on out," Al insisted.

"Did you ever get used to… you know, being alone, away from your home?"

Al stopped pounding the metal and looked at her. He reached up with his left hand and tugged on his beard a bit. "Missing your family?" he asked.

Kyra shook her head. "It isn't that. It's just…"

Al smiled softly and removed his work gloves before coming around the anvil toward her. "You used to know where you belonged, who you belonged with, and what you were supposed to do, and now you don't," he said.

"How did you figure out what to do?" Kyra asked.

Al reached out and took her hands in his. "I don't know what you're feeling, exactly, but for me things never felt right at home. Most dwarves love the tunnels. They thrive on the smell of rock and dirt, and they feel right at home in the darkness. I never did. I always went outside to see the sky. I loved the forge, but I couldn't stand to work it in the depths of a mountain. It was… suffocating." Al sighed and then shook his head as his eyes broke from hers and looked off to the distance. "My father couldn't understand it, said it wasn't natural. We had a bit of a falling out when neither one of us could bend to the other. When I left, even though I had never felt at home, I still felt lost. Here I was, a lone dwarf in a world of tall folk. Some of them accepted me, many didn't. I had to fight for my right to buy a forge, and then I had to fight for orders. I worked harder than anyone else ever had, and even then I failed several times. Buktah was the seventh town I started a smithy in, did you know that?"

Kyra shook her head.

Al nodded. "Failed many times before finding success. I think the fates were testing me, making me prove that I wanted it, deserved it. That way when I finally found my place I would treasure it. A lot of folks get bored with what they have, and they throw it away. Not me, I worked too hard to get this forge, and I don't intend to give it up, not ever."

"Do you ever miss your old home?"

"Sure, sometimes, but it gets easier with time. You'll find your place, if you keep looking, and once you do you will understand what I mean. Home isn't the place you were born, it's where you feel like you belong. Just like family isn't always blood, it's everyone who accepts you and loves you enough to help you become the best version of yourself. Here in Buktah, I found acceptance. The people judged me by my work, not by my race, or the fact that I didn't conform with the usual dwarf's notions of living in a mountain somewhere. That's when I found my purpose. I met people who connected me with the army. I create the equipment that gives the soldiers the best chance of survival they can hope for. Truth be told, the work might be considered beneath a dwarf of my skill level, but I love it. Occasionally I still get to make some very fancy weapons or armor, but on the whole my life revolves around helping people fight for the life they want." He let go of her hands and then pointed a stubby finger at her face. "That's why I was so eager to help you and Kathair when you came to me for help. That's what I live for. It's the opportunity to help that makes me feel like I have finally found my home, the place in the world where I belong."

Kyra nodded. "Thank you, Al. I had a feeling you would understand."

Al smiled and held his arms out wide for a hug. "That I do, Kyra, and believe you me, it will get better. I promise. Someday soon you will find the place you belong, and you will know what you want."

The two hugged and then said their good-byes. Al went back to his work, and Kyra retired to the inn for the night.

She found Mindaugas already lying upon his bed, nearly asleep. She closed and locked the door behind her, and then went to her bed and read while she waited a while to make sure Mindaugas had fallen into a deep sleep before trying to conjure her portal again. Once he was snoring, Kyra got up and created her portal. She glanced back at the large man when the silvery light crackled and popped to life, but Mindaugas didn't wake. Instead he turned over to face the wall and began to snore heavily.

Kyra breathed a sigh of relief and then stepped through the portal. This time, she emerged inside her mother's old study at Caspin Manor.

A wave of grief punched her in the stomach when she saw the room. Nothing was as before. The exterior wall had been removed, and someone had been adding onto the room, extended the floor out beyond its normal bounds. The makings of a fine orrery were being pinned in place, dangling from the ceiling by brass chains and containing jewels that represented the known planets and moons around Terramyr. She saw her mother's desk shoved into a corner, with books heaped over it haphazardly, some of them obviously being bent out of shape in the pile. Along the northern all was a fresh mural depicting something that resembled the tales of Terramyr's creation, with Icadion holding a ball of blue and brown in his hands while standing on the rainbow bridge that would connect the world to the heaven city of Volganor.

"How could he do this?" Kyra whispered. She knew how Lord Caspin felt about her as a daughter, but if he had cared for her mother at all he could have cleaned the room and set it back to the way it was to respect her memory. Why change it like this? Lord Caspin wasn't even a believer in the Old Gods, and had demeaned others who had professed to believe in the old ways. She shook her head as tears welled in her eyes. This was just another way for him to separate himself from them, she knew. Erasing her mother's study and replacing it with something that meant so little to him, but would be fancy enough to show off to his guests when he entertained. It was little more than a status symbol.

She wanted to say something, but she couldn't find the right word to suit the man that had once been her father. How could he so completely turn his back on them both, as if they had never been a part of his life? It was hardly Kyra's fault that she was actually the daughter of a vampire. For that matter, it wasn't her mother's fault either. Even as powerful a sorceress as she had been, her mother couldn't defeat the vampire that had kidnapped her. Could Lord Caspin's ego truly be so frail that he couldn't see past it?

Kyra moved to sit on a workman's stool near her mother's desk and let herself think through it all, processing the emotions as best she could while confronted with the mess around her. Then, when she was able to wipe away the last tear from her face, she rose up and searched through the pile of books. She had found the help she needed in here once before, so she was certain she could find the spell to open her ancestral home in the woods.

She spent at least an hour digging through books and notes before finally giving up for the night. She would have to return another time, and with a more methodical approach. Next time, at least, she wouldn't be overwhelmed with memories and shattered dreams. She had already come to terms with the fact that this was no longer her home, but she felt that more keenly now than ever. Once she had the final clue from her mother's old study, she would never again have a need to return to this place.

Kyra stepped back through the open portal and crawled into bed, completely unaware that Mindaugas' eyes were open, watching her when she returned.

Chapter 4

Kathair and Wendin walked along the wooded road, on track to reach their destination an hour before sundown. Wendin had said very little during the journey, but Kathair knew that was his way. The elven warrior had always been short on words, even when he'd served as a page in Telstian's house when Kathair was very young. Still, Kathair was unaccustomed to traveling multiple days without at least some conversation, and he was more than eager to hear what Wendin had been up to the last couple of years.

As they rounded a corner in the road, Kathair attempted yet again to start up a conversation. "Have you ever been to Lugtoliv?" Kathair asked.

Wendin shook his head. "No."

"Telstian said it's a nice little village, woodcutters mostly."

Wendin nodded, but didn't respond.

"What was your assignment before Telstian sent you with me?" Kathair said, trying a different angle.

"I was watch commander at Dunerian Redoubt."

Finally, a whole sentence! Kathair smiled. "Did you like it there?"

"Indeed."

Kathair frowned. "Did the Tarthuns ever attack while you were watch commander?"

Wendin shook his head.

Kathair thought for a minute. He had to ask something that would require a more detailed answer. After a moment, he had something he was sure would get the large elf talking. "If the Tarthuns did attack Dunerian Redoubt, what strategy would you use to repel them?"

Wendin smiled. "I would kill them."

Kathair snorted. It wasn't the kind of answer he was hoping for, but it was a typical Wendin response. More than that, it was probably the most accurate response Wendin could give. Direct and to the point. "What would you do if you were outnumbered one hundred to one; I hear they can come in large hordes sometimes."

Wendin smiled wider. "Dunerian Redoubt is built in the narrowest part of the pass leading east. Their numbers would not matter. We would prevail."

Kathair nodded and gave a sigh, letting the conversation fall. The two continued onward for several hours in silence, watching the animals and birds in the forest around them as the sun peeked through the dense canopy of leaves above to guide their way.

After crossing a small river via a log bridge patched with moss along the railing, they came to the base of a hill, atop which sat the village they sought. The wooden wall of poles tapered to spikes surrounding the buildings was broken by a single gateway guarded by a large, wide-shouldered man. He looked to the two of them and offered a wave.

"What brings you two out this way?" he asked as they drew near.

Wendin stepped toward the guard and handed him an official writ of passage from the Tualdern Council.

The guard furrowed his brow and shook his head. "Sorry, mate, but I don't read. I just keep the riff-raff out."

Wendin gave a nod. "Then allow me to pass along the respect and greetings of the Tualdern Council."

"The council?" the guard echoed. "Sounds like you are on important business."

"We are here to seek a man by the name of Magnus. He is a northman, like my ward here."

The guard turned and eyed Kathair carefully. "Aye, I know Magnus. What does this boy have to do with him?"

Kathair almost spoke up, but Wendin answered first.

"Magnus knew his father, and we have come to ask a few questions."

"I see," the man said with a nod. "You should know before you come in, we don't have any inns. We aren't as large as the fancy cities farther inland. You might be able to rent a stable for the night though, or perhaps Magnus might put you up for the night if you need."

Wendin went back to being his silent self, answering the guard only with a respectful nod.

"Magnus' house is on the far side of the village. Go past the town hall and you'll see his cottage behind that. He has a rose bush on the left side of his door. Can't miss it."

Wendin gestured for Kathair to move along and the two walked into the town.

A low grunt to his right alerted Kathair to a rather large pig pen with a few sows inside. They were much larger than any pigs he had ever seen before, weighing several hundred pounds by the looks of them. "They're covered in a lot of hair," Kathair commented, noting the thick, curly hair covering them from snout to tail.

Wendin smiled. "Mangals," he said.

"They have a richer flavor than the pigs grown throughout most of the Middle Kingdom too," the guard at the gate called out.

Kathair looked back to the guard and waved to acknowledge him. "It's a bit weird seeing shaggy pigs." He was accustomed to the short-haired breeds, but had never imagined pigs that looked as though they were covered in sheep wool. "Can they use the hair for anything?" Kathair asked. Wendin must not have heard him, for he was already walking onward. Kathair hurried to catch up. They passed several more pigpens with large mangals inside. Several chickens roamed the dirt street, pecking at bugs here and there. There were also a fair amount of goats nibbling at the patches of grass. A few people meandered around the town, some fetching water from a well, others pulling and pushing hand-carts full of wood. None of them paid much attention to Kathair or Wendin, though.

When the two reached Magnus' cottage, they found a tall, blonde haired woman sitting outside on a stool while a young girl with curly dark hair played with a wooden doll nearby. The woman looked up at them, and then her blue eyes settled on Kathair and she gave a nod.

"I wondered when you would find us."

Kathair stopped and his brow drew into a knot above his nose. "You recognize me?"

The woman gave a sideways nod. "I can spot a northman easily enough, and I doubt any other northman would ever come looking for us."

Kathair looked to Wendin, but the large elf only gestured toward the woman with his hand. It seemed the talking would be left up to Kathair. "I have some questions," he said.

"Magnus will be home soon," the woman said. "He usually arrives home before dark. We can all talk then."

The little girl looked up and pointed at Kathair. "Boy!" she shouted with a giggle.

The blonde woman scooped up the child and nuzzled her. "Very good, Brenna, that is a boy," the woman said with a hint of amusement in her voice. She turned to Kathair and offered a mostly flat smile. "I am Alva. Come inside and rest your feet." She turned and pushed the door open. Wendin motioned for Kathair to go first.

Inside, the house smelled of lavender and honey. Braids of garlic hung from a ceiling beam, along with what Kathair assumed were various dried herbs. A single table occupied the main room of the house, situated near the stone hearth. In the back was a single bed big enough for the whole family to share. A chest sat at the foot of the bed, sealed with a heavy iron lock.

"Have a seat," Alva said as she moved to set Brenna on the bed. "I can put on some tea if you wish."

Wendin gave a nod.

"I have chamomile and mint, which would you prefer?"

"Chamomile," Wendin said.

Kathair nodded in agreement.

"We sweeten ours with honey," Alva said. She took a kettle to the fire and prepared the tea while they waited. She had only just poured the tea when the door opened and in walked a very large man holding a woodcutting axe over his left shoulder.

"Alva, I hear we have guests," Magnus said.

Kathair turned around to regard the man. He stood nearly as tall as the doorway itself, only barely clearing the top without ducking, though he did have to turn sideways to fit his shoulders. His dark hair was cut short, but he had a long beard held styled with a single braid from the chin, clipped with a silver ring.

"Magnus," Kathair said as he rose from his seat. "I am Kathair, the son of—"

"Yes, I know," Magnus said. "Your father was a dear friend of mine, and I have bounced you on my knee nearly as many times as I have Brenna." Magnus set his axe down and closed the distance between them in two strides. He reached out and placed his hands on either side of Kathair's jaw, turning the young man's head side to side, and then up. Kathair tensed, but Wendin seemed at ease, sipping his tea and hardly watching the interaction.

"What are you—"

"Just checking," Magnus said.

"For what?"

Magnus smiled and let his hands fall to Kathair's shoulders. "To see how you have grown since I last saw you. There used to be a wine-colored birthmark just under your chin, did you know that?"

Kathair shook his head.

"Well, glad to see you grew out of it; not everyone is so lucky." Magnus untied the collar of his shirt and opened it up to reveal a strawberry shaped mark just below his neck. "Here's mine. Brenna has one on her left shoulder, though it's fading. Alva used to have one right on—"

"Magnus Olferson, if you wish to live through the night you will stop right there."

Magnus' smile faded as his cheeks reddened. "Sorry love," he said. He turned back to Kathair and gave a wink. "Some are more sensitive about it than others. Anyway, I have been waiting for this day for a long time."

"Waiting?" Kathair said. "I thought you were hiding."

Magnus' smile disappeared altogether. "Northmen don't hide, Kathair Lepkin, and I trust that you won't repeat such a notion under this roof."

Kathair frowned. "It's just, we had to search for you. No one knew where you were."

"There's good reason for that," Alva cut in as she handed her husband a cup of tea.

Magnus looked at the tea and then set his cup on the table next to Kathair's. He walked around and took a seat with his back to the hearth. "We were there," he began. "We travelled with you, your father, mother, and another three families from our home village."

"What?" Kathair asked. "I didn't know there were so many northmen here in the Middle Kingdom. I only recently heard about you from Telstian. Where are the others?"

"Dead," Magnus said. The words resounded like thunder in the small cottage. Silence filled the room afterward for a few moments until Magnus sighed and shook his head. "We were attacked on the road. It was an ambush from the start. We were surrounded on all sides. Arrows dropped out of the sky without warning, and then the warriors charged us from the tall grasses. We had no idea they were there."

"Who were they?"

"Blacktongues," Magnus replied. "Vile, disgusting creatures who live only to murder and sow the seeds of chaos on this world. Some say they are cursed, that they gave up their ability to speak in exchange for inhuman strength and agility. Others say they are the offspring of Hatmul himself, the unholy union of the god of the underworld and an ogress. Whatever the truth is, they were too strong for us all." Magnus intertwined his fingers and rested his hands on the table. "Your father was the best warrior I had ever seen, and your mother as well. They fought valiantly, as did our brethren, but in the end they were cut down. Alva and I had been tasked with protecting you." Magnus reached out and placed a hand over Kathair's. "I didn't want to leave him, you must understand. He made me swear I would get you to safety." Tears welled in the big man's eyes and he shook his head, staring away from Kathair and clenching his jaw.

"The Blacktongues followed us for three days," Alva said. "If not for Telstian and his cohort of soldiers, we would have been overtaken." Magnus nodded and leaned back in his chair to wipe away the tears. Alva walked to him and cradled his head against her hip as she continued. "Telstian saved us all, but one of the Blacktongues escaped. Telstian was the one who thought it would be best for us to…"

Kathair nodded, understanding what she meant.

"We moved many times," Magnus said. "Big cities, small towns, and even camping in the mountains alone. We never stopped. Sometimes we were lucky, staying as long as a year or two before we were discovered. A few times we had to fight off a blacktongue or two, but we have managed to survive."

"Why did they attack?" Kathair asked.

"You don't know?" Magnus asked, his eyes wide.

Kathair shook his head. "Telstian said you would know."

Magnus looked to Alva, then back to Kathair. "Your father was supposed to become the Keeper of Secrets."

Kathair's mouth fell open.

Wendin leaned forward, setting his cup on the table and sliding it away. "Are you certain?"

Magnus nodded. "He received a letter from the priests at Valtuu Temple. That was the reason we came to this land. Each of the families that accompanied him were loyal to him. He was our chieftain. He told us to stay in the north country, but we couldn't abandon him. We had served his family for generations, and we would serve you now, should you wish it," Magnus said with a stoic nod.

Kathair shook his head. "Why didn't Telstian mention any of this?" He turned to Wendin. "Surely he must have known. If not at the time of the attack, then he would have learned it afterward."

"He did," Magnus said. "Though I suspect he sent you to us for another reason entirely."

Kathair leaned forward and set his hands on the table. "What other reason could there be?"

Magnus knitted his brow and looked at Kathair with deep, dark eyes. "Kathair, we were betrayed. Not only your father, but all of us."

"What do you mean?"

"Someone back home must have alerted the Blacktongues of your father's invitation. It was well known in our city."

Alva cut in. "A northman is responsible for the ambush."

Kathair sucked in a breath and looked to Wendin.

The elf gave a nod, and then took over. "We wish to bring those responsible for the murders to justice. Telstian sent several spies, but was never able to uncover the traitor's name. Do you know who is responsible?"

"I have an idea," Alva snarled.

Magnus nodded. "Malech Cridhe is the one I would suspect, though I have no proof."

"Where is this Malech?" Wendin inquired.

"In the north country. He never left, as far as we know."

Alva said, "Find Malech, and you will find clues to who he was working with. You can count on that."

"It had to be someone here in the Middle Kingdom, who else would care about who became the Keeper of Secrets?" Magnus said.

Kathair folded his arms and leaned back in his chair. "What do we do?" he asked Wendin.

"If you are going to go north, you will need our help," Magnus said. "Most people who go there travel by sea to the lowland beachhead, but then you would face the orcs. Even if you managed to get through their lands undetected, you would have to travel through the forest, and it's teeming with savage elves."

Wendin bristled. "We do not refer to them as elves," he said.

Magnus held up a hand. "No offense meant. That is just what we call them because of their pointy ears and affinity for bows and living in the woods."

Wendin arched a silver brow and took in a slow breath, but he didn't press the matter further.

"So how do we reach our destination?" Kathair asked.

Magnus sighed. "I had hoped you wouldn't take on the journey until you were a few years older. Even with our help it won't be easy."

"I am not afraid, and I have been raised to fight."

"Spoken as a true northman," Alva said.

"I have a map. We can use it to find a special place in the cliffs east of the lowland beaches. It will bring us close to our homeland, though it will still be within the forest where the savage el—" Magnus stopped himself. "Where there are still dangers," he corrected.

"That will do," Wendin said. "We leave at dawn."

Magnus looked to Wendin. "You can't go," he said. "Malech will see you coming from miles away. He'll disappear before we can reach him."

"Will he not recognize you?" Wendin countered.

"We will blend in better," Magnus said, pointing to himself and Kathair. "But, if you could take Alva and Brenna back to Tualdern—"

"I cannot," Wendin interrupted.

Magnus slapped the table. "Why not? Every time we asked Telstian for help he has refused! For the last many years he has left us on our own. Why not help us now?"

Wendin offered an understanding nod. "As I mentioned, we have sent many spies north in the years past. Many of them have perished. Telstian fears there may be a traitor among our own people as well."

"Oh—Icadion strike me down!" Magnus shouted. "Now you tell me?!" He jumped up to his feet and pushed Alva back from him. "We need to leave. It isn't safe here. If there is a spy in Tualdern, then we may already be discovered!"

"I assure you, we were not followed," Wendin said.

"That you know of," Magnus argued.

Wendin held up a hand. "I can escort you to Valtuu Temple. Alva and Brenna will be safe there."

Magnus turned and arched a brow. "The temple? They too have turned us away in the past."

"Telstian has made arrangements," Wendin said. "He is not without heart, and knows the sacrifice you have made, and those yet to come."

Magnus nodded. "Very well, but we should not stay here tonight. We should leave immediately."

"I can help you pack," Kathair offered.

Magnus shook his head. "No need, we always have our emergency packs ready." Magnus and Alva opened the chest at the foot of the bed, then pulled out two large backpacks and a strange looking harness that fit around Alva's front. Once the harness was secured, Brenna was set into it.

"We're ready now," Alva said.

"Let's move," Magnus added.

Wendin stood from the table and put his own backpack on again. "Very well."

"We travel alongside the roads, but not on them," Magnus directed. "No one should see us leave." He motioned for everyone to follow him. Kathair gathered his equipment and rushed to the back of the house. Magnus pushed a large armoire away from the wall and then undid a series of bolts and locks to reveal a secret door that led into a tunnel. "This will take us several hundred yards away from Lugtoliv, and open into the forest. From there we can head north without anyone noticing our departure."

Wendin nodded, and the group descended a flight of stairs and made their way into the tunnel.

Magnus led the way, followed by Alva, carrying Brenna, then Kathair. Wendin secured the doorway and brought up the rear. A musty dampness wafted up into Kathair's nostrils as they snaked through the narrow tunnel, guided by a small torch Magnus had ignited just after entering the underground passage. None of them spoke, not even Brenna. Alva cooed softly whenever the young girl fussed, but the only other sounds were those of their feet padding over the hard-packed earth. As Magnus had said, the tunnel ended at a flight of stairs several hundred yards from the house.

The large man went to the iron door and slipped a thick key into the lock. He turned it three times to the right, each revolution bringing with it the metallic scraping of bolts and clicking of gears. The iron door then opened outward to yet another door, this one made of wood with an iron plate set about eye-level. Magnus went to the second door and took hold of a small handle on the iron plate. With a pop of dust, the plate slid to the right, allowing Magnus to look out. Kathair couldn't see whether this door led to the outside or to yet another doorway, but Magnus closed the plate and gave a nod.

"No one has been inside. The seal on the outer chamber is still intact."

Alva breathed a sigh of relief and patted Brenna's back. "All right, my darling, time to be quiet now. We're going for another walk."

Kathair wondered to himself how many times Alva had said something similar to little Brenna throughout the years. While he had enjoyed safety and relative freedom, they had lived a life of secrets that he could not imagine, and it was all to protect him. "Magnus," Kathair called out.

Magnus opened the wooden door and turned back to Kathair. The two shared a look while Kathair tried to formulate the right words to convey his appreciation. Magnus smiled, as if feeling what Kathair wanted to say.

"It's all right, Kathair," Magnus said. "Everything is all right."

Kathair offered a smiling nod and then the group pushed into the outer chamber. Magnus moved up close to the third wooden door and inspected several strips of red silk ribbon that had been placed across the doorway so as to break if anyone had found and opened the door.

"Are they all intact?" Alva asked.

"They are," Magnus replied. He then turned to Wendin. "When I open this door, there will be a few boards just outside holding up dirt and mounds of grass that we put in place to conceal the entrance."

Wendin moved up close to the door while Alva and Kathair stood a few feet away. The door opened and just as Magnus had warned, an avalanche of wood, dirt, and grass fell through the doorway. Wendin and Magnus made quick work of the mess, clearing the path for the others, then they exited and found themselves on the east side of a rather large hill set deep in the thick of the forest. Magnus extinguished the torch and the group turned northward, navigating by moonlight.

*****

Tauron squatted upon a thick pine branch midway up the tree, scanning the village before him in the stillness of the night. Two guards stood at the gate, but only one of them was awake. The other was slumped over a table snoring. Tauron turned to his left, peering around the thick pine to another blacktongue. Seeing his gaze, she offered a nod, acknowledging that the time had come, and then leapt down to the ground below, and ran back to where the others waited. Tauron then readied his bow, a gnarled weapon crafted from layers of bone and wood. He nocked a two-pronged arrow to the string and took aim at the alert guard. He would be the first to die tonight, followed shortly thereafter by his lazy comrade.

The blacktongue commander aimed his arrow and took the shot. A faint, yet sharp whistle trailed after the double-pronged missile as it sailed across the sky to find its mark in the guard's left eye. The guard's head jerked backward, and then the man's knees faltered and his body collapsed into a heap. The slumbering guard caught Tauron's second arrow in the neck, his body jolting to the side before his arms fell limp.

Tauron dropped from his place in the tree and crept through the tall grass toward the gate. He didn't bother looking behind him for the others. He knew they would all be moving into position. Blacktongues were masters of infiltration, and unlike the rigid knights of the land who led their ranks by shouting orders and sounding trumpets, the blacktongues worked in silence, each fully capable of carrying out their tasks and changing with the needs of battle autonomously.

The commander sneered when he found the wooden gateway to be open. Not that a locked gate would have stopped them, but this was almost too easy. Tauron slipped through the gateway, his feet gliding silently over the dirt as he crept to the first house on his left. He tested the door and again found no lock between him and his prey. His right hand went down to grab his dagger, a wickedly curved blade with jagged serrations on the back that would make a mess of the largest of foes with a single stab. He pushed the door inward and found an elderly couple lying in bed. It wasn't the target he was sent for, but it made no difference. Each blacktongue had been assigned a series of houses to search, and the target would be found in one of them eventually. Until then, there could be no witnesses left behind who might alert neighboring villages to trouble if they found murder victims. Eventually some trader would arrive and discover what had transpired, but that would be several days away at least, and by then the Blacktongues would be long gone.

Tauron padded softly with his bare feet toward the sleeping couple. The firelight from the hearth danced upon the dark tattoos swirling over his forearm as he prepared to strike. Two quick thrusts and the elderly couple was sent into the next life. Their blood spilled out onto their mattress, quietly pooling between them.

The blacktongue commander then exited the home. Across the street he saw two blacktongues exiting other houses. They each saw him and gave a single horizontal slash of their left hands through the air. They hadn't found the target either. Tauron moved to the next house, finding a single man inside with a rather robust belly protruding from under a tunic that looked as though it had never really fit. He dispatched him and moved to the next house, and then the next. No alarm was raised as the blacktongues brought their work of death to the village, moving from home to home, leaving none alive.

At last, Tauron came to a house that was empty, though a lingering fire struggled to stay alive in the fireplace, sending thick smoke up through the chimney. Bowls and cups were on the table. Tauron lifted a cup to his nose and sniffed. *Chamomile tea.* His eyes darted around the house, taking in everything in a matter of seconds. The blankets on the bed were disordered, and there were a pair of wooden toys, a small horse and a pig, nearby on the floor. The target had been here.

Three other blacktongues entered the house.

Tauron ignored them and went to a large armoire, noticing that it wasn't fully sitting against the wall. Scuff marks along the floor appeared fresh as he bent down and wiped a tattooed finger across them. He stood and twisted the armoire away from the wall, revealing a large door with several locks. A grin stretched his thin lips. He went to work with his lockpick tools as the other blacktongues gathered around him. Within half a minute, he had the door open and was stepping into an open stairway leading to a dark tunnel. His grin widened and his heart pumped faster. *Perhaps this will be an enjoyable hunt after all.*

Chapter 5

Several hours after Kyra and Mindaugas had bid farewell to Al and left Buktah, Mindaugas suggested they stop for lunch. Having skipped breakfast in favor of getting a jump on the day, Kyra happily obliged, leading her horse off the side of the rode into a small clearing filled with ferns. Mindaugas pulled out a fistful of jerky, which was hardly anywhere near the total amount he had purchased from the butcher in Buktah, thanks to Kyra's enchantment put on his saddlebag.

"Have you ever tried elk?" Mindaugas asked.

Kyra shook her head. "No."

Mindaugas handed her a piece of the leathery meat and watched eagerly. "Go on, taste it. You'll love it."

Kyra took a bite and began chewing. It wasn't as tough as she had anticipated. It had a slight gaminess to it, but not overwhelmingly so. In fact, it was rather pleasant the more she allowed the flavor to wash over her tongue. "It's good," she said with a nod. She took another bite.

"I have three whole pounds of elk," Mindaugas said. "I love the stuff. I have other kinds too: deer, beef, he even had some turkey." Mindaugas shoveled a whole piece into his mouth at once and began chewing sloppily while rummaging around in his saddle bag for the rolls he had purchased from a baker. He came up with two perfectly golden, albeit a tad squished, rolls. He offered one to Kyra and then scooted back to lean against the trunk of a tall tree while he ate. "So," he said once his mouth was clear. "Where did you go last night?"

Kyra stopped chewing and swallowed hard. "I…" What was she supposed to say? She stole books from the man she had known as her father for nearly all her life? Or perhaps that she was only trespassing so she could find the spell to unlock her ancestral home that had been obtained from Lord Caspin by leveraging the man? Perhaps if she mentioned that Master Orres and Headmaster Herion had helped her secure certain promises and possessions from Lord Caspin that might go over better, but before she could decide how to explain, Mindaugas jumped in for her.

Mindaugas smiled. "Don't worry," he said. "I'm not here to judge you, but I do want to keep you safe. You should tell me where you go, especially if it's far away, or dangerous."

Kyra sighed. "Caspin Manor," she said.

Mindaugas' smile melted into a slight frown. "I thought he disowned you recently."

Kyra nodded. "He owes me a few things," she said. "Or, at least he did. I went to retrieve them."

"That's where you got all those books, am I right?" Mindaugas laughed and waved the notion away before she could answer. "That's not really any of my business. I was never any good at familial relations myself. I ever tell you I have two brothers?"

Kyra shook her head.

Mindaugas took a bite, chewed a few times, and then swallowed so he could continue. "Two brothers who haven't spoken to me in over twenty years. Not even at our mother's funeral."

"I'm sorry," Kyra offered.

"Don't be." Mindaugas shrugged. "They never really understood me, and I never cared to listen to their pig-headed world views. In any case, all I am trying to say is that if you think Lord Caspin owes you some books on top of everything else, I would understand. Just, don't try and sneak off next time, understand?"

"All right," Kyra said. "But I plan on using the portal again tonight."

"He owe you more books?" Mindaugas asked.

"No, but I haven't finished searching my mother's study. I'm looking for...something."

Mindaugas arched a brow and took another bite of elk jerky.

"I'm not trying to cause any trouble," Kyra clarified.

Mindaugas grinned. "As you say." He took another bite and leaned his head back against the tree, closing his eyes while he chewed. "Too bad you can't conjure us a portal to get to Valtuu Temple quicker."

Kyra smiled. "I have to know the place well enough to envision it in my mind and anchor the portal at both sides. Without a direct memory, I can't make the connection."

Mindaugas shrugged. "Oh well, I suppose a bit of horseback riding through the country won't be terrible either." He winked and tore off another hunk of jerky.

They spent another ten minutes resting and eating their fill before mounting their horses and resuming their journey. They traveled until an hour after dark, and then spent the night in a cave Mindaugas knew of. The Keeper of Secrets set up a few defensive traps at the entrance and then kept watch for another hour while Kyra returned to her mother's study to search for a way to unlock her manor. Mindaugas called to her through the portal before she was able to discover anything of use. As she had promised, she returned through the portal and the two went to the back of the cave and got into their bedrolls.

The next day the two of them spent another seven hours on horseback before they finally came around a bend and emerged from the forest to see a tall structure in the distance, surrounded by a great wall. The central tower was styled like a pagoda reaching toward the sky.

"Is that Valtuu Temple?" Kyra asked.

Mindaugas nodded. "It most certainly is."

"It's beautiful," Kyra said.

Mindaugas nodded. "It's one of my favorite places in all of the Middle Kingdom."

The thick outer walls of white stone rose up, topped with battlements enclosed by a green tile roof. At each corner a square tower rose from the ground, half again as tall as the wall, with red and gold flags flying over them. Kyra could see that each corner of the pagoda style roof on the tower was fashioned into the head of a dragon. She looked beyond the wall to the tower in the center and guessed by the number of stories that it stood at least seventy feet high.

"I can see why you like it so much, it's amazing. I've never seen anything like it."

"And, if you like books, then the library will more than satisfy your thirst for knowledge. It has all sorts of books on magic; anything you could ever want to know." Mindaugas prodded his horse gently and pumped his eyebrows once. "Race you to the bottom of the hill. First one to that sign post just before the gate wins."

Kyra grinned and kicked her horse into a gallop. The horse sprinted down the road toward the gate. She leaned down low, holding tight as she pulled away from Mindaugas. The thought crossed her mind that if she could use magic to make things lighter, she could use a similar spell to make Mindaugas feel heavier to his horse. She turned and whispered the words to just such a spell and then grinned as her lead grew with each passing second.

If one spell was good, then two would be better. Kyra grinned and summoned a tailwind while making herself feel lighter to her own horse. Soon she was more than ten yards ahead of the Keeper of Secrets. Trees whipped by on either side and the stale air took on a fresh quality as her hair flew backward. The horse deftly avoided a brown puddle in the road and then leapt over a small bit of brush covering part of a fallen log as she solidified her lead and eased into a less grueling gallop.

"You're using magic!" Mindaugas shouted from a ways back.

Kyra shook her head and laughed. "No need!" she shouted over her shoulder. The priests might have known she was lying, but Mindaugas would have no way of proving it. Within seconds she turned her horse to the left at the signpost. "I win!"

As she came closer she could see more detail built into the walls and the tower. The outside walls were not plain white, as she had thought. She could now see yellow, white, gray, and even a few darker stones set into the wall. Within a few seconds she realized that the colored stones were set in a weaving pattern that nearly resembled a serpent slithering along the wall.

"I still say you cheated!" Mindaugas shouted as he reached the sign post and turned down the short road leading toward the large double doors.

Kyra ignored him, intrigued now by the temple itself. She noticed many protrusions on the doors themselves. They weren't spikes like she had seen in Buktah, but large, round bumps of metal that almost looked like the tops of helmets. "Strange," she commented aloud. "What purpose do those serve?"

"Some people touch them for good luck," Mindaugas said as his horse came to a stop near the door on the left. He reached out and slapped one of the black knobs. "Perhaps the next time we race I'll make sure to get some extra luck."

Kyra laughed. "Luck has nothing to do with it. My horse is fast, and I'm lighter."

Mindaugas nodded and hopped down from his horse. "Not to mention your magic."

Kyra shrugged. "I don't know what you're talking about."

"Wait here a moment," he instructed. "I'll get a priest to verify your claims." Mindaugas chuckled, obviously pleased with himself. Then he turned and opened the door on the left, sticking his head through for a moment to look around before entering the temple grounds, closing the door behind himself.

Kyra looked up to the battlements on the walls, but saw no one. She then inspected the towers, but again saw no one. "Maybe they're all inside eating." She reached down and patted her horse's head. After a couple of minutes, the doors opened and Mindaugas stepped out, walking next to a priest that she didn't recognize.

The priest was shorter than her, perhaps just over five feet tall, but the white beard beneath his bald, liver-spotted head told her he was far older than either her or Mindaugas. The priest stopped and tilted his head, letting his gray, sightless eyes settle upon her.

"This one has a strong aura," the priest said.

Mindaugas nodded. "She will be a great ally in our fight against those that seek the book.

The priest narrowed his eyes and reached up to stroke his beard. "There is something else," he said.

Kyra stiffened in the saddle. She knew the priest could see the part of her that was different, the energy gifted to her by her vampire father. Would he judge her for something beyond her control?

"The prelate will want to see her himself," the priest said quickly. He moved toward Kyra and stretched out his arms. He took her left hand gently and clasped it warmly in his hands. "Miss Dimwater, my name is Sal Vinder. I am one of the high priests here at Valtuu Temple. Please, allow me to extend my warmest welcome to you."

Kyra nodded, but remained silent. Despite his greeting, she was still unsettled by the way he had looked at her. "Will the prelate feel the same?" Kyra asked pointedly.

Sal smiled and helped her down from her saddle before releasing her hand. "Yes, I believe he will, however, not all of the other priests will. Though it pains me to say it, I cannot hide the truth from you for that is against my nature. Many of the younger priests will see you as a threat." Sal took in a breath and shrugged. "Many of them have been training and studying for years and they will recognize the difference in you. However, they are not yet enlightened enough to know that a person's genealogy does not account for character. Just as there are many who would categorize different races as better or worse than others, some of the priests here will judge you to be unworthy. However that is neither your fault, nor problem. Let weak minds think what they will, and you focus on your mission."

Kyra smiled, finding Sal's honesty refreshing. "What do you see?" She reached over with her other hand and put it atop Sal's. "You said you see something different. What did you mean, then, if you do not see me as unworthy?"

Sal smiled wider and gave a single nod. "Because of my gift of True Sight, I can see all that swirls within your aura. I can see the colors of your moods and thoughts, the truthfulness of your words, and I see that you have equal parts from two races. More than that, I can see the magic that runs through your life energy. I see the power stemming from your human mother, and I can see the strength flowing from your vampire father. But do not worry. I will judge you only by your actions and integrity, as I am sure you will judge me the same."

"You aren't scared?" Kyra pressed.

Sal shook his head. "As I said, I can see your intentions before you ever voice them. You bear no ill will toward me, nor anyone that I can see. So no, I do not fear you. Now come, I will send someone to tend to the horses. They are not permitted on temple grounds inside the walls, but they will be well cared for."

Kyra turned back and reached to unfasten her bag full of books. Mindaugas grabbed his saddle bag of jerky, which he had somehow managed to empty of all but two pieces despite the large quantity that it had contained thanks to her spell. He looked inside, his hand scraping the bottom, and took out one of the last pieces to chew on.

The three walked up a set of stone steps and into the temple. Sal and Mindaugas talked of his recent journeys, giving an accounting of various investigations that the Keeper of Secrets had conducted before returning to Kuldiga Academy for Kyra. While they spoke, Kyra took in the grand murals in the large ante chamber. She knew enough history to recognize the battle of Hamath Valley. The painted images depicted the horror well, with humans and dragons on both sides of the bloody conflict. Wizards cast spells and dragons breathed their fire as human and dwarf warriors fought on the green fields below.

"It was supposed to be our final victory," Sal said, pulling Kyra from her thoughts. "But we could not stop the power of Nagar's Blight. The best we could do was destroy his army and take the source of his power from him."

Kyra turned to Sal. "You can see the painting? I thought you could only see auras."

Sal held his arms out to his sides. "The paint used in these murals is infused with a magical essence, allowing us to see even more than the colors and images you see. We can hear the cries of battle, and feel the loss of death."

Kyra frowned. "Every time you walk through this room?"

Sal nodded. "This is hallowed ground, Miss Dimwater. The temple is built upon the very spot where Hiasyntar'Kulai, the Father of the Ancients, lay bleeding after the Battle of Hamath Valley. It was here that he made the decision for all remaining dragons to leave the Middle Kingdom until Nagar's Blight could be defeated, thus making it safe for dragons once more. It was then that our order was born. Those of us who continue the fight should never forget what has already transpired, lest we become slothful in our duties to prepare for that which is yet to come." Sal turned back around and continued walking through the ante chamber. Kyra hurried to catch up with the others, wondering what it might be like to hear and feel the awfulness of war instead of seeing just a painting. Ultimately, she was glad her other senses could not partake of the sorrow.

They wound their way through a couple of corridors before being shown to living quarters.

"We do not have a lot to offer in the way of luxury," Sal began, "but we have everything you will need."

"Thank you, Sal," Mindaugas said. "This will do fine."

"We have taken the liberty of bringing in a partition to divide the room for more privacy," Sal said, pointing to a large folding partition set near the center of the room.

Mindaugas frowned. "I'm sorry, but there are plenty of rooms in the temple. Can't she have an adjoining room that would afford her privacy?"

Kyra watched as Sal's smile faded. "I will bring it up with the prelate once more, but my understanding is that the high priests were concerned about allowing her too much privacy."

"She is not dangerous to anyone here," Mindaugas said, his usually calm demeanor turning hard.

Sal bowed his head. "Keeper, it is not my place to override the prelate, but perhaps you can speak with him."

"I intend to," Mindaugas said. "She is to be treated as a guest, and a friend."

Sal nodded and inclined his head even further. "If it were up to me, I would have already furnished a private room for each of you, I assure you."

Mindaugas sighed and nodded as his hardened expression melted. "I know you would, Sal. Sorry, I shouldn't take it out on you, but I am not happy about this."

Kyra, already conscious of the trouble her presence was causing, jumped in. "It's all right, Mindaugas. I don't mind."

Mindaugas looked at her and folded his arms. "At least have a few more partitions sent in."

Sal nodded. "Of course."

"Kyra, go ahead and get yourself situated. There are a few things I need to discuss with Sal, and the prelate. With any luck, I will have a new room prepared for you by the time I return, if not sooner. Then, perhaps later today we can go to the library."

"That sounds good," Kyra replied. "I have a few books I can read until then."

Mindaugas and Sal exited, closing the door behind them.

Kyra set her bag of book onto the bed meant for her and began pulling out the categorized bags within. When she found the one she wanted, she opened the bag and reached inside to find a book entitled *Planes and those who Walk Them*. "All right," Kyra said to herself. "Let's see what kind of ideas this one has." She cleared space on the bed and then jumped onto it, tucking her legs under herself. Hoping she could find something, anything, that might help Leatherback, she spent the next two hours reading about various planes and dimensions tied to Terramyr. Some promised ruin and death, while others were fabled to hold vast treasures. Most of them were categorized as being too difficult for a mortal to find. Some of them, like the Astral Plane and the Plane of the Dead, she had heard of before, but neither of those would provide refuge for Leatherback. She needed to find a place for him that would provide everything a dragon needs to survive: food, open skies, and freedom from Nagar's Blight.

She continued reading through the pages until she came upon a section about Viverandon, the mythical home of the Satyrs. At once she became excited, for she hadn't seen Njar during her final encounter with Severin, despite the fact that Njar had promised to be there. Worse still, she hadn't seen him at all afterward either, nor even received a message from him. She feared he was injured somewhere, or perhaps trapped. Whatever the case was, she had a sickeningly heavy feeling in the pit of her stomach whenever she thought of him.

The book spoke of Nonac, a great tree that guarded the way into the peaceful lands controlled by the satyrs. According to the book, Nonac was sentient, and could not only use its limbs and roots to attack would-be intruders, but it kept a history of Viverandon and the satyrs. Its leaves could be used in balms and ointments, as well as in rituals to portend the future in some cases. Yet, despite these interesting facts, there was no mention of how to get past Nonac. There was a brief mention of a password rumored to be used by those deemed worthy enough to be called friends of the satyr, but the author of the book bluntly stated that they not only didn't know the password, but they doubted its existence as no human had ever reported finding the place.

"Sorry, Njar," Kyra said as she finished the section on Viverandon. "Perhaps I will find better clues in the library here. I'll find you though, I promise."

*****

Asteri, a young satyr with white fur, stood outside Njar's home. The sky above her seemed alight with red and orange hues that were unnatural to the otherwise controlled climate within Viverandon. A harsh wind blew in from the west, carrying with it the blackened leaves that fell from Nonac. Her father, a large brown-furred satyr with broad shoulders and thick arm muscles that would make even the largest of humans envious, emerged from the house and shook his head.

"He hasn't returned," he said. "There has been no trace of him for several weeks now."

Asteri nodded. "Father, I am ready," she said.

"No, not yet, perhaps the others will find something. Nikilaus is trying to meditate, calling upon Mother Terramyr for guidance."

It was the first time Asteri had ever heard fear in her father's voice. "I will be all right," she insisted. "But I have to go."

"Njar should be the one to go."

Asteri stepped in close and embraced her father. "I will be careful."

"At least let me come with you," her father said.

Asteri shook her head. "No, father. You must stay here. Without Nonac's protection, we are vulnerable. You must stay and lead the warriors in case of attack."

Her father snorted.

"I am the restorer, and so the duty falls to me." She almost let it slip that Njar had told her of the dragon he had helped a young human girl tend to in the forests of the Middle Kingdom. Not telling him created knots in her stomach whenever his eyes locked on hers, but telling him would be much worse.

"The only remedy for Nonac is found far in the northern country. It is not a safe place."

"And yet, if I do not go now, Viverandon may lose the ability to hide itself."

"But you cannot go alone!"

"Father, you know that I must. The cure rests in the ancient tomb of the great trees. Only the one chosen as the restorer can enter, and I will have an easier time being undiscovered if I go alone. I will have to travel through some human lands on my journey, and some orcish lands as well."

"That is precisely why I should go with you, or at least someone should."

"Father… no other satyr can blend in the way I can."

Her father grunted and gave a single nod. "Very well, Asteri. Go. Fulfill your duties, but be quick. If you are not back in three months, then I will lead the warriors to your rescue."

Asteri squeezed him harder and then broke off to return home and gather her supplies. Three months would give her just enough time. First, she would go to the grove Njar had spoken of, and then after she had determined his fate, she would travel to the ancient tomb to find Nonac's cure. She could only hope that the dragon Njar had so often told her about had not succumbed to Nagar's Blight and attacked him. She could deal with humans and orcs, but a dragon was something entirely different. A chill ran down her spine as she thought about how easily a dragon might make a meal of her. She pushed the thought away as she stuffed the last of her equipment into her bag.

She lifted it up and then closed her large, golden eyes. A portal opened in front of her, displaying a green field dotted with yellow flowers. A mist gathered around her body, changing her furry form to that of a human woman in her twenties. Since the spell was mostly an illusion, she felt no pain as the magic completed its work. Her real form remained as it always was, but no one would see her true self. Even if she looked into her reflection she would now see a blonde haired woman staring back at her. No other satyr could perform this kind of magic, for it was a special power passed down from restorer to restorer, to use only in times of great desperation.

Asteri took in a breath, trying to steady her nerves before stepping through the portal.

This was a time of great desperation.

Chapter 6

Kathair and the others stopped for camp just as the sun was dropping from the sky. They had marched through the forest at a grueling pace all through the night, and without so much as stopping for breakfast or lunch. Brenna had eaten a couple of hard biscuits and dried fruit, and almost appeared oblivious to everything around her except for the fact that that her big bright eyes kept glancing through the trees and she hardly made a sound except once to cough and another time to ask for more fruit. Kathair and the others had eaten similar bits of food while continuing their escape.

The group's pace never slowed, despite crossing several streams and winding through thick patches of trees and underbrush. Kathair nearly had trouble keeping up, and was surprised to see that even Wendin seemed impressed by their endurance. Wendin once offered to carry Brenna, but Alva wouldn't have it, insisting on carrying the young child herself. Magnus and Alva hadn't even begun to breathe heavily when the group made their way up into the foothills for the night, a testament not only to northman strength, but also to the hard life they had lived since arriving with Kathair's father.

"Kathair, come here," Magnus said. The large man pulled a small hand shovel from his backpack and held it out. "Dig a hole, twelve inches in diameter and two feet down."

Kathair took the shovel and did as he was told, stabbing the tool into the soft earth and stirring up old pine needles, beetles, and bits of fibers from bushes long dead. Magnus then went to work cutting a long, slender sapling and removing the sprouting branches. He fashioned the tip to a point while Kathair continued digging. Once satisfied with the tool, Magnus started thrusting the makeshift spear into the ground at an angle from a few feet away, digging toward Kathair's hole.

"What are you doing?"

"Firelight can be seen from far away if it's set atop the ground. However, if you dig a pit for us to build a fire in, the light will be contained, but we need air to get to it, and that's what my hole will provide."

"I will go and find us meat," Wendin said. The elf didn't wait for anyone to respond. He turned and disappeared into the trees easier than a doe might vanish from view.

"He's a good friend," Magnus said.

"Not really a friend," Kathair said. "More of a servant for Telstian, but he is kind and thoughtful enough."

Alva came near and dropped a pile of wood near Kathair. "I'm going to set Brenna here," she said. "There is a stream nearby. I'll get some fresh water."

Magnus nodded and shot his wife a smile. "Don't be gone long," he said, letting his eyes linger on her form as she turned and walked away. The large man noticed Kathair watching him and blushed just enough to turn his cheeks a slight pink. "She is a wonderful woman," he said.

Kathair smiled and finished hollowing out the pit. He reached for some wood, but Magnus told him to wait until the air shaft had been connected to the pit. Brenna picked up a stick and swung it playfully at a nearby bark beetle. Kathair took up another piece of wood and softly tapped Brenna's.

"Careful, she may be small, but she—"

Magnus' warning came too late. Brenna stood up and whacked Kathair across the shoulder, and then chopped down on his hand.

"Ouch!" Kathair said, pulling away and rubbing the red spot on his hand. "I yield!" He dropped his stick and put his hands up.

Brenna smiled and held her stick up victoriously. She then turned and ran to her father. The big man scooped her up into a hug.

"Did you beat that big old kid over there?" Magnus said, nuzzling her with his nose. "That's my girl!"

Kathair walked over and took Magnus' digging stick and finished the air shaft while the big man played with his daughter and started teaching her the names of trees and bushes. His manner was much softer than Telstian had ever been with Kathair, but then perhaps that was the difference between a familial bond and that of an adoptive parent. That, or maybe it was because Telstian was an elf. Whatever it was, Kathair wished he had known his own father. He had come to like Magnus quite quickly, and couldn't help but imagine that his own father would have been similar.

After the fire pit was finished, Kathair went about arranging the wood to fit within the pit and lit the fire, careful not to let the flames rise higher than the hole was deep. He continued to break apart smaller sticks and bits of wood until he had the beginnings of a thick bed of embers to cook upon. Then, he stood up and brushed himself off.

"Kathair, go and see if Alva is ready with the water," Magnus said.

Kathair turned and walked in the direction he had seen the woman walk. He followed a narrow game trail through the woods and around a thicket of tall thorny bushes before finding the wide stream Alva had spoken of. He looked up and down the stream, but didn't see her. He checked the ground for tracks and found her footprints near the water's edge leading higher into the foothills, and followed them. After a quarter mile he came to a sizeable pool, held in place by a combination of natural elevation leading to a choke-point and a beaver's dam that reduced the outlet's flow.

He heard the splashing of water and looked toward the center of the pool where Alva rose from the water. Her long, blonde hair was slicked back over her head and shoulders. Kathair blushed and turned away before the rest of her emerged from the water.

"I'm sorry," he said. "Magnus sent me to help with the water."

"It's all right, Kathair," Alva called out. "I am covered, you can turn around. The waterskins are near my backpack. Fetch my cloak from the pack and then you can take the waterskins back."

Kathair tried to use his peripheral vision to locate her belongings. He dared not turn around as she had said, for clothed or not he still felt he had intruded upon something he shouldn't. He kept his eyes to the ground and walked toward the backpack. He dug inside for the overcloak and then stood up and held it out. He could hear Alva splashing through the water and coming toward him.

"Kathair, I have my undergarments on. Magnus wouldn't have sent you if I was indecent."

Kathair nodded, but kept his eyes to the ground. "I should hurry with the water," he said. He felt her pull the cloak from his grasp, and only then did he feel comfortable. "The fire is already going hot, and Wendin went out for some food. I suspect he should be back very soon."

"That is good," Alva said. "Before you take the water, you should know that I am impressed by the young man you have grown into," she added. "I knew your father well and see much of him in you."

"What was he like?" Kathair asked, turning around and facing her.

She smiled, reaching up to squeeze the water out of her hair. "Kind, fiercely loyal, and smart—smarter than any northman I ever knew besides."

Kathair smiled and opened his mouth to ask another question, but something caught his eye on the other side of the pool. He couldn't be certain, but he almost thought it was a person. He leaned to the side, peering around Alva, but he saw nothing there, not even a shivering branch or other sign of disturbance. The young man's ears twitched, catching a faint whistling sound.

Alva stumbled forward and the whistling stopped with a sudden *thabump*.

Kathair reached out to steady her, but she pushed him away with wild eyes. "Go! RUN!"

Kathair drew his sword and moved to step around her, his eyes scanning the forest for danger. Alva reached for his sword and twisted it from his hand.

"I said RUN! Warn the others!"

Another whistle sailed toward them. This time, Kathair shoved Alva to the left, saving her from a second arrow that only narrowly missed him before sinking into a nearby tree, popping the bark off in several directions. Alva pushed Kathair with a strength that seemed impossible for her size, sending him several yards back.

A figure dropped from a tree overhead. Kathair noted the tattoos covering the man's mostly-naked body. The black, swirling symbols seemed to pulse with a dark energy that put a knot into the pit of Kathair's stomach. Alva cut the man down with Kathair's sword. The woman then glared at Kathair with eyes that implored him to run. Several more tattooed figures appeared on the other side of the pool as Alva pulled a crossbow from inside her backpack and turned to give them battle.

Kathair wanted to stay, but he knew she was right. Not only were they outnumbered, but he could see the black arrow shaft protruding from her back. He doubted she would live much longer no matter what he did. The only thing he could do now was make sure that Magnus and Brenna survived the attack. He turned and ran as fast as his feet would carry him through the forest. He tore through bushes, ignored slapping branches that left stinging welts over his arms and face, and barreled over a large hill until he nearly stumbled his way back into the camp.

By the time he reached the firepit, Magnus was standing with sword in hand and nearly chopped Kathair in half.

"Where's Alva?!" Magnus shouted.

Kathair could hardly breathe, let alone respond verbally. He thumbed over his shoulder. "Ambush…men…with…tattoos."

"Blacktongues!" Magnus started to push past Kathair, but Wendin appeared around a tree and stopped the large man in his tracks.

"Three more coming from the south, nearly upon us." Wendin's scimitar was not only out, but dripping with dark crimson blood.

"ALVA!" Magnus cried out.

A blacktongue jumped out from a pair of trees on the other side of camp, rushing toward Kathair with a hand axe and dagger at the ready.

Magnus turned on his heels and let out a yell that echoed off the pines and hills around them. The large man intercepted the blacktongue, cutting the man's left arm off with one swing of his sword and then leaning into a powerful headbutt that knocked the wiry blacktongue to the ground. Magnus quickly flipped his sword in his hands and drove the point down into the blacktongue's chest.

Wendin moved to engage a second blacktongue. His scimitar clashed angrily against the blacktongue's blades. Kathair watched, almost in a daze, for he had never seen swords move so quickly. The blades blurred through the air, neither fighter able to score a hit on the other.

The rustling of leaves and branches forced Kathair to turn around.

A tall, thin woman came toward him. Like the others, she was covered in tattoos and wore only enough clothing to cover the essentials. A thick, black tattoo striped across her mouth, giving her white teeth an eerie quality as she sneered.

Kathair reached for his sword, but only then realized that it was at the pool with Alva. He looked around frantically, seeing only the sapling they had used to tunnel the air shaft to the firepit. He seized it and readied himself as the woman rushed him with a pair of daggers. Kathair flipped the thick sapling around, leveling the dirt-smeared tip at the blacktongue and trying to study her movements.

She was wild, animal-like, as she struck out with savage swings and danced around Kathair's slow parries. He only just managed to keep her out of striking distance, but she was quicker than him, and would easily end his life if he made a mistake.

Out of the corner of his eyes, Kathair noticed two more blacktongues rushing the camp. Magnus engaged them both, and Wendin was still fighting the other. There would be no help for Kathair. He was on his own, using a makeshift spear that he didn't have sufficient training in, though he doubted it would hold up for long anyhow.

The blacktongue woman sliced and hacked at the spear, jarring Kathair to the side and nearly bringing him within reach of her deadly blades. Her ghostly smile widened with each passing second. Kathair stabbed forward, missing as the lithe woman dodged to the side. She answered with a series of quick thrusts and slices that wrenched the spear from Kathair's hands. She stepped forward and landed a solid barefoot kick on the young man's chest, sending him backward into a thick pine trunk.

Then, just as the blacktongue advanced to finish the fight, Brenna jumped from nearby bushes and hurled a small rock. It struck the blacktongue without any real damage whatsoever, and then Brenna shouted nearly as loudly as her father had, and raised the very same stick she had used to hit Kathair earlier. The blacktongue turned toward the child and snarled. She took only a single step forward before Kathair sprang into action. A fire welled up in the young man's chest, giving him strength and speed he had hitherto been unaware of possessing. Somehow, he slipped past the blacktongue's daggers and tackled the woman to the ground. His left hand snatched her right wrist and drove her arm down, pinning a dagger to her breast as he sat up and pummeled her with his right fist. She lashed out with her free hand, but the dagger only grazed Kathair's chest as he ducked backward. Then he leaned forward, pressing the pinned hand down harder so that the blade in the blacktongue's right hand bit into her flesh. She let out a scream, and then Kathair grabbed her free hand and pushed it down until he had both her hands crossed over her chest. She snarled and fought back with everything she could, but Kathair had her overpowered. Brenna disappeared back into the bushes and a moment later there was a quick flash of silver that removed the blacktongue's head from her shoulders. The woman's strength went out from her body and Kathair jumped back to see Wendin standing over them both.

"The fight is over," the elf said.

Kathair looked over to Magnus to see the man inspecting a slice across his left arm, with three blacktongues lying dead at his feet.

"I have to find Alva," Magnus said.

Wendin sheathed his scimitar and helped Kathair to his feet.

"I'll watch Brenna, you go with Magnus," Wendin said.

Kathair went with the northman through the forest and back up to the pool. Kathair could hardly keep up with the man as he sprinted through the bushes and around the trees, calling out for his wife the whole way up to the pool.

The two emerged from the tree line to find Alva kneeling over two blacktongues, their bodies twisted from battle and spilling blood across the ground.

"ALVA!" Magnus dropped his sword and ran to her, nearly bowling her over as he crashed to the ground beside her, skidding on his knees and wrapping his arms around her. "Alva! I'm here, I'm here."

Kathair stopped and watched from a few yards away, scanning the pool and trees for any additional blacktongues.

"I stopped these…" Alva said weakly. "Others followed Kathair…"

"I know," Magnus said, his face streaming with tears as he gently rocked his dying wife. "We got the others. It's all right now. It's over."

Alva reached up with a bloody hand and caressed Magnus' cheek. "I was lucky to have you," she said.

"I'm the lucky one," Magnus choked out through his tears. "Stay with me, Alva."

Alva shook her head and leaned into the big man's chest. "It's all right," she said. "It's my time."

"No!" Magnus cried.

"Take care of our little girl." Alva said.

"Not without you!" Magnus said.

Alva tilted her head back and looked up at him. "Promise me."

Magnus shook his head as the tears stole his ability to speak.

"Promise…" Alva insisted.

Magnus sniffled and swallowed. "I promise."

Alva smiled and leaned back into his chest.

Kathair watched as the few seconds seemed to stretch into hours, and then her hand grew weak and slid from Magnus' cheek, leaving a thin double trail of blood along his skin. Magnus cried and held his wife tighter to his body, and then he looked up to the heavens and shouted something in the ancient northman tongue that Kathair no longer understood. The two of them remained at the pool for a long while before Magnus found the strength to stand. Neither of them said a word. Kathair gathered the backpack and waterskins, and Magnus carried his wife's body back to camp.

Kathair watched, with tears filling his eyes, as Brenna tried to wake her mother, failing to understand what her father was trying to explain. After a while, Wendin put the harness on his chest, placed Brenna in it, and then went for a walk outside of camp, giving Magnus the time he needed to tend to his wife's body. Kathair, knowing the traditions of his people, went to work locating several birch trees and cutting them down by torchlight as the moon rose high into the sky. After limbing three trees, he had what he needed to build a respectable pyre. He cut through the logs at the halfway point, and then again cutting the smaller halves in two so that he had nine birch logs. He arranged them into a pyre, and then placed the limbs around the stacked logs.

When he returned, he found that Wendin and Brenna were tucking into their bedrolls, and Wendin was telling the young child a story about how the stars were made. Magnus sat beside his wife's body, with her cloak covering her for the night. Kathair couldn't fall asleep for hours, and doubted whether Magnus slept at all, but when the morning finally came he helped Magnus with the final preparations. Magnus laid Alva's body atop the birch pyre and Kathair gathered some additional dry wood, placing it around the base.

Kathair then lit the torches they would use to start the fire, and waited for Magnus to speak. By tradition, it was his right to speak the final prayers, but the man stood there in silence, staring at his wife's face while holding her lifeless hand.

"She was my everything," Magnus said after a while.

Kathair remained quiet, not wanting to insult the man, or Alva, by saying anything inappropriate.

Magnus turned to Kathair and put a hand on the lad's shoulder. "It isn't your fault, you know," he said as his watery eyes locked with Kathair's.

Kathair felt his stomach sink into the ground below him. He hadn't even considered his part in Alva's death. Only now, as her loyal husband was offering forgiveness, did Kathair realize that it was, in fact, his fault. Had he not come searching for them, she would still be alive. Brenna would still have her mother, and Magnus would still be working and making a living for them in the village, safe and hidden away from the blacktongues.

"Kathair," Magnus said, jolting Kathair from his thoughts. "It is not your fault. Do you hear me?"

Kathair shook his head. "I…" his words failed him. He couldn't bring himself to voice what he felt.

"The blacktongues are responsible for this, and they alone shall be blamed."

Kathair tore his face away and looked down to the ground as tears welled in his eyes. "No, if I hadn't come…"

Magnus placed a hand on either shoulder, turning Kathair back to him. "The blacktongues attacked us long before, and stole your parents from you. Now they have come again, and stolen my fair Alva from me. Do not let a wedge of grief drive us apart. We are northmen, and we must band together now."

Kathair could hardly believe what Magnus was saying. How could the man not blame him?

"Kathair, we must be as one blade, forged in the losses we have suffered, and ready to stab at the heart of these wicked men." Magnus took the torches from Kathair and turned to the pyre. "If the All-father is listening, then let Icadion bless us with the strength we need to avenge the fallen. Let not their innocent blood lie in the earth, crying helplessly while those responsible for their suffering go unpunished." Magnus lit the base of the pyre and then lifted his head to the heavens. "Icadion, send Nagé to collect Alva's spirit, for she is more pure than any other soul to have lived upon Terramyr. Let not the gates to Bifrost remain closed to her. Allow her passage, so she may rest in the halls of our ancestors in Volganor."

It wasn't the traditional prayer expected at such times, but Kathair thought it more than fitting. He stepped forward and took one torch back for himself. "As one blade then," Kathair said. Magnus looked at him and nodded.

The two stood as the crackling fire grew and consumed the pyre and Alva's body. The jet smoke billowed upward, darkening the sky and smothering the scent of the pines. Kathair then offered up a silent prayer of his own. *Icadion, let my father's spirit guide and strengthen me as we hunt those black-hearted dogs that would murder our kin.*

*****

Asteri walked through an open field, her hands drifting lightly over the tall grasses so that the tips brushed against her skin with their coarse seed pods. Her eyes scanned the area about her, but it was her hands that led her feet as the various energies rose up from the ground to touch her palms. Like any other satyr, she could smell the deer that had recently grazed here, but as a restorer, she had a special connection to the very world itself, and could sense trails that even the most keen of predators could no longer find. The human girl, whose energy had left an imprint both upon Njar and upon the Pools of Fate, had been through this field not too long ago. Asteri could feel it.

Terramyr's energy flowed up all around the satyr, guiding her to a large citadel with high towers and thick walls. Though she had never set eyes upon the place, she knew it by sight and reputation. She let her eyes linger upon Kuldiga Academy for a few moments. Her father's warnings echoed in her mind. There could be trouble here. Sorcerers of all levels would likely be within Kuldiga Academy's walls even now. It was not a place for any satyr.

Still, perhaps Njar had been captured here—though she did not sense his energy—or at the very least she could find the girl he had befriended. She needed answers if she was to restore Nonac to health, and she needed them quickly. It was this last fact, the continual seepage of time, that decided her plan. What other choice was there but to enter the academy and find the girl?

She walked toward the southern gate and found it open with no guard standing watch. Asteri walked through the gateway to find several dozen young human males practicing with swords.

"One!" shouted a rather large man with a barrel for a chest, and arms the size of young trees. The young men in front of him swung their wooden practice swords horizontally. "Two!" the man shouted. The men each took a step back and brought their blades up as if blocking an enemy's strike. Asteri thought it best to skirt around the practicing swordsmen, but their instructor caught sight of her and called out. "Visiting days aren't for two weeks," the man said.

Asteri gathered herself and held fast while the large man approached. *Don't show fear. He can't see my true form.* "I need to speak with someone about a friend."

The large man shook his head. "I'm afraid no one is allowed to have visitors today. Like I said, the end of the term isn't for two more weeks."

"She might be in danger," Asteri insisted. "Please, allow me to speak with the headmaster."

The large man folded his arms over his chest and narrowed his eyes on her. "You wouldn't be talking about Miss Kyra Dimwater, would you?"

Asteri blinked. *How could he have guessed?*

"I'll take your silence as a yes," the man said. He gestured for her to follow him a few feet farther away from the waiting apprentices. "Anything concerning her can be shared with me. Besides, if she is in trouble, better to tell me than Headmaster Fenn anyhow. He isn't overly fond of her."

Asteri, falling into her role of concerned friend, asked, "Why is that?"

The large man reached up and scratched the back of his head. "On account of how she cast a couple of nasty spells at his wife." The man shrugged. "I don't think she meant to, exactly, but it happened nonetheless."

"Where is she now?" Asteri pressed. "I need to talk with her."

The man shook his head. "She isn't here. She went off a couple days ago with a small party to Valtuu Temple for some field research."

Asteri frowned and let out a sigh. She knew all about Valtuu Temple and the priests there. It was one place she could be certain her illusion spells wouldn't hold up. "Is there any way we can send a message to her?"

The man nodded. "I can send a messenger falcon."

Asteri scrunched up her nose. "Falcon? Don't humans, er, I mean to say aren't pigeons more common?"

The man chuckled. "Not around here. Haven't used carrier pigeons for centuries. Too many hawks and falcons in these parts that make easy meals of carrier pigeons. We use falcons, but don't worry, they're reliable and swift. Give me a letter, and I can send it off this afternoon."

Asteri nodded. "Is there a place I can find some paper?"

The man nodded and then turned to his apprentices. "Light sparring until I return. First start with the Waler Drill, then after each have had turns with that move onto two-on-one drills. I'll return in fifteen minutes." Turning to Asteri he said, "Come, I will show you the way."

She followed the large man to a doorway through which he only fit by turning slightly to the side. They walked through a large hallway, decorated with busts and tapestries along the walls, until they came to another door. The man pulled out a set of keys and opened the doorway.

"This is my office, a bit different from my old office, but at least it's on the ground floor." He turned and smiled. "A lot of other instructors here fight over the higher floors, each wanting a better view, but I like being lower to the ground. Makes me feel more connected to the world." He scoffed and shook his head. "And I hate stairs, so there is that."

Asteri found herself chuckling at the man's humor, momentarily forgetting just how dangerous a situation she was in. She followed him into the room, noting how it smelled of cinnamon with a hint of body odor. To her left stood a bookshelf filled with books, but the layer of dust on the covers told her that he hadn't read any of them for some time. To her right stood several armor and weapon stands, each with highly polished items displaying a wide range of styles.

"My collection," the man said when he caught her staring. "I have spent several years acquiring them."

Asteri nodded. "They're…nice."

The man pointed to a rather large sword with a blade as long as she was tall. "That one is the prize of my collection. I call it the giant-slayer. It was a special commission, forged in the northlands for a warlord by the name of Wulfgar Demson. If you believe the legends, Wulfgar was born of a demon mother who seduced a northman father and was prophesied to be the end of all dragons. Of course, the trouble was he was born three hundred years ago, and the Battle of Hamath Valley was five hundred years ago, so he arrived a little late to the battle I suppose." The large man clapped his hands and the rubbed them together. "Either way, I have his sword now."

Asteri forced a smile.

"Now, here is the paper. Write what you wish to tell Kyra, and I will have it sent right away." The large man set a piece of paper on his desk and slid a quill and inkwell next to it.

"You haven't told me your name," Asteri said as she moved to the paper and began to write.

"Master Orres," he said. "But, you can call me Feberik. Any friend of Kyra's is a friend of mine. So, what's all this about then?" He leaned closer and peered down at the paper.

"It's private," Asteri insisted. Feberik frowned, but took a step back and gave her space. She turned to the paper and wrote:

Kyra,

I'm looking for Njar. We need to speak. I'll be in the grove.

~A

friend

She rolled the paper and then spotted a wax seal to stamp upon it.

"Technically speaking, if you put my seal on it, I should know what it says," Feberik said, his right eyebrow arching suspiciously.

Asteri nodded and handed him the sealed letter. "Please see that it is sent right away. I must be on my way. I don't want to be caught out on the road at night."

"At night?" Feberik echoed. "Didn't you come with someone? I suspected you had a carriage waiting."

"I'll be fine," Asteri replied. She started to walk by the large man by he reached out and grabbed her arm. His thick fingers gripped her hard. She jumped and made a noise that sounded somewhat like a goat's bleating when it is frightened.

Feberik cocked his head to the side.

"Sorry, you startled me…" She glanced down to his massive hand, trying to decide whether to use her magic to free herself. He was many times her size and physical strength, but she doubted he could withstand her spells. On the other hand, attacking him would mean he wouldn't send her message. Her heart thumped in her chest, her breathing quickened. Then, just as her left hand started to weave a spell, the man let go and stepped back.

"I apologize, I didn't mean to hurt you, it's just, you shouldn't be out on the roads alone, even in the daytime. Please, tell me which house you are from, and I will arrange for a carriage to take you home."

House? The poor fool thinks I am a noble. She shook her head. "No house, Master Feberik," she said quickly. "Just a friend from a nearby village. Please, it's no trouble. I walk the roads all the time. I'll be fine, I assure you."

Feberik started to open his mouth, and then a sly grin came over his face and he wagged a finger at Asteri. "I understand.

You're like Kyra, aren't you? I bet you have a whole gaggle of spells up your sleeve. Am I right?"

Asteri quickly realized the man wasn't speaking down to her, but rather with admiration. She nodded. "I have several spells at my disposal. I promise, no bandits or other predators will harm me, but I do hate to travel by night, so I must go now."

Feberik nodded and stepped aside. "That's one weapon I will never be able to add to my collection," he said as she walked out. "It's a shame too. I'd love to conjure up a flaming sword or perhaps a magic arrow."

Asteri bid him farewell and quickened her pace, retracing her steps through the hallway and out into the courtyard. The young men were all engaged in sparring practice, a couple of them sitting on the sidelines nursing shoulders and heads that had red and purple welts she could see from where she was walking.

Humans and their love of war. What good will ever come from such a foolish race?

Chapter 7

A knock at the door pulled Kyra from her studies. She closed a book on vampires and set it to the side as she rose from her bed. The knock came again, more insistent this time.

"Come in," she answered.

A short man with white eyes pushed the door open and stepped into the room. "My name is Tigran, and I am the librarian here at Valtuu Temple. I have been asked to escort you to it." His blind eyes studied her from head to toe. Had he not been a priest of this particular order, Kyra might have taken offense at where his gaze seemed to linger, however, knowing that he was blind to the physical and was likely inspecting her aura, she squirmed just a bit, wondering whether he could see more of the vampiric darkness inside her.

"Come along, young one," the priest said, wrinkling his nose and turning to the side and gesturing for her to join him.

"Thank you," she offered as she passed through the doorway.

The priest closed the door and led her down a series of corridors that dumped them into a narrow staircase leading down below ground level. As they walked, Kyra couldn't help but wonder what the silent priest thought of her. She had never seen him before, but it seemed he was on the side of those that didn't appreciate her presence in the temple. A group whose numbers seemed to grow with each priest she met. Only a handful of priests were like the first she had met, showing her kindness and going out of their way to make sure she understood they welcomed her. The others weren't hostile per se, but their coldness and quiet, reserved demeanors told her everything she needed to know about them. Even the prelate had kept his distance, allowing her to stay but never personally introducing himself to her.

Kyra pushed the thoughts from her mind, soothing herself by remembering all of the great things she had done. With Kathair's help, and Leatherback at her side, she had conquered garunda beasts, shades, and all manner of evil creatures seeking to destroy her, and everything around her. Honestly, the priests should be thanking her, not treating her like some sort of embryonic monster waiting for its birth to unleash horrors upon the world. Her thoughts lingered on Leatherback for a few moments. She hoped he was all right. Khefir had promised to watch after him, but Kyra's worries grew with each passing day. Nagar's Blight was powerful. Based upon everything she had read, it might be true that even Khefir wouldn't be able to shield the dragon from the curse. She had to find a safe place for him.

In that moment, she found herself keenly aware of how much she missed Kathair as well. If he had been at her side, instead of this judgmental priest, he would lighten her mood with a joke or two, followed with a healthy dose of optimism and faith that would keep her spirits up and her mind focused on the task at hand. He had been a most helpful friend in anything she had sought to do, from hiding Leatherback from Kuldiga Academy, to solving her mother's murder. He had been there nearly every step of the way. But now, he was gone.

She wondered how he was doing. Was Telstian able to help him solve the mystery he was working on? She wished she could go to him. Even if she couldn't help, if she could just talk with him. It would make them both feel better.

"Here we are," the short priest barked out, ripping Kyra from her thoughts.

She looked up to see a large set of double doors and smiled. At least she had finally been given access to the books here. Even with Mindaugas advocating for her, it took several days for this moment to come as there had been plenty of opposition to allowing someone of Kyra's nature to have such free access to their guarded prophecies and ancient texts. From the grimace pulling the short priest's jowls down, Kyra understood that he was one of those who had fought against it. A flash of heat rushed through her chest. She had had enough of such men judging her.

Kyra walked up to him as he pulled open the door on the right. "Why did you decide to become a priest?" she asked pointedly.

The priest arched a brow and tilted his head. "Whatever do you mean?"

Kyra grinned. "I know that people like Sal Vinder become priests because of something in their hearts that compels them to help people, just as some people become knights in order to protect the weak. Yet, some knights seek to take power for themselves with the sword. Likewise I can't help but wonder if it isn't the promise of power that draws some priests in as well."

"Power?!" the priest shrieked. "What in the name of the Ancients are you on about? A priest does not have power similar to a knight's."

Kyra shrugged. "Three priests came to Kuldiga Academy to judge both me and my friend Leatherback—"

"The dragon is dangerous, for the curse might warp him. Just as the darkness in you might warp you as well."

Kyra shot the man a nasty and hard look, narrowing her eyes and stepping closer to him. "Precisely. You, as a man, are fully capable of similar evil, yet no one takes it upon themselves to pre-judge you. They defer such condemnation until such time as you act upon the temptations plaguing your heart. You are no different than any other man in the Middle Kingdom. Yet, as a priest, you have the power to forget the darkness swirling within your soul and focus solely upon what you perceive to be evil within my own. Despite the fact that I have not hurt any innocent person, you treat me as though I am a demon."

The priest bristled and took in a breath, but Kyra was not about to let him interrupt her.

"As I said, I wonder if that kind of power didn't beckon to you because your arms were too weak to use a sword and gain power in other ways."

The priest opened his mouth, but no audible response emerged. Kyra walked by him and into the library, leaving the short priest in the hallway and turning her attentions to the many rows of shelves standing before her. Even the library at Kuldiga Academy seemed dwarfed by the massive chamber before her. There were several times the number of shelves here, and each of them were at least twice as tall as the bookshelves at the academy as well.

"By the stars," she whispered. "It would take a lifetime to absorb everything here, perhaps even more." She descended three carpeted stairs and walked to the first row, her left hand stretching out to graze the spines on the first shelf as she read their titles. There were many subjects of interest, but none so far relating to pocket dimensions or other planes of existence. She found a few texts in Peish, the language of the dwarves, and many written in Taish, the language of the elves. She briefly admired the way their script differed from that of the Common Tongue, and couldn't help but wonder how many of the dwarven texts might speak of dragons, for she knew that the Ancients themselves had created the dwarves in the Middle Kingdom from the very stone of the mountain they still occupied. Surely the dwarves would have much wisdom of interest to her and Leatherback. She quickly scanned over the titles, but didn't see anything that looked to deal with dragons or other dimensions.

The short priest closed the door, sending an echo through the room that changed the pressure in the chamber as well. "The Keeper of Secrets requested that you be given unfettered access to as much of our records as possible."

Kyra looked up, noting the sour expression still lingering on the man's face.

"You may study any of the books in this outer chamber, but you may not go into the inner library." The priest pointed from atop the stairs toward the back of the chamber. Kyra turned and looked, spying a large golden door after a few moments.

"What's in there?" she asked.

"Prophecies written by the mystics, and they are not for the likes of you."

Kyra clenched her teeth to keep from voicing the responses swirling in her head after hearing such an insult. Still, she made sure to turn back toward the priest and stare at him until he shifted uneasily on his feet.

"What I meant, was that no one but the prelate may use them. They are written with a magic that only we can decipher. Even I may only read the most basic of texts in that room."

A pathetic attempt to backtrack, Kyra thought, but she let the matter drop without further argument. No doubt the priest had already seen the anger flourishing in her aura, and that is what had made him try to amend his statement. It was then that she realized that the librarian wasn't simply a weak-minded priest, as Sal had warned her about. This priest was blinded by his fear of her power, and that drove his dislike for her. She shook her head, almost pitying the man, and called out to him.

"Where can I find books on Hammenfein and other dimensions and planes?"

The blood seemed to drain from the priest as his mouth fell open.

"Mindaugas did mention the kinds of books I would be studying, did he not?"

The priest closed his mouth and gave a single nod. "Yes, yes, of course. Over here." He shuffled down the stairs and made his way to a row of shelves toward the far left side of the room. "The first three sections here deal with not only Hammenfein, but the histories of the Old Gods. As for other planes, some books here will speak of the Plane of the Dead. Others will cover the Astral

Plane. Those you will find in section four on this row, since the other planes are more a result of the Great War than anything else, they are filed after the histories of the Old Gods."

With a slight bow of his head, the librarian then turned and walked to a desk situated atop a small landing overlooking the entire library from the back, giving him a full view of the entrance and the forbidden chamber that held the books of prophecy.

Kyra moved to the first section and scanned book titles. She found several tomes about the creation of Terramyr. Each one varying in size by several pages from the others and listed alphabetically by title. "All-Father's Gift," she said, reading the first title aloud. "Bifrost's Connections, Cursed Races and their Origin." Kyra paused and put a finger on that one, knowing that it would speak of orcs and other creatures created by Khullan. With any luck, it would also speak of Hammenfein and possibly some of the dimensions connected to it. She pulled the book and tucked it into her arm before continuing to read more titles aloud. "First Races and Icadion's Promise, Genesis of Terramyr, Humans and the First Kings, Sozdal." Kyra wrinkled her nose. "Why wouldn't anyone include other dimensions with this section?" Weren't any of the other dimensions connected to the original creation? She moved on to look for more appropriate books. At the end of the first section, sitting under a thick layer of dust on the bottom shelf, she found a book with a title that intrigued her: Hammenfein and the Ghosts of Hell.

At a glance, she could tell it was several hundred pages long. It was as good a place to start as any, so she ripped it from the shelf, leaving a trail of dust that flittered to the floor. Kyra blew the top of the book and then moved to a desk near the wall and opened the first page.

The author, identified only by the name Feistos wrote a short foreword after the title page. Kyra read it aloud, "Few have ever delved into the mysteries of Gaia's Tear, and fewer still have ever emerged from the mouth of Hammenfein to tell the tale. Most of the foolish souls who make the attempt while still alive are either killed along the way, or lost to the various savage tribes in the shrouded lands beyond the treacherous peaks of the Nahktun Mountain Range. Those who survive the journey will find that Gaia's Tear, the volcano that serves as the portal to Hammenfein from our world, is itself a trap filled with brittle walkways that mislead adventurers down false paths that break, thrusting the unwary fool down into the lava pools below, or they are caught by unimaginable beasts that prey upon any living thing careless enough to risk the descent.

"For those lucky and foolish few who reach the bottom unharmed, they must then contend with the Hellhounds that guard the gates below, and the labyrinths beyond. To be clear, I am not speaking of the fabled dogs with burning fur that are twice the size of a man, though those certainly exist, but instead I am referring to Hatmul's army of orcs. Some say the Hellhounds are undead, others say they are spirits imbued with the power to take life, and others still insist the orcs are reanimated into a state of immortality, so long as they serve Hatmul honorably. I do not know which of these theories is correct, despite having seen several Hellhounds with my own eyes. I do, however, know that orcs must earn the right to serve as Hellhounds. In life, they are the most ferocious, savage creatures ever to set foot upon Terramyr. They place their bloodlust above all else, wishing only to serve Hatmul as generals in their afterlife. This makes the Hellhounds the most dangerous army to ever exist upon Terramyr, for it grows every day with the death of every orc. Should it ever be unleashed upon the world above, then I have no doubt Hatmul would become the ruler of all Terramyr within a matter of days.

"At the risk of appearing blasphemous, I do wonder if perhaps the great Icadion erred when he cursed the orcs and their cousin-races. Perhaps, if He had instead allowed the Cursed Races to inherit Volganor and find rest in Heaven upon death, the orcs might not plague us so viciously upon Terramyr as mortals, nor would they strive to become Hellhounds in the afterlife. For if the Great War was enough to force Icadion to shut Bifrost and separate us all from Volganor's grace, offering only the Plane of the Dead as substitute, then how much greater still would be the sorrows of man if the Hellhounds were ever unleashed upon us?

"Think on these things, and bear in mind as you read this account of my travels that I have been to Hammenfein. I not only survived the journey there, but outwitted Hatmul himself, something even the goddess Kyra failed to do. I won my freedom, and thus the ability to create this record for all to see. Take heed and do not dismiss my warnings, nor trifle with Hammenfein nor any of its secrets. There is a power there that threatens to destroy us all. Hatmul is not the obedient guardian of hell that he appears to be. He is a treacherous god, filled with spite and more cunning than the slyest of men. If you are reading this as preparation for your own attempt to delve into Hammenfein, I implore you to turn back now. Nothing good will come of it, and though I am proud of this account, for I think it is of great worth to all who read and understand it, I wish that I had not sojourned through the mouth of hell, for its ghosts still haunt me, and I fear my soul is irreparably tainted by my transgressions."

Kyra sat back and cocked her head at the book. She didn't necessarily plan on trying to reach Hammenfein, but her understanding was that Khefir, Hatmul's brother and collector of damned souls, had opened a small pocket dimension within Hammenfein to harbor Leatherback. Had she made an error? Would Leatherback's soul become tainted by his time there as Feistos believed his had been?

Or perhaps Feistos spoke of something else that he had done either in Hammenfein or as a result of being there. There was no way to be sure, but her curiosity was piqued beyond a casual interest, and she found herself devouring the book page after page, her eyes running over each word as her mind caught onto the sentences and held them for her to ponder later.

As hours ticked away, she learned a great many things, some possibly useful for Leatherback, others not so much but interesting nevertheless. Only when the librarian approached her desk did she stop to look up from the book.

"It's late," he said. "I'm going up for dinner. Didn't you hear the bell?"

Kyra shook her head. "No, I was too busy reading."

The priest looked to the book and sighed. Had she been in a normal library, he would not have known what she was reading, for he could not see as she did with her eyes, but every book in this collection was imbued with magic, allowing the librarian not only to see the shape of each book, but also to read its words as well.

"Come," he said. "It's late, and no one is permitted in the library without my presence."

"Will you be here tomorrow?" Kyra asked.

The librarian arched a brow as if to ask why she would bother with such an obvious question.

"What time will it be open?"

"I open the doors after breakfast, every day of the week. In case I am sick, my apprentice will take over for the day. During my lunch break and subsequent meditations, sometimes my apprentice is able to open the library and other times the chamber will remain closed."

Kyra nodded. "Thank you." She closed the book and scooped it up into her arms, ignoring the frown appearing on the librarian's face. "I'll be sure to bring this back tomorrow."

The librarian grunted and led her to the door.

Kyra retraced her steps back to her room, skipping right by the mess hall and abandoning the idea of supper altogether, her mind grumbling for sustenance far louder than her stomach complained for lack of food.

When she reached her room, she could see that Mindaugas had both come and gone, for his sword was propped against his bed but he was nowhere to be found. She figured he probably had gone to supper like everyone else, and didn't give it another thought.

She jumped onto her bed, bouncing the single pillow onto the floor, and then crossed her legs under her and reopened the book she had been studying. She studied until the fading sunlight only barely cast its rays through her window, then she paused just long enough to snap her fingers, sparking a flame to a nearby candle. Unsatisfied with it, she looked up to a candelabra standing in the corner near her bed and magically lit its candles as well. Then she pointed her nose back down to the pages, absorbing them as quickly as her eyes would move across the words.

She read for another hour after sunset, and then stopped after reading a passage about a strange plane mentioned within one of the chapters. Feistos called it Sudragaru, and mentioned it was a place he was able to take refuge in while on his journey through the shrouded lands. The passage describing it spoke of trees, vast hills, and many caves in which one could safely rest. It mentioned a few dangers as well, but advised the reader that these could be avoided by sticking to the caves and building a large fire. Feistos felt the plane safe enough that he wrote down the incantation he personally used to reach it.

Kyra smiled and shook her head. If this plane was far enough away from the Middle Kingdom, it could provide Leatherback with safety. She read over the incantation several times, and then closed her eyes and spoke the words.

The candles around her flickered, their light faltering and throwing shadows all over the walls and floor. A chill gripped the air, slithering around her body as the bed melted away from her. She didn't fall into the portal so much as float gently through the darkness. It was like diving into a pool, except she could still breathe as the cold air pulled her downward into Sudragaru.

After a few moments, she landed softly on a grassy hillock overlooking a winding stream running at the base and snaking off into the dense forest before her. Kyra stood and turned around. Behind her stood jagged, gray peaks devoid of any trees or bushes that she could see. The area was bright, but there was no sun in the sky, only a pale blue expanse that stretched over the hills and forests.

"This isn't bad," Kyra said. A smile pulled the corners of her mouth upwards as she skipped lightly down toward the stream. She looked into the clear water, admiring the stones within the liquid, and then she turned toward the forest. She narrowed her eyes on the trees, and then slowly turned around, surveying everything around her as an uneasy feeling started to take hold.

The trees, mountains, and sky were all very beautiful, but something was missing. There were no butterflies or bees flittering about the flowers on the hillock. There were no fish in the stream. There were no birds singing in the forest. Everything was still.

The hairs on her forearms stood on end as a prickle of cold rolled through her. She prepared a magical ward with her left hand, and a fireball in her right just in case. She walked toward the forest, searching for the caves spoken of in the book. As she moved deeper into the forest, the air around her darkened considerably. She looked up to see a thick canopy of green above her, blocking out much of the day's light. She wondered then, whether it was late in the day or early. It was strange to think that while the sun had set and night covered the area around Valtuu Temple there was still light in this place. Did that mean it was far away from the Middle Kingdom, or simply that the rules governing light and dark were different?

A crunching sound brought her to a stop next to a tall oak tree. She looked around, but saw nothing where the sound had come from.

A low growl came from the bushes on her left.

Kyra turned, her ward and fireball at the ready. She couldn't see what was making the noise, but she knew better than to press her luck. She backed away, her eyes glued to the bushes. After a couple of moments the growling stopped and the bushes swayed a bit as if an animal moved from behind them.

The young sorceress felt the hairs of her neck stand on end. Something was here, and it was not happy with her presence.

Once she emerged from the forest, she recited the incantation again. Within moments she returned to her bed in Valtuu Temple, safe from whatever had been growling.

"Where were you?" Mindaugas asked from across the room.

Kyra looked up to see the man standing in the open doorway and holding a plate of food in his hands. "I was told that you hadn't eaten, so I thought you might like some food."

Her stomach snarled and knotted on the left side as the aroma of roasted chicken reached her nostrils. "Yes, I would love some."

"Were you at the manor again?" Mindaugas pressed, holding the plate up out of reach as she approached him.

"Oh… no. I was…" Kyra held up a hand and went back to the bed for the book. "I read about another plane in this book and thought—"

"Kyra, you shouldn't be jumping into other planes by yourself. You never know what you might find."

Kyra smiled and shrugged. "Yes, I realize that. It's just, this one sounded like a good place for Leatherback."

"Did it?" Mindaugas asked, his tone softening considerably. "Well, what is it called?"

"Sudragaru."

Mindaugas' right brow jumped up as his face contorted into something between a snarl and frown. "Sudragaru?"

Kyra drew her brow into a knot above her nose. "Yes," she said. "Feistos said that it was a harmless enough place, so long as you take fire with you, and I have many fire spells."

"Feistos… ugh." Mindaugas shook his head and set her plate down on a small table near the center of the room. "I'm not sure Feistos is the best judge of danger."

"Sudragaru was harmless enough," Kyra said. "I found a lovely forest and stream at the base of a large grassy hill."

Mindaugas nodded. "Kyra, Feistos was a master of fire sorcery. When he says something is safe as long as you have fire, it would be like me saying a town is safe as long as you have a sword. It isn't so much the weapon, but a man's particular mastery of it that makes them safe. No offense, but your skills are still amateurish at best when compared with the likes of Feistos. You might be thinking you need a fire spell large enough to keep a bear at bay, but he is likely talking about something that could evaporate a water elemental."

Kyra frowned. She didn't dare mention the growling animal she had nearly encountered.

"Besides, there isn't just the danger of you entering a plane and being set upon by something there, but your travel to and from might unleash something *from* there and bring them *here*."

Her frown deepened. She hadn't considered that. "I thought you wanted me to study other planes," she said, not knowing what else to say in light of his response.

Mindaugas patted the air. "I do, Kyra, I most certainly do. But I want you to be safe too. Research all the places you like, but before you explore them, you should discuss them with me. I can then talk with the prelate and we can put together an expeditionary team of sorts."

"I don't think many priests would want to come with me into other planes."

Mindaugas laughed and shook his head. "Probably not many, no, but Sal would, and a handful of others would as well. That would be enough too. Their special sight would allow us to see dangers from afar off, and my skills would help as well."

"Don't discount my magic," Kyra put in.

"Exactly. With my blade, your magic, and their sight, we would be far better prepared to explore new planes."

Kyra nodded.

"So, will you promise me that next time you will let me come along and bring a few priests?"

Kyra's frown faded away, replaced by a toothy grin. "I can promise that."

Mindaugas nodded and then gestured to the plate. "I have a meeting I need to attend. I won't be back until late."

Kyra watched as the large man moved to retrieve his sword. "You need your sword for the meeting?"

Mindaugas snorted. "Most meetings I attend do require that I be prepared. The life of a Keeper is never dull." He turned and flashed a quick smile and then disappeared out the door before she had the chance to say anything else.

The young sorceress went to the table and ate her food, then prepared for bed and fell asleep.

As she slept, a chill filled the room, and she found herself dreaming of the grassy hill with the stream at its base. In her dream, she stepped to the edge of the water and dipped her hand in to drink. The cool water rushed down her throat and chilled her very soul. She looked at her hands, watching helplessly as they turned a pale gray. Her heart slowed and her breath turned cold, freezing before her with each exhale. She stood away from the water and moved to the forest for shelter.

As before, there were no animals nor other signs of any life except for the trees and bushes around her. After walking for some time, she came upon a small cave and, remembering Feistos' words, went inside to find refuge from the cold. The air outside grew so dark she couldn't see more than a foot in front of her, so she used her magic to light a large fire at the cave's entrance. She conjured a second fireball in her hands to explore the cave's depths. It wouldn't do any good to block off the entrance if there was something dangerous lurking in the back of the tunnel.

She walked for several minutes as the cave meandered in what she thought was the direction of the jagged mountains she had seen in the distance behind the grassy hillock. Moss patches marked the damp stone walls around her, but there was no sign of animal tracks. When she finally found the end of the cave, she was relieved to see that there were no wild bears, or water elementals or anything else, just a solid wall of rock.

Kyra started to turn back toward the entrance, but a cold draft rushed about her body, coiling around her legs and blowing her hair in several directions. A voice called to her on the breeze, but she couldn't make out what it said. The words were harsh and foreign to her, barely louder than a whisper.

"Who calls for me?" Kyra asked.

The voice answered in words she didn't understand. The breeze snaked around her left wrist and then seized it, extinguishing the fireball in her hands as it laughed at her. The darkness was infinite, swallowing her entirely, but she was quick to bring a new fireball in her right hand. In front of her, there was some sort of being. It was silvery and slightly transparent, as if the breeze itself had taken corporeal form. She blasted it with the fireball.

The being hissed as the fireball ripped a hole in it. Kyra broke from its grasp and conjured two more fireballs, launching them just as the creature lunged for her. The spells knocked the creature into the stone wall. With what sounded like a heavy exhale, the creature faded into the air, disappearing from sight.

Kyra conjured a ward spell around her whole body and ran for the tunnel entrance.

Something knocked against the protective shell on the right.

Another blow hit the left side.

A third attacked from above, smacking the shell several times. In the light provided by the ward, Kyra could just make out three of the air creatures. Each of them took turns attacking her defenses as she ran through the cave. As she approached the entrance, the fire she had set in place burned hot and bright. She knew the ward would protect her from the spell, and since the fireballs had seemed to work against the first air creature she decided to run through her fire barrier.

She leapt into the flames and grinned as the air creatures hissed and fizzled away.

Just as the creatures disappeared, she heard the strange voice again, but this time it spoke in Common Tongue, harsh and raspy like something inhuman trying to form words that Kyra would understand.

"There is no escape," the voice said.

Kyra moved out of the fire and tried to run, but then the same growling she had heard before stopped her. A massive, gray wolf emerged from around a thick oak, his head held low and his hackles up as he snarled. It was larger than any wolf she had ever seen or heard of before, his shoulders even with the bottom of her ribs.

"No escape!" the voice shouted. Something crashed into the right side of her protective shell. Golden light erupted from the crack now spreading through her spell. Her defenses were weakening. Another hit like that and the ward would be gone.

Kyra tried to work her hands, but her eyes were glued to the wolf's. It snarled at her, stalking toward her slowly, calculating its approach with an intelligence she could feel in the pit of her stomach.

Another blow slammed into the ward on the left side. An explosion of golden light tore through the darkness. Kyra fell to her knees, her breath knocked from her lungs by another blow that struck her in the stomach. Her eyes widened as the wolf lunged forward, mouth open and fangs ready to deal death.

Chapter 8

Kathair woke in the middle of the night, sitting upright and peering into the darkness. Magnus slept nearby, holding baby Brenna in his protective arms while Wendin sat upon a low branch in an oak tree, watching the darkness around them for any sign of danger. The young swordsman stood up and quietly walked to the oak while rubbing his left shoulder.

Wendin gracefully descended from the tree. "No sign of them since the first attack," the elf reported.

Kathair nodded, glancing back to Brenna and letting out a sigh. "If we hadn't come to them…"

Wendin set a hand on Kathair's shoulder. "Magnus is not a man to flatter others' egos. Believe him when he says he does not blame you."

"And what if I can't help but blame myself?"

The elf gave a squeeze of his hand. "Kathair, it is impossible to explain the evil desires and plans others thrust upon us. A good man wouldn't understand the mind of one who imposes his will through violence even if we could explain it. But, the one thing we must never do is blame ourselves for the evil in others. The Blacktongues are to blame, and they alone. They murdered your father and mother, as they murdered Alva and seek to take away your life still."

Kathair heard the words, but had trouble internalizing them. The fact still remained that Magnus had succeeded in protecting his family until the very night Kathair showed up at their doorstep. "Why are they so relentless?"

Wendin took in a breath and stood silent for a moment. "The Blacktongues never act alone. Someone leads them."

"Is it Malech? The traitor from the north?" Kathair asked.

Wendin shook his head. "Doubtful. I suspect he works with the mastermind for some sort of reward. The real enemy is the man who pulls the strings. It is him we must find if we are to stop the Blacktongues. For as long as he lives, their contract will stand in force and they will continue to hunt you."

"But why? If they were scared that my father would become the Keeper of Secrets, then why hunt me after they killed him?"

Wendin offered a rare smile. "Kathair Lepkin, you have a part to play that will shape the Middle Kingdom, and the whole of Terramyr itself. They cannot afford to allow you to fulfill your destiny."

Kathair wrinkled his nose. "I am just me," Kathair said with a huff. "What can one man do?"

Wendin grabbed Kathair by both shoulders and bent down close so their eyes met, just inches apart. The elf's hot breath fell upon Kathair's face as he said, "Never underestimate the value of a virtuous man, for his actions can alter fate far more effectively than any other power on this plane."

The young swordsman nodded. He wasn't sure he wholly agreed, but he wanted the conversation to be over. Wendin, seemingly satisfied, went back to the tree and resumed his watch. Kathair walked a few yards away from camp to answer the call of nature that he had suddenly become aware of. Then he went back to sleep.

When the morning broke over the forest, Wendin and Magnus were already breaking camp and rationing out dried meat and biscuits. Brenna was playing in the dirt, her little fingers wound tightly around a stick.

"Momma," she said. The single word wrenched Kathair's stomach into knots, and he found himself refusing breakfast and struggling to keep from vomiting.

The group made their way through the forest, emerging from the trees just after noon and finding themselves on a hill overlooking a valley to the north. In the center of the valley stood a massive tower.

"Valtuu Temple," Wendin said, pointing to the structure. "You and Brenna will be safe here."

Magnus held his daughter tight and started down the hill without a word. Kathair and Wendin were quick to follow. Kathair had never seen the temple before, but he remembered the three priests that had come to Kuldiga Academy to ensure Leatherback never succumbed to the curse that befell all dragons in this land. It was hard to forget them, the way their gray, blind eyes could pierce a person's soul and see every intention of their heart. They had made him terribly uneasy then. So much so that he questioned the idea of hiding Brenna and Magnus here.

The citadel walls stood tall and thick like that of any castle, but there were no soldiers patrolling the battlements. The massive double doors stood closed to the outside, with strange knob-like protrusions covering them, but there were no guards.

As the group neared the doors, Wendin marched forward and gestured for the others to stop. The elf gently brushed one of the knob-like protrusions with his right hand and then used his fist to knock. "I am Wendin, servant to Telstian Do'Urgro. I have come seeking refuge for friends of the cause."

Kathair looked to Magnus, wondering what might be going through the large man's mind. The doors opened and a short, bald man emerged, smiling wide and holding his arms out and approaching Wendin eagerly.

"Wendin! It is a pleasure to see you once more."

Wendin bowed his head and the two embraced. Kathair tilted his head to the side at the sight, for never in his life had he ever seen Wendin hug anyone before. The bald priest then broke the embrace and looked to Magnus and Kathair.

"I can see your journey has been hard. Come, come," he said while gesturing quickly. "Let's get you all inside. We can talk later, but for now let's get you a room."

Wendin offered thanks as the group was shown into the main courtyard. "Sal, did Telstian send word of our arrival?"

The priest nodded. "I received a message by falcon a few days ago that said you might choose to come this way. I have already prepared quarters for you and spoken with the prelate. You will be given anything you need."

Kathair followed everyone up a large set of stone stairs, noting a pair of guards at the front entrance. Their eyes were the same as any other priest Kathair had seen before, but they carried themselves quite differently, with shoulders squared and chests out, each holding a tall staff-like weapon with a massive blade on top. The guards looked at Kathair and the others with their gray eyes, nodding as the group entered the temple.

The young swordsman stopped in the front room, amazed by the mural inside. Dragons, humans, and dwarves were locked in a grand battle, but there was more to it than that. The images almost seemed to move. Kathair turned slowly, taking it all in. Then, his eyes fell upon a massive golden dragon. No sooner did he gaze into the image's eyes than he felt a sharp pain in his head. Screams of the dying filled his ears. Clashing swords and exploding dragons' breath overcame his senses, and he fell to his knees, crying out as the strain caused a trickle of blood to run from his nose.

Wendin and Sal were quick to help him to his feet and pull him from the room, but Kathair was unable to remain conscious.

The next time he opened his eyes, Sal and two other priests were standing over him, chanting soft words and holding their palms out over his chest and head. He could feel a rush of warmth flowing through him, comforting and peaceful. His head still ached, but it was a dull pain that he could ignore now, thanks to the priests and their apparent healing powers.

"Thank you," Kathair said.

Two of the priests turned and exited the room, while Sal remained with Kathair.

"It is not usual for northmen to react the way you did," Sal said.

Kathair shook his head. "I don't know what happened. I was looking at the mural, and then…"

Sal nodded and took a seat on the bed next to Kathair as the young man sat up and put his feet on the floor. "The mural is painted with magic, so that the priests can witness the destruction of Hamath Valley each time we enter or exit the temple."

"Every time?" Kathair asked.

Sal nodded. "We can hear the cries of battle, feel the dragon's fire, and smell the stench of magic and scorched dirt and flesh. It is meant to remind us of our duties, and the cost for failure." Sal put the back of his hand to Kathair's forehead. "However, our initiates spend much time in preparation before they are allowed to walk through the chamber, and even then they have a priest escorting them so they are not overwhelmed."

"Why didn't Magnus or Wendin feel it?"

Sal shook his head. "Most who are not of our order do not experience the chamber's magic. They see only a mural. Even after one has been granted the gift of True Sight, which is what causes our physical blindness while granting us the ability to see energy and magic, most do not feel the chamber's effects as keenly as you did."

"Will it happen again?" Kathair asked.

Sal smiled. "I will help you the next time we pass through the chamber. You will find the effects bearable, I promise."

Kathair shrugged. "Where is Magnus?"

Sal took Kathair's left hand and held it firmly. "Kathair, I don't think you understand what this means," the priest said, ignoring Kathair's question. "You have a great destiny, and what happened in the front chamber confirms that."

Kathair snorted and shook his head. "Wendin tried to say something similar."

Sal squeezed Kathair's hand. "I will come back for you tomorrow morning. The prelate will want to speak with you, as will Mindaugas Reif." Kathair's eyes shot open wide. He knew that name. He had seen the Keeper of Secrets back at Kuldiga Academy, though he hadn't spoken to the large man much. "There is much you don't know." Sal patted Kathair's hand and then stood up from the bed. "Before we get to that, there is someone else that has been begging to see you."

Kathair was about to ask who, but Sal called out for the other two priests and the door swung open. The young man's heart skipped and nearly leapt into his throat. Kyra rushed in, covering the room in just a few paces. Kathair barely had enough time to stand before she wrapped him in a tight hug that nearly squeezed the breath from his lungs.

"It's good to see you! They told me what happened in the forest. I'm so sorry."

Kathair melted into her hug, taking comfort in his friend's support. "I'm glad to see you too," he said after a bit.

"I'll leave you two to get reacquainted," Sal said.

Kathair pulled back from Kyra's hug and let her hands slide down his arms until they were both holding hands. "I didn't know you would be here," he said.

Kyra smiled wider. "Mindaugas brought me so I could study in the library. I have some ideas that might help Leatherback."

Kathair stiffened and glanced to the priests standing outside the still open door.

"No, no, it's okay. Everyone here knows of him, and is anxious to help him as well."

"Really?" Kathair asked.

Kyra nodded. "The whole order cares about Leatherback very much." Her smile faded then and she paused as if there was something else she wished to say.

"Then what's wrong?" Kathair asked.

Kyra shook her head. "It's nothing. Come, I have something I want to show you." She started to turn away, but Kathair held her fast.

"Do they mistreat you?"

Kyra huffed and smiled faintly. "You were always blunt."

"Because of your father?" Kathair guessed.

"It's understandable. They fear—"

"They're fools," Kathair cut in. One of the priests turned around and stared through the doorway at him. Kathair met the gray eyes with a steely gaze of his own and then added, "If the priests are too blind to see you for who you truly are, then they are fools indeed, and I will be happy to help them see the light."

The priest turned back around and turned his gaze to the hallway.

Kyra put a hand on Kathair's cheek. "I'm fine, really. It's okay."

Kathair shook his head and looked back to her bright eyes. "No, it really isn't." He lowered his voice so only she could hear him. "I mean it, you tell me which one of them so much as misspeaks to you, and I'll be on him faster than a bullfrog jumps a lazy fly."

Kyra giggled. "Kathair Lepkin, you of all people should know that I can handle myself."

Kathair shrugged, but couldn't stop a playful smile from catching the left side of his mouth. "And you should know I don't like my first name."

"Well, don't be rude, and I won't have to call you by your full name then."

Kathair laughed. "It isn't rude to stand up for what's right."

Kyra turned and dragged him by the hand. "Come on, put away your childish impulse to fight and let's go read some books."

Kathair made a point of groaning, but they both knew it was only for show. Truth be told, he was delighted to help her with any books she wanted to read. They spent a couple hours in the library, discussing various theories about Sudragaru and other possible planes and dimensions they might be able to use to rescue Leatherback. Then, after an early supper they retired to Kyra's room.

Mindaugas was sitting at a small table in the center of the room. He looked up at Kathair and gave a short nod.

"Hello, Master Reif," Kathair said.

"Kathair, good to see you again. I'm sorry about the troubles you faced on your way here," the Keeper of Secrets replied.

Kathair felt a pang of guilt strike his gut. He didn't know what he felt worse about, the fact that Alva was dead because of him, or that he had so quickly forgotten her murder and allowed himself to think of Kyra and Leatherback during the past couple of hours. "Me too," he said as the guilt turned into a wave of melancholy that threatened to drag his very body into the floor.

Mindaugas stood up from the table and moved to place a hand on Kathair's shoulder. "I know what it is to lose people. I have lost many that were close to me, and many more still who were under my command."

Kathair nodded, but couldn't think of anything to say.

"All we can do is continue the fight and hold them in our memories," Mindaugas said. The large man then sighed and grabbed Kathair under the chin to bring the young man's eyes up to his own. "You mustn't blame yourself. I heard the reports from Wendin and Magnus. Neither of them blame you, and both would willingly do everything all over again to ensure your safe journey."

"That doesn't help," Kathair said.

"It will, in time. Keep Alva in your memory, but don't let the grief of her death overwhelm you. She wouldn't want that."

Kathair pulled away. "You speak as if you know her."

Mindaugas smiled. "I do," he said. "I have known them both for many years. We met shortly after your parents were murdered." Mindaugas patted Kathair's shoulder. "Keep moving forward, Master Lepkin. Move forward and keep up the fight."

Mindaugas gave him another pat and then turned back to sit at the table.

"I was going to take him to the manor," Kyra said.

Mindaugas nodded. "Leave the portal open."

Kathair followed her to her bed and sat down beside her.

"We don't have to go now," she offered. "If you need some time…"

Kathair shook his head. "No, it will do me good to get out of here for a while." He flashed a smile to prove himself, and then added, "Let's go. I want to see your house."

Kyra smiled and squeezed his hand. Then she turned and cast a spell that opened a portal. Through it, Kathair could see an overgrown flower garden flanking a dirt path leading up to a wonderful house. Kyra stood up and tugged on Kathair's hand. The two walked through the portal together, appearing just forty yards away from the house.

Kathair smiled as he took in the fresh air. "So, take me to this locked door and let's see if I can't open it."

Kyra led him to the front door. "I have tried everything I can think of, it doesn't open." The two walked up to the front door, flanked by walls of river rock teeming with ivy, and Kyra slipped her key into the lock. Kathair watched her turn the key and then frowned when the knob refused to turn.

"That doesn't make any sense. Is there a spell keeping it sealed?"

Kyra shrugged. "I thought of that, but I don't know how to undo it, or even figure out if there is one."

The two walked around the building, trying to open the wooden shutters only to find them solidly locked as well. When Kathair saw an outbuilding, he pointed to it and said, "Maybe there's a ladder inside."

"Thought of that, but that building is locked as well."

Kathair frowned. "Well, what about that window there?" He pointed to a second story window above them. "You could stand on my shoulders and test the shutters."

Kyra smiled and nodded eagerly. "Let's try it."

Kathair placed his feet slightly wider than shoulder-width apart and squatted down, holding very still while Kyra stepped on his right leg and then up to his shoulders. She wasn't heavy, but she kept most of her weight on the balls of her feet, digging into Kathair's shoulders a bit. He reached up and grabbed her ankles.

"Lean forward and walk your hands up the wall for balance as I stand up."

Kathair stood slowly, allowing Kyra enough time to balance herself. At full height, she could just reach the bottom of the shutter. She pulled on it. For half a second it looked as though the plan would work. The shutter moved away from the window, but it abruptly stopped about two inches out, locked to the other half of the shutter and refusing to budge any further.

"Icadion's beard," Kyra grumbled.

"We can try the other upper windows. Maybe someone forgot to lock one of the shutters."

"I doubt it," she replied. Still, the pair walked around the house repeating the process at each upper story window until all of them had been confirmed locked.

"Is there a letter, or note perhaps, that explains how to open it?"

Kyra flapped her arms out to the side. "If there is, I haven't found it."

Kathair found a stump that had been carved into a sort of seat with a tall back and sat down. "I'm sure we can think of something. I mean, it's your ancestral home. If there is magic, it has to answer to you."

"Unless Lord Caspin is the one who sealed it," Kyra said.

"I didn't know he had magic."

Kyra shook her head. "He doesn't, but he might have paid someone to lock it up. After all, it was given to him as a wedding present for marrying my mother. He's the kind of man who would have wanted it kept to himself."

"That's not right," Kathair said.

"A lot isn't right about him," Kyra replied. She moved toward the stump-chair and motioned for Kathair to scoot over. He slid to the side, giving her enough room to sit with him. The two shared several silent moments leaning on each other while Kathair wondered how to get into the house and enjoyed the peaceful surroundings.

After a half hour, Kathair heard something. He stood up and looked off in the direction of the portal.

"What is it?" Kyra asked.

Kathair held up his left hand and his right went for his sword. When it wasn't there, he realized that the priests had removed his sword belt in order to help him after his incident in the entrance chamber. His eyes darted around and found a thick fallen branch. He picked it up, quickly snapping the lateral branches and then breaking off the top third to create a jagged point.

Kyra stood up and prepared a fireball in her hand. She and Kathair had faced enough enemies together that they didn't need to speak. Kathair walked toward the tall roses, his eyes scanning the ground nearby and then moving to the dense trees of the forest beyond the flower garden. Kyra moved into position just left and behind, watching his flank and as ready as he was to strike out at any danger.

"No escape," a voice called from the trees. The raspy words sent chills down Kathair's spine, but what bothered him the most was the fact he couldn't find the enemy.

Had a Blacktongue found them? Could that be possible? How would they think to lay a trap here? Or was it something else? Something that wanted to avenge Severin's death perhaps?

A cold breeze picked up, bending the roses and rustling the leaves on the trees.

"No escape!" the voice said, louder this time.

Kathair held his stick ready, but still he couldn't locate the aggressor. "Is this part of the locking spell that secures the manor?" Kathair asked, doubting so even as he voiced the question.

"No," Kyra said.

Kathair noted the hesitance in her voice and turned back to look at her. Gone was her normal confidence, replaced by an expression of worry, and Kathair knew they were in trouble. "Go to the portal," he whispered. "I will cover you."

"With a stick?" Kyra shot back. "I have magic, I should cover you."

"Kyra…" the voice whispered.

Kathair froze. This time the voice was behind them, and it knew her name. "It isn't after me," Kathair said. "It's after you. Go, now!" Kathair wheeled around as something formed from the wind. It vaguely took on the shape of a man, but it had no substance to it. Kyra let loose her fireball, blasting a hole through the creature's chest. Kathair let his instincts and training take over. He rushed toward the creature, slashing and hacking with his stick. The weapon passed through the air, cutting the silvery form only to have it reform as soon as the stick passed.

"Kyra, light my stick on fire!" Kathair shouted. Just as the air-creature swung for Kathair's head, the stick burst into flame, covered with magical fire that burned hot and blue. Kathair parried with his now-magical weapon and found that this time the creature hissed and recoiled upon touching it. "Go, I'll deal with this!"

Kathair stabbed his flaming stick forward, piercing the creature where a man's heart would be, and then it vanished. He turned around to see Kyra running down the dirt path between the flowers toward the portal. She let out a scream as several more air creatures formed next to her. Kathair sprinted toward her as she pelted the beings with fireballs that kept them at bay.

The young swordsman rushed toward the closest air creature and cut through its middle, dissipating the magic that held it together.

"There is no escape, Kyra!" the same voice hissed.

Kathair vanquished a second creature as Kyra blasted two more of them with her magic.

A wolf stepped out from behind the open portal, its head low and fangs bared. Kathair called out a warning and rushed forward. He dropped his stick and placed both hands on Kyra's back, then he shoved her as hard as he could toward the portal a few feet in front of them. As she flew toward the portal, another air-creature reached for her at the same time the wolf came around the portal and lunged. Kathair gasped, hoping he had launched her fast enough. Fortunately, the air-creature only managed to swipe through her dark hair as she sailed into the portal and landed safely on the other side.

The wolf and air-creature collided. The air-creature dissipated and then reformed several yards to the side.

"You!" the voice snarled. "How dare you interfere!"

Kathair reached down for his flaming stick. The wolf locked eyes with him. Kathair's legs felt as though they had turned to stone. He could hardly breathe, let alone move. The wolf stalked closer toward him as the air creature watched from afar.

The young swordsman struggled against the magic holding him in place, but couldn't find the strength to break free. The wolf stepped ever closer, its teeth bared and its hackles forming a ridge of spiky fur along its spine. Kathair's eyes looked past the wolf and through the portal. Mindaugas was helping Kyra to her feet, but they hadn't closed the portal yet, she was working her magic to keep it open. Only the wolf stood in his way. In that moment, a wellspring of fury erupted in his chest and he swung his stick, the magical flames roaring and flashing just a couple inches in front of the wolf.

"What? How can you break the paralysis spell?" the voice shouted. The air-creature charged toward him, but Kathair paid it no mind. He waved the flaming stick twice more until the wolf shied away and leapt out of the dirt path. Kathair then sprinted for the portal. Two more air-creatures appeared in front of him, but Kyra attacked them, sending streams of fire through the portals. Kathair leapt the last two feet and would have bowled Kyra over had Mindaugas not caught him first.

Kyra then closed the portal and the two stood in the room panting for breath.

"Someone had better explain what in the fiery pits of Hammenfein just happened, and it better be a right good explanation," Mindaugas demanded.

Chapter 9

Hatmul sat on his throne deep in the heart of Hammenfein, far below the surface of Terramyr and away from its troubles. Sleeping to the right of his golden chair was a leopard of red spots and black fur, twice the size of any related animal living in the mortal realm above, and four times as vicious. To his left, a woman cooed in his ear. She was a recent addition to his captive souls, and was very pleasing to look at, with all the right curves and eyes that seemed to be made of liquid mahogany. In life, she had been some nobleman's wife, but had earned her place in Hammenfein by murdering some poor soul who had learned about her affairs.

For now, Hatmul entertained himself by allowing her to stay at his side, though time would tell how long she could hold his interest before being cast back into her torment. She plucked a pomegranate seed from a bowl and playfully placed it into his open mouth. She reminded him slightly of someone else, someone he had held captive long ago.

He reached around her waist and drew her close to him. She bent her head downward and the two kissed.

"My Lord," a tall orc said as he pushed open the heavy door of the throne room.

Hatmul pulled away from the beautiful dark-haired woman and stared at the intruder. "What is it, Morek?"

The muscular orc quickly knelt and bowed his head. "I would not disturb you, my prince, except that there has been a disturbance in Sudragaru."

Hatmul removed the woman's hand from his chest and stood from his throne. "What kind of disturbance?"

Morek lifted his face. "Someone has found and entered it."

Hatmul clenched his fist. "No!" He spun on the dark-haired woman and waved her away. "Go back to your cell," he commanded. The woman pleaded with her eyes, but that only served to stoke Hatmul's anger. "Now!"

An orc guard stepped forward and seized the chains that ended in an iron circlet around the woman's neck. Whimpering, she was led from the throne room via a side door.

Morek rose to his feet. "It might be nothing, my prince, but I wanted to inform you immediately."

"Summon my brother," Hatmul commanded.

The black and red leopard rose to sit on its haunches. It snarled a toothy yawn and then sat motionless, its jade eyes falling upon Morek and making the orc quicken his steps as he backed out of the throne room.

"Of course, of course," Morek said. He closed the door and the sound of running footsteps echoed in the halls beyond.

Hatmul descended from his dais and walked toward a tall scrying pool. "Sudragaru has been dormant for a very long time," he said. He thought of using the scrying pool now, but thought it better to wait for his brother. He wasn't kept waiting long, however, for less than a minute later a dark cloud formed in the center of the throne room.

Yellow streaks of lightning snaked across the dark cloud as it grew several feet in diameter.

"I am here, brother," Khefir called from within the cloud. A moment later, a skeletal hand reached out from the darkness, followed by a foot stepping forward. The cloud dissipated behind him, leaving the robed skeleton in full view. His glowing eyes fixated on Hatmul for a moment, and then Khefir bowed low and deep, sweeping both arms out to his sides. "How may I be of service?"

"Khefir," Hatmul began. "Your sudden appearance may be impressive to mortals above us, but here I find it rather bothersome. Why not walk through the palace like everyone else?"

Khefir rose form his bow and shook his head, his jaw clicking as he spoke. "When the mighty Hatmul calls, I prefer to come immediately. Walking would take longer."

Hatmul sighed and let the matter drop. "Khefir, it has come to my attention that someone has disturbed Sudragaru."

Khefir approached, his bony feet clicking along the stone floor with each step. "Do you know who?"

Hatmul shook his head. "That is what I want you to discover. I needn't remind you how troublesome it was the last time someone used that plane for their own purposes."

Khefir nodded. "Feistos…"

"I do not want a repeat of that instance," Hatmul said. "You must not only find the person who disturbed Sudragaru, but you must uncover *how* they came to find it in the first place."

"I will, my prince," Khefir said.

"If I am not mistaken, I had charged you with destroying all mention of the plane," Hatmul said. Khefir paused, and most certainly would have blushed had he still had a face of flesh. "Do not fail me," Hatmul added.

"Of course not, my prince," Khefir said with a bow of his head.

"Speak with Morek, he alerted me to the disturbance. Find out what you can from him and then be on your way."

Khefir nodded. "By your command, brother." A dark cloud enveloped the skeletal being and took him from the throne room.

Hatmul stared at the cloud until it had fully vanished, and then he turned to his scrying table. For a moment he thought to open a channel to Sudragaru himself, using the scrying table to survey the plane, but he decided against it, knowing that Khefir would uncover the details quicker than he would be able to without knowing who had unsealed the plane. "Don't fail me brother," Hatmul repeated. He waved a hand over the black waters held within the scrying pool and surveyed the new souls that had been brought down to Hammenfein. At a glance, he could see their guilt as easily as Khefir could. Most were murderers and thieves of various races. Others were orcs, goblins, trolls, and other cursed races. Some of those were guilty of crimes worthy of an eternity's damnation, but most were only guilty of being what they were when Khullan had formed their races.

"My army grows day by day," Hatmul said, studying the new souls. "Icadion should never have cursed the races my father made, for they will be his undoing."

Hatmul then turned away from the scrying pool and barked an order to one of the orc guards. "Go and fetch me a woman."

The orc gave a dutiful nod. "Shall I bring the one that was here moments ago?"

Hatmul shook his head. "She bores me. There is a new woman who was brought today. She is tall, with bronzed skin and red hair. Fetch her, and then see to it that the new orcs are sorted according to strength and assigned to their appropriate units. Khefir will be out for a while, but I do not want to waste valuable training time."

"As you command."

*****

The prelate, a tall man with a full head of dark hair and piercing blue eyes sat cross-legged on a quilted chair. He quietly nodded after hearing Mindaugas' account of what had happened. Lining the council chamber were seven other high priests, and Wendin sat in the back of the room far behind the Keeper of Secrets. "Could you identify the creatures?" the prelate asked.

Mindaugas shook his head. "No. They seemed to be weak to fire, as I said, but they had no real corporeal form."

The prelate nodded as other priests shared hushed whispers amongst themselves.

"It was the girl, she attracts evil," one of the priests said.

Mindaugas took a breath and bit lightly on the tip of his tongue to keep from saying something he would later regret.

Instead, he turned an angry face at the priest, knowing full well that his emotions would convey the message.

"The Keeper of Secrets is blinded by his hope to ally with the dragon," the same priest said. "He does not understand the dangers he is bringing into our walls."

"And yet, my word counts for more than yours, Errgan," Mindaugas said. "You would do well to hold your tongue, for you are the one who is blind."

The prelate stood up, putting a hand in the air to quell the argument before it blossomed further. "Each of us seeks to conquer the evil within our souls, is this not so, Errgan?"

Errgan bowed his head and ceded the point.

Mindaugas smiled, but the prelate turned to him next. "Mindaugas, you may be the Keeper of Secrets, but you are not infallible. It is the way of humans to err. Be careful that you do not let your affection for the girl cloud your judgment."

"She is honest of heart," Mindaugas said, refusing to back down. "Surely, you would see this for yourself if you would speak with her in person."

"I must echo his sentiment here," Wendin said. "Both the boy and the girl are of honorable stock. I may not have your vision, but I can see it as plainly as if it were written upon their hearts."

The priests murmured amongst themselves. Mindaugas grinned, knowing that they had been offended by the elf's words, for he was not supposed to speak in such councils, yet none of them had the courage to quiet him.

"Wendin, your assessment is taken with great respect," the prelate said. "I have known you and Telstian for many decades, and there are few whose opinions I would hold in higher regard." This quieted the priests in the room. "Still, we must ascertain whether the girl did indeed attract the creatures, or whether this incident was a simple matter of being in the wrong place at the wrong time."

Wendin bowed his head in response.

"I will admit," Mindaugas began, "there is a possibility that Kyra accidentally alerted the creatures to her presence when she recently tried to access another plane, but she has promised not to access any additional planes or dimensions without my explicit permission."

"Yet these creatures follow her even in this plane, it would seem," Errgan cut in.

The prelate clapped his hands twice. "The council is adjourned. I will speak with these two in private."

Errgan blushed, his fists clenching and jaw shut tight.

Mindaugas made sure to wave to the priest as he left the room, which started a mumbling rant from the high priest just before the door was slammed closed.

"That was not necessary," the prelate said, beckoning Mindaugas and Wendin to approach closer.

"No, but it felt good," Mindaugas said. "I've never been one who can stomach men like him."

"Arrogance," Wendin said with a nod.

Mindaugas smiled. "He understands." He thumbed at the elf warrior, smiling wide in vindication.

"He has redeeming qualities," the prelate said. "Besides, I dare say there are a great many here who felt similarly about you when you first arrived to take your post as the Keeper of Secrets."

Mindaugas' smile faded and the large man shrugged. "Point taken, I suppose." Eager to move the conversation along, he said, "Shall I summon Kyra and Kathair?"

The prelate shook his head. "No," he said, with a tone much harsher than before. "I have something I need to ask of you both."

Wendin and Mindaugas exchanged glances, then turned and each gave a dutiful nod.

"As prelate, I have the responsibility of reading the great many prophecies given to us by the mystics. I need not tell you how important these are, nor how complicated they can be to interpret or dangerous to abuse."

"Of course," Mindaugas said. "Kyra has not tried to access the prophecies, I can swear to that."

The prelate shook his head. "That isn't what I am saying. Listen, and listen well. There are a great many prophecies that talk of those two."

"Kyra?" Mindaugas asked.

The prelate nodded. "We must tread carefully here, for Kyra and Kathair can become forces for good, or they can become the worst scourge ever to befall the kingdom."

"Kathair would never betray the Middle Kingdom," Wendin interrupted.

"Perhaps not now, no, but it is possible," the prelate insisted. "I cannot share the prophecies with you, so I must ask you to trust me."

"Surely you can show me," Mindaugas said. "I am the Keeper of Secrets, after all."

The prelate shook his head and folded his arms. "This goes beyond even your privileges, Mindaugas, for the prophecies encompass more than Nagar's Blight, or the cursed book that holds the magic that twists dragons. Kathair and Kyra are bound by the fates in such a manner that even the slightest misstep will result in disaster for all of us. The two of them must be kept alive at all costs, for to lose either one will ensure the other's downfall as well."

"I will protect Kathair with my life," Wendin promised.

"And I won't let any harm come to Kyra," Mindaugas pledged.

The prelate nodded. "They must also be kept apart," he added.

Mindaugas frowned and looked to Wendin. "Apart?" he echoed. Wendin shrugged. "I don't understand," Mindaugas said. "What do you mean?"

The prelate sighed. "They share a bond that is very dangerous. If they are allowed to grow that bond, then events will unfold that will turn them against us at this temple, against dragons, and against the kingdom itself."

Mindaugas was speechless. What harm could come from teenagers growing close together?

"Mindaugas, as the prelate, I am within my rights to issue specific orders if they involve our prime directive."

Mindaugas stiffened.

"For now, I will not issue the order, but I advise that you separate them as soon as possible. They should not study together, and they must not be allowed to travel together at this time." The prelate turned to Wendin. "I have made arrangements for baby Brenna. If Magnus wishes to travel with you to the north, then his child will be looked after. Alternatively, he can stay with the host family until he has recovered from his wife's murder."

Wendin gave a bow. "My thanks."

"But you must leave tomorrow morning. Kathair must depart, and he cannot return so long as Kyra remains here." Wendin stiffened, and Mindaugas could tell the elf wasn't happy, but the warrior didn't object.

"I thank you, for your hospitality and kindness. I would not want to take advantage of your goodness. We will be gone with first light."

*****

"What do you mean?" Kyra asked.

Mindaugas slumped onto his bed and bent over to tug at his boot. "Kathair has to move on. The prelate spoke with Wendin about it. They leave in the morning."

"But…" Kyra didn't finish her protest. She had only just barely reconnected with him. She wasn't ready for him to leave yet. "It's because of the creatures that attacked us, isn't it?"

Mindaugas shrugged. "That's part of it, I imagine."

"That wasn't his fault."

135

Mindaugas nodded. "I understand," he said. The look on his face told her there was more to it than this, and that he didn't agree with it.

"You bent the rules once before to tell me about Kathair, remember?"

Mindaugas shook his head. "I could disobey Headmaster Fenn because I am not under his authority. In this case, it is the prelate of Valtuu Temple making the decision. All I can say is he has his reasons."

"Reasons! Hmph!" Kyra spun around and slammed a fist into her open palm. "Then at least let me say goodbye." Mindaugas sighed, but didn't protest, so she took that as permission to see him. She went to her book bag and reached deep inside for a certain stone, then she hurried out of the room before Mindaugas could change his mind. She raced down the hallways until she came to Kathair's room.

The door was open. Two priests were speaking with Wendin while Kathair packed a backpack on the far side of the room. One of the priests turned to look at her, his gray eyes scrutinizing her, searching for her intentions. Wendin came to her rescue, placing a hand on the priest's shoulder and turning him back to the conversation at hand. Wendin then shot her a wink and gestured with his head for her to enter the room. Kyra smiled and went to Kathair.

"Mindaugas just told me," she whispered.

Kathair frowned. "I'm sorry if I caused trouble for you."

Kyra reached out and grabbed his hand. "No, it isn't that at all, I promise. Here, take this." She slipped the stone into his hand and then curled his fingers around it. "It's a summoning stone. You hold it in your hand and focus on my name, and it will show me where you are. Then I can open a portal and visit you anytime we want."

Kathair smiled. "Thank you." He deposited the stone into his pocket. "I'll be sure to keep it safe."

"Good, because I am not going to lose you again like I did when Master Fenn sent you away."

"Actually, it's funny you mention the headmaster. I'll be setting out for the old headmaster's house tomorrow morning."

"You're going to visit Herion?"

Kathair nodded. "Wendin said that Herion has some connections that can help us charter a ship to reach the northern territory. Telstian trusts Herion, so that means Wendin does as well."

Kyra frowned. "But wasn't Herion the one who burned Telstian's letter in the first place?"

Kathair shoved a shirt into his backpack. "At the time, he thought I wasn't ready to learn of my parents' murder. Telstian wrote the letter for me to read when I graduated from Kuldiga Academy, and gave Herion strict instructions not to let me read it before then."

"I guess Telstian hadn't figured you would be returning sooner than that."

Kathair laughed. "No, it was quite a shock when Fenn sent me back. Telstian turned white as a sheet, then he flushed so red I thought his face would explode. He was angrier than I had ever seen him. He thought I had been expelled for misconduct."

"Well, that's almost what happened," Kyra put in with a wink.

"Miss Dimwater," one of the priests called out. "It is late, shall we escort you back to your room for the night?"

Kyra glanced over her shoulder. "No, I'm fine, thanks."

The priest stepped toward her and held out a hand. "I think you misunderstand. These two are going to sleep shortly, as they will be leaving before the sun rises. We should leave them to rest."

"I'll call you," Kathair said. "When I can," he added.

Kyra turned back and flashed him a smile. "You better. Good friends are hard to come by, you know."

Kyra went back to her room shortly thereafter, with two priests following behind her until she closed her door. Mindaugas was already lying on his bed, one arm flopped over his eyes and the other hanging limp over the side. He wasn't snoring full bore yet, but she could tell he was long gone. He went to her bed and pulled out a book she had taken from the library earlier that day. Kathair had actually been the one to find it. It had surprised her that he had been so quickly able to shake off the attack at the manor and refocus on researching possible safe havens for Leatherback. She had not quite been able to concentrate since the manor.

Until now.

She opened the book and found that it had very little to do with other dimensions. Instead, it detailed Viverandon, Njar's home. It had whole chapters devoted to Nonac, the guardian tree that prevented outsiders from reaching the satyr's sacred home. Then, sometime just after midnight she found a passage that discussed a particular gateway that could lead a person to Viverandon through a secret passage, altogether bypassing Nonac.

Kyra glanced to Mindaugas. The slumbering warrior had hardly stirred since she entered the room, but just to be sure she magicked the partition between them so she could attempt to open a portal. As he focused her mind, zeroing in on the target destination, she remembered her promise to the Keeper of Secrets. She hesitated, nearly pulling her hand back, but ultimately decided to go ahead with the spell. She wasn't going anywhere dangerous. This was a path to Viverandon. One that few knew about, but nevertheless a safe path to friendly territory. There were no warnings as there had been in the text about Sudragaru. And, Njar was still missing. She had to find him.

She opened the portal, wincing when small streaks of electricity sizzled across the rift.

Mindaugas snorted, then turned to face the opposite wall.

Kyra slipped through the portal, closing it behind her to ensure Mindaugas wouldn't wake during her absence. As with other portals, the air grew cold while she traveled over great distances. Unlike her other spells, however, she felt herself curving through space, as if sliding down a long chute with bends and twists. The journey took much longer than normal as well, nearly a full minute. She had just begun to panic when she emerged through the other side, falling a few inches to land in the middle of a pine forest. An owl hooted above her, then took flight upon its silent wings and disappeared in the darkness.

The moonlight failed to pierce the forest canopy, so Kyra summoned a ball of light and began to take in her surroundings. Shadows danced around the trees with each step as her mage light chased away the darkness within a twenty yard radius. Rodents and other nocturnal creatures scurried away from her, quietly vanishing into the underbrush. She turned around several times, looking for any clue that would lead her to Viverandon, but there was nothing to find. The forest stretched on in every direction farther than she could see even with the help of her mage light.

She knew enough about Viverandon to understand that the whole territory was imbued with magic that allowed it to move to different locations. Perhaps that was what had happened. She sighed and kicked at a pinecone on the ground. Perhaps the route she used had worked at one time, but now no longer reached Viverandon. Or, maybe it would reach Viverandon if the satyr's land passed close enough to where this portal had opened up for her. Whatever the truth was, she was alone in a dark forest, with no sign of Njar or Nonac.

Determined not to waste a trip until she was certain her attempt had failed, she walked for another mile through the trees. She kept a fireball spell at the ready in her mind, just in case, but she felt no hostile presence. There were only the small animals and the plants around her. Confident in her security, she magnified her mage light until it scattered the darkness entirely, making the forest almost as bright as it would be at mid-day. Another mile farther and she decided there was no more point to continuing. The book had been wrong. This was certainly not a backdoor to Viverandon.

"I should have just gone to bed," she muttered. She turned and started the spell to summon the return portal, focusing on her room in Valtuu Temple, but the magic fizzled as she spoke the incantation. A wisp of smoke rose from her outstretched hand, but no portal opened. She tried again, with the same result.

"I told you there would be no escape," a familiar voice called out.

Kyra's heart quickened. She summoned two fireballs in her hands and then conjured a ward around her. Her eyes scanned the trees with the help of her mage light, but neither the air creatures nor the wolf had appeared yet.

"Show yourself!" Kyra shouted. "Who are you?!"

"You don't know?" the voice taunted. "You really shouldn't meddle with things you don't understand." The raspy voice began to laugh.

"Twice you have attacked, and twice I have beaten you," Kyra shouted. "Come at me again and I will destroy you!"

The voice laughed louder. "Twice?" An air creature formed in front of a tall pine and pointed at her. "I count three encounters."

"Three?" Kyra echoed.

"But it doesn't matter whether we have three or three hundred battles. You woke me Kyra, and I will not rest again until I have devoured you."

Kyra's mind quickly recounted the encounters at the cave and the manor. What did the voice mean by three times? Her eyes widened with sudden realization and her mouth fell slack. "You mean…"

"That's right, Kyra, your nightmare was more than just a dream. We are connected, you and I."

Kyra let out a yell and threw the first fireball, connecting with the air creature and knocking it back toward the pine. She threw the second just a moment later, obliterating the creature entirely. She summoned two more fireballs just as she heard the familiar growl coming from behind. The young sorceress turned and saw the same gray wolf coming around a tree. Its fangs were bared as always, and its big eyes fixated on her.

"Well, come on then!" Kyra shouted. "You want to fight, then let's fight!" She threw her fireballs at the wolf. The animal dashed behind another tree, deftly avoiding the attack.

"Kyra!" the voice shouted as something collided with her magical ward. The force altered the pressure inside the protective shell, making her ears pop and ring. She spun around and summoned a column of fire with both hands, shooting it out at whatever had attacked her, but this time she missed. The air creature had circled around with her and hacked at the ward relentlessly. Kyra decided on a different tactic, turning and summoning a thunderclap to disorient her attacker. The spell knocked the creature back, nearly throwing it to the ground. She followed that with a fireball thrown from her left hand and a bolt of lightning from her right. The two blasts hit the creature simultaneously and extinguished it.

"This is the end, Kyra!" The voice began laughing louder now as seven more air creatures formed around her.

Try as she might, she couldn't fend them all off at once. She blasted two only to have the other five rush her, bashing her protective shell over and over until it began cracking. Golden light exploded from each new fissure as the spell weakened around her. She managed to destroy three more, but just as she was getting the upper hand several new air creatures appeared.

Then the wolf came back into view.

Its eyes locked with Kyra's just as her ward shattered.

The air creatures started to close in as she desperately summoned a wall of fire to hold them off. She closed her eyes, trying to maintain her focus lest the fire wall collapse.

The wolf howled.

The air creatures screamed and hissed.

A massive thunderclap extinguished Kyra's spell and knocked her to the ground. Her ears rang and her vision blurred from the force of the blast. She could just make out four air creatures that had survived her fire wall, but she couldn't summon more than a spark to her hands. Her focus was drained somehow, and her magic refused her call. The air creatures moved in for the final blow, and so did the wolf. Kyra could hardly think. She grasped a nearby stick, but was kicked in the side by one of the creatures. The air left her body, and she was certain the fight was lost.

The wolf lunged in, but to her surprise it didn't attack her. Instead, the wolf's jaws closed on an air creature and the magical apparition screamed in agony as the wolf tore it asunder. It moved on to the next air creature, taking a defensive stance over Kyra as if protecting a pup.

More air creatures appeared around them, growing in numbers with each passing second. Even despite the wolf's heroism, it appeared as though the battle was going to end very badly for them.

A purple bolt of lightning struck the ground, forcing the air creatures back. The wolf continued to shield Kyra as a black cloud formed over the ground where the lightning had struck. An acrid odor filled the air, and then a bony hand emerged from the cloud.

"Back, Feistos! Back to your cage!" someone said.

Kyra pushed herself up to a sitting position and stared at the cloud. She couldn't believe her eyes when Khefir stepped from the swirling black mists, lightning and fire flowing from his bony fingers and destroying several air creatures with each blow.

"Khefir!" the voice protested. "You can't deny me!"

Khefir produced a gnarled staff of ebony and then struck the ground twice. Lightning blasted the forest around them and purple flames rose in a dome, trapping all of them inside with the Collector of the Damned. "Feistos!" Khefir shouted. "Kneel before me!" Khefir stamped the staff on the ground once more and deafening thunder roared through the sky.

All of the air creatures flashed different colors, then were pulled together, merging into a single being that was forced to kneel in front of Khefir. Only this time the body appeared to be solid, instead of made of air.

"You can't do this to me!" the man shouted.

Khefir stretched his staff out to the kneeling man. "Feistos, I banish you back to Sudragaru, and hereby seal the rift that loosed you."

"You can't deny me!" Feistos screamed. "She trespassed! She owes me her soul!"

Khefir touched the staff to Feistos' head. A golden spark burned into the man's forehead as he knelt helplessly, screaming and crying out in protest. "Go back to the prison I made for you, Feistos." Black tendrils broke through the ground around Feistos and wrapped around him as the spark in his head turned into a flame that seemed to torment him without actually consuming his flesh. The tendrils pulled him through the dirt and soon the screaming faded.

Kyra sat motionless, her mouth open and her magic drained. How had Khefir found her? And why had he come? Their deal was for Leatherback's safety, not hers. Had he come to collect her soul, knowing that she was about to die?

Khefir turned to her, his jaw clicking with each word that came out of his fleshless mouth. "Kyra, I might have known it was you."

Kyra tried to speak, but nothing came out. The wolf bowed its head and moved away from her, somehow making her feel even more vulnerable.

"You went to Sudragaru."

Kyra nodded. There was no point in lying to a god.

Khefir leaned upon his staff, his glowing eyes boring into her very being. "You are searching for another place to take Leatherback to, am I right?"

Kyra nodded again.

"You must stop this," Khefir said. "When you opened Sudragaru you not only loosed Feistos' soul, but you alerted my brother to your actions as well."

"Feistos?" Kyra echoed. "But, it was his book that said I should go to Sudragaru. He described it—"

Khefir shook his head. "It was a trap. Feistos made those books with magic to lure the unwary to Sudragaru so he could consume their soul and be released. He was caught sneaking through Hammenfein, and my brother banished him to Sudragaru as punishment rather than keep him in Hammenfein itself."

"But why?"

Khefir laughed, his jaw clicking and jerking with the expression. "Feistos was a unique kind of sorcerer. He fed upon spiritual energy. To keep him in Hammenfein would be akin to giving him an eternal feast. So, my brother sent him to a plane where no other soul existed, condemning Feistos to an eternity of starvation."

Kyra nodded, then looked to the wolf, who had lied down a few feet away and seemed fully at ease now. "I thought the wolf was with Feistos."

"Silverfang is the only creature native to Sudragaru. He holds powerful magic, and has at times aided me." Khefir tilted his skinless skull to the side and watched the wolf for a moment. "It seems he has taken a liking to you."

"It's a good thing too," Kyra said. "He saved my life."

"Much more than that," Khefir said. "He saved your very soul. Feistos would have consumed your essence entirely so that nothing would have remained. It is a fate far worse than death."

Kyra felt a sour knot form in her stomach at those words.

"Come, we cannot waste time. The priests are looking for you," Khefir said.

"The priests? I haven't even been gone an hour," she said. "I'm sure no one misses me."

Khefir held out his left hand and Silverfang approached him to receive a pat on the head. "No, Kyra. An hour has passed in this plane, but back at Valtuu Temple it has been two days and twelve hours. Kathair and Wendin have been rushed away from the temple, and the priests have been searching your books for clues to your whereabouts."

"No, Kathair wouldn't leave if I was missing."

"They didn't tell him," Khefir said. "The priests sent him on his way at sunrise, and you were not discovered missing until Mindaugas woke an hour after that."

"No, it can't be. The book was on my bed. They would have found it."

Khefir nodded. "In fact, the book you used to conjure the portal to this plane is here."

Kyra checked herself for the book, but didn't see it. "No it isn't, I would know if I was holding a large book."

Khefir stamped his staff on the ground once and the three of them appeared in the very spot where the portal had deposited her when she first arrived. There, sitting on the ground where the portal had closed, was the book. "You see, in order to leave this plane, you have to use the book. That's why its magic brings it with the traveler."

"That's why my spell didn't work when I tried to conjure the portal," Kyra guessed.

Khefir nodded. "It has to do with the time distortion. Because each minute here is an hour back in the mortal realm, a precise spell is needed to exit this plane. Surely you noticed how the portal was different than others you had used."

Kyra said she had. "I thought this would take me to Viverandon."

"The time distortion in this plane was useful for that a long time ago. At the time this book was written, Viverandon traveled in a predetermined path through the mortal plane, using its magic to remain hidden. If a person spent seven days in this plane, they would find themselves aligned with Viverandon, and could travel to it without facing Nonac. However, such is not the case anymore. Njar's predecessor fixed that weakness centuries ago."

Kyra sighed. "I had to try."

"Perhaps you should listen to Mindaugas," Khefir offered. "He will help you in your research, but you have to be willing to develop patience. Magic is not a sprinting race, it is a lifelong pursuit." Khefir held out his left hand and the book floated up to land in his hand. "Now, I have to send you back before my brother realizes you were here. I promised to keep Leatherback safe, and I can't have my brother discover you for it would endanger Leatherback."

"How is he?" Kyra asked.

"He is well. Now come, I must take you back." Khefir pointed at a space in the air with his staff and created a portal back to Valtuu Temple. Kyra could see her room. Next to her bed stood Sal Vinder, another priest she knew as Errgan, and Mindaugas. They each turned, weapons at the ready, and then froze when they saw her. A gentle force pushed her through the portal and she found herself standing just inches away from Mindaugas a moment later.

"By the Ancients!" Errgan screamed just before running from the room.

Kyra turned to see Khefir reach his bony hand through the portal. He snapped his fingers and the book the Feistos wrote about Sudragaru answered his summons by bursting into flame.

Khefir then pulled his arm back and closed the portal.

Mindaugas was whiter than fresh snow, standing completely still.

Only Sal dared move, approaching Kyra with a questioning expression on his face.

"I…" Kyra started to explain, but what could she say?

"I misjudged you," Sal said softly. "You have defiled our temple." The words cut Kyra more painfully than any blow Feistos had landed.

"No, Sal, it isn't what it looks like... I was looking for Viverandon."

"You consort with devils," Sal said with a shake of his head. He held up his left hand. "Be gone!"

A flash of light ripped her form the room and deposited her outside the temple walls. Warning bells sounded around the complex, and priests scurried about the grounds. Within moments, two guards armed with guandaos emerged from the large green double doors and then shut them. They crossed their weapons, making it entirely clear that she was no longer welcome.

Chapter 10

"What news?" Rheddis asked.

The single Blacktongue bowed his head and held out a clean dagger, the sure sign of failure. Had the Blacktongues succeeded, the dagger would have the target's dried blood upon it.

Rheddis tossed his goblet aside, splashing wine across the stone floor. "The boy yet lives?"

The blacktongue nodded.

"Did any of your comrades survive?" Rheddis asked.

The blacktongue shook his head.

"Fools, the lot of you. I delivered the boy into your hands! How could you fail so miserably?"

"Magnus' wife is dead, but the others live," the blacktongue responded. "They escaped the town through a tunnel."

"And how many witnesses in the town will tell of your failure?"

"None, my lord. No one in the town survived."

Rheddis snorted. "You massacred an entire town, but failed to catch your true target?"

The blacktongue took the dagger and pointed it inward, pressing it to his bare, tattooed chest. "I have shamed myself."

Rheddis nodded. "That much is true, but your death will accomplish nothing." He stood up and took several steps toward the assassin. "Where are they now?"

"I followed them as far as Valtuu Temple, but I could not get close to them because of the priests."

Rheddis stroked his chin. "Yes, their true sight would have caught you long before you approached their walls. You were right to end the pursuit there."

The doors at the far end of the chamber opened and in walked an old man with a long beard. He walked with a staff, the bottom tapping along the stone floor with each step. "Rheddis, I believe I know where they are heading."

Rheddis eyed the man carefully. It had been years since he had last seen him, but he recognized him despite the wrinkles of time that now creased his face. "Darin, come in," he said with a slight nod. "I am glad to see you in good health."

Darin grunted. "I'm too old and stubborn to let my health go bad. I have urgent news."

Rheddis nodded. "Yes, I assumed you would have."

Darin came to stand next to the blacktongue and looked down at the man. "I tried to warn you that Kathair was not to be taken lightly. He may be young, but he is strong." He looked back to Rheddis. "The elf warrior who travels with him is one of the very best as well."

Rheddis shrugged. "I have heard of Wendin, but we will not fail again."

Darin wrinkled his nose and cleared his throat. "I received word, they are traveling to northward."

Rheddis stiffened. "Do they suspect us?"

"Of course not. They know that blacktongues hunt them, but not who commands the assassins. They will try to make haste for the northern territory. I suspect they will go to Herion's house for help. After all, Wendin knows him, and Herion was headmaster of Kuldiga Academy when Kathair started there."

Rheddis nodded. "Yes, I suppose it's a good possibility they would go to him. He is not far from Valtuu Temple either."

"More than a possibility," Darin said. "It's a certainty. He dug into a pocket and pulled out a long, yellowed parchment. "This is letter details some contacts I have up north. Kathair and the others will need a ship, so we should try to cut them off before they can cross the sea. If they find Malech, then we will be found out. Beyond the name of my contacts, this will give you your instructions. I have some specific places I want to position our assassins. We cannot afford another failure." He glanced back to the blacktongue, who still held the dagger to his chest as if anticipating Rheddis would change his mind. "I'd send a lot more this time," Darin said, thumbing at the assassin.

Rheddis arched a brow. "And we can trust your contacts to keep their mouths shut?"

"As I said, they owe me several favors," Darin said with a shrug. "Besides, they know to double cross me is to sign their own execution orders. Now, all you have to do is get your men in place before Kathair and his protectors reach the sea. I'm certain Herion will assist them with some sort of portal so the group can outpace your assassins, but I can create a portal as well, and get the blacktongues to their positions."

Rheddis smiled. "Very well." He turned to the blacktongue. "Icadion's beard, put the dagger away. Go assemble your new team." He held the letter out for the assassin. The tattooed man sheathed his dagger and snatched the letter, offering a thankful bow before turning and running toward the door.

"Have them meet outside at the western field," Darin called out to the blacktongue. "I'll meet you out there and create a portal that will put you just a short distance from the town Herion is likely to send them to. I don't want the targets to escape again."

The blacktongue stopped just long enough to turn and offer one more bow before rushing out of the chamber.

"You could have sent me instructions," Rheddis said once they were alone. "Why risk being seen?"

Darin smiled. "I have another issue I wanted to discuss with you." The old man leaned heavily on his staff, narrowing his eyes at Rheddis. "I have an informant near Valtuu Temple. Of course, he told me everything about Kathair and Wendin, but I also heard that Kyra was expelled from the temple grounds."

"Truly?"

Darin nodded. "Apparently, Khefir appeared in the temple with her, dropping her off through some sort of portal and stealing a book from the temple as well."

"The Collector of the Damned appeared *inside* Valtuu Temple?" Rheddis asked. "And Kyra was involved?"

Darin's smile widened. "The priests expelled her then and there. They refuse to hear Mindaugas' arguments also, claiming that she is never to return."

"That is interesting," Rheddis noted. "But, what do you want to do about it?"

"For now, nothing, but I want to keep a close watch on her. Do you think you could manage that?"

"I can assign two blacktongues to her—"

Darin shook his head and waved the notion off. "No, Rheddis, I want *you* to handle it yourself."

Rheddis bristled. "Me? I am not some lowly errand boy that you can—"

"You forget your place," Darin said, his voice taking on an edge that Rheddis knew bordered on deadly. "You will see to this yourself."

"And who will take command in my absence?" Rheddis asked. He wasn't so much worried about ongoing duties as he was concerned with his position.

Darin shook his head. "I'm not ousting you, if that's what you think, Rheddis. Kathair is priority one, and so long as the blacktongues don't muck it up again, it will be dealt with. Kyra is priority two. I can't trust this mission to anyone else. You know how valuable she is. In the right hands, she could be quite useful. But, despite the recent expulsion from the temple, Mindaugas travels with her, and I can't have him filling her head with the wrong ideas. She needs… a more subtle hand to guide her."

"So I am to watch and report?" Rheddis asked. *Hardly seems worth my time, regardless of her powers.*

"That's part of it, but not all," Darin said. "I want you to orchestrate a meeting, try to ingratiate yourself with them. Then, when the time is right, kill Mindaugas and take her in under your wing."

Rheddis' eyebrows shot up. "Kill the Keeper of Secrets?"

"He is an obstacle, always will be. If we strike now, there won't be any suitable replacements. Besides, with Kyra expelled from the temple he is too angry to think strategically at the moment. He's blinded by the temple's insulting treatment of his new protégé. He won't be as guarded as he otherwise would be. More than that, the temple won't want to go looking for him any time soon. We have to act quickly. With any luck, Kathair and Mindaugas will be dead within the week, and Kyra will be ready for our guiding wisdom."

Rheddis grinned. "I understand," he said with a confident nod.

"And Rheddis, don't fail."

*****

Khefir stepped through the black smoke and entered his brother's throne room, finding Hatmul sitting upon his throne with two women flanking him in scanty dresses that hardly covered their voluptuous curves. In that moment, Khefir felt a pang of anger, seeing his brother still able to enjoy the gifts a body brings to those who have them. Even the dead women found reprieve, for Hatmul could give them corporeal bodies at any time he wished, which gave him his pick of any woman that came into the fires of Hammenfein. Khefir, on the other hand, could never have a body again, as it was taken by Icadion, with powers that no other god could come close to reversing.

"My brother, I have news," Khefir said.

Hatmul pushed one of the women from him and peered around her hip. "I have mentioned how I hate your random appearances in my throne room, have I not?"

152

Khefir bowed his head to maintain the appearance of a reverent servant. "And, as I have reminded you, my lord, this is the fastest way for me to travel. I wish only to serve you well, and bring you my discoveries in a timely manner."

Hatmul sighed and sat up. The two women moved to cling to his shoulders, and this time the god of hell let them stay. "What is it?"

"I have dealt with the intruder," Khefir said. "Feistos somehow deposited one of his books with the priests at Valtuu Temple."

Hatmul lurched forward and spit upon the floor, the liquid hissing as it melted into the stone. "Curse those dragon-lovers. They would be the ones to hold such an artifact." He raised a finger, pointing at some indescript point in the distance. "They seek to thwart me, they always have! Curse those priests and curse the Ancients! They never belonged here!"

Khefir nodded. "The priest released Feistos, but I have imprisoned him once more and sealed Sudragaru."

Hatmul sighed. "Good. And what of the priest? I don't suppose you could collect their soul and bring them here?"

Khefir shook his head. "No, my lord. The priests are not corrupt, and very few have ever subjected themselves to your rule through deeds done in the mortal realm."

Hatmul drove a fist into his waiting palm. "Very well. What of the book?"

Khefir swept his bony arms out to the sides. "I entered the temple and took it myself. No additional copies survive."

Hatmul jumped from his seat, nearly throwing the two women back. "You entered Valtuu Temple!?" He clapped his hands and the evil grin on his face stretched so wide his lips turned white across the tops. "I wish I had seen their faces!"

Khefir bowed once more. "If there is nothing else, my lord?"

Hatmul shook his head. "No, that is all. You have done well, brother. I shall remember to reward you accordingly."

Khefir nodded and disappeared through a cloud of smoke. *And I shall remember to reward you accordingly.* Khefir transported himself not to another location within Hammenfein, but to the pocket dimension in which he kept Leatherback. The dragon had grown considerably since Kyra had entrusted him to Khefir. Fortunately, there was still no sign of the blight within the creature.

"Kyra?" Leatherback asked when Khefir stepped into view.

"Not yet," Khefir said. "She is well, but I have not found a place to relocate you where the both of you will be safe."

The dragon snorted blue flames and laid its head down on its crossed forelegs as its tail thumped against the rocky ground.

"She is searching in places she ought not, and it has aroused my brother's suspicion," Khefir said. "I am afraid we will need to relocate you to another place. If he should find you, there would be no end to your torment."

Leatherback let out a long, slow groan that rumbled deep within his throat.

Khefir stepped close and patted the dragon's snout. "I will keep my promise to her, and to you. I am doing everything within my power to help, but I cannot move you, not yet. My brother would detect it if I moved you across Terramyr, or if I traversed any of the planes he is aware of with you in my custody. But, there may be one place he would not look."

Leatherback's large eyes narrowed as a plume of smoke snaked out from his nostrils.

"Ivarglendar," Khefir said. "It would be dangerous, of course, but it might still be safer than remaining here."

"Sky?" Leatherback asked.

Khefir looked up to the red clouds of fire and smoke above them. He couldn't see the thick slabs of granite above the clouds, but he knew they were there. The dragon wanted to fly, needed to in fact, but that would not be possible here. Neither would it be possible in Ivarglendar. "No," Khefir said. "I'll return soon." With that, he walked into another cloud of smoke and emerged in his own chambers, a meager room with little more than a bed, a table and chair, and a large bookshelf filled with various tomes older than most of the races that lived upon Terramyr.

"One day, brother, I will repay you the kindness you have shown me." Khefir stroked his index finger of bone along his left ulna. He could still remember the time when his body had been whole. His muscles had been full of strength, his heart had beat wildly, and many there were in the Heaven City that thought Khefir the more handsome brother. Not so anymore.

Khefir removed his ragged cloak, daring to stand in his room as a naked skeleton. He looked down, his sight magically preserved by Icadion those centuries ago when his flesh had been stripped from him, and studied his bony legs and hips. By all accounts, he was now nothing more than a monster, the very embodiment of death itself, and the Collector of the Damned.

But he was not the real monster. That title rightfully belonged to his brother, Hatmul. One day, he would make the other gods see the truth. Somehow, he would expose Hatmul for who he truly was. When the timing was right and the evidence aligned with Icadion's will. Until then, he would do what he could to frustrate Hatmul. If that meant keeping a dragon in a special pocket dimension until the beast was old enough to be unleashed on Hatmul, then so be it. The dragon had no sign of the taint yet, but even if he ultimately succumbed to it, Khefir could use the dragon against his brother. One way or another, he would have his revenge, even if it took another thousand years of planning.

*****

Mindaugas hadn't spoken since before Kyra had been expelled from the temple. His usual, jovial self was replaced by a quiet, stern face and hard glances cast in her direction whenever she tried to break the silence. They retraced their journey, heading for Buktah on their way back to Kuldiga Academy. Only when they stopped to make camp for the night in the forest did Mindaugas break his silence.

"A message came for you, just before you were found with the…" his voice trailed off. "Well, before Khefir appeared with you."

"He saved my life," Kyra said.

Mindaugas shrugged. "We had a deal, and you broke it." The large man reached into his pocket and pulled out a piece of paper.

Kyra took it from him and opened it, reading its contents quickly before folding it and putting it into the fire Mindaugas was building. "Khefir saved Leatherback too," she said.

Mindaugas kicked at the dirt, his hands on his hips as he turned away from her, shaking his head and mumbling something she couldn't quite make out. After a moment, he turned around once more and jabbed a finger in the air. "You are trifling with powers you cannot even begin to comprehend!"

Kyra bristled. "I understand them, and so did my mother. It was her notes that helped me make the arrangement with him."

"And what did that demon ask for in return? Your soul? Your allegiance? By the gods! Maybe those other priests *were* right. You are dangerous, Kyra Dimwater."

A tinge of pain stabbed at her, but she didn't let it take root. Instead, she absorbed the hurt and replaced it with anger. "I have been betrayed by every man who has ever claimed to care for me, save only two. If you wish to join the lot of them, then do so. I don't need your help, and I don't need your approval."

"I am the Keeper of Secrets!" Mindaugas shouted. "It is my responsibility to ensure the safety of this realm. Can you not see the danger you have brought to the Middle Kingdom?! Answer my question, what did Khefir take from you as payment to harbor Leatherback?"

"You aren't the only one who can keep secrets," Kyra fired back. "I won't tell you."

"You will, this instant!" Mindaugas made a step toward her, but the young sorceress raised her hand and summoned a barrier between them, thickening the air so that he could not reach her.

"You and Sal have both forgotten, it is not a person's powers that makes them evil, it is what they choose to do with their abilities. I don't have to explain myself to you." With that, she turned and opened a portal, only this time she was not going to her manor. She went to the special grove of aspens Njar had created and stepped through. She closed the opening behind her, leaving her books, her horse, and everything else back at the camp with Mindaugas.

"Kyra?" a voice called out.

Kyra turned and saw a beautiful young blonde who appeared to be of similar age. "You sent the letter?" Kyra asked.

The young woman nodded. "I did."

"But..." Kyra eyed the woman from head to toe. "You aren't what I expected."

The young woman smiled. "The trees here are beautiful."

Kyra caught on quickly, realizing that the young woman was testing her. "Njar planted the grove for Leatherback, to stave off Nagar's Blight."

The young woman's smile widened. She closed her eyes and the human form melted away as water running over thick glass, revealing a young female satyr with white fur and large, bright eyes. "My name is Asteri, I am the restorer."

Kyra gave a bow of her head. "Kyra Dimwater."

Asteri motioned for Kyra to sit nearby. "We have not seen Njar for some time," Asteri said.

"Nor have I," Kyra replied. "I was surprised when he didn't come to my aid during the last battle with Severin. I thought perhaps he was injured, or unable to use his portal. Until I received your letter, I had hoped he was in Viverandon."

Asteri shook her head. "No. He is missing, and Nonac is sick."

Kyra narrowed her eyes. "Nonac? The guardian tree?"

"Yes. It has become diseased, and if not healed soon it will die."

"What will happen to Viverandon then?" Kyra asked.

"Then Viverandon will cease to be protected from this world. It will stand in one place as any other city, easy to find and attack. We satyrs are not prepared for such vulnerabilities. We have always depended on Nonac to protect us, moving us from place to place so none could find us except for the guests we choose to allow."

Kyra nodded. "I have been to the Pools of Fate," she said. "Njar took me once. I was able to see much of your beautiful home. If there is a way I can help—"

Asteri smiled. "Part of my mission was to ascertain whether you had betrayed him."

Kyra stiffened and shook her head vigorously. "Njar is one of my truest friends, and he only ever sought to help me and Leatherback."

Asteri held up a furry hand and nodded. "I know that now, I only mention it so you understand. He would never abandon us, so I feared the worst."

"I understand," Kyra said. "If anyone here understands betrayal, it's me."

Asteri tilted her head to the side.

"Long story, but my father disowned me, my tutor turned out to be an imposter who was trying to use me for his own gain, and just last night I was expelled from Valtuu Temple after being promised that I could conduct my research there."

"You search for a new home for Leatherback?" Asteri guessed.

Kyra nodded once more.

"Where is he? Is he safe?"

Kyra took in a breath. "He is safe for now."

"And the taint?"

"No sign of it yet, but I am worried about it constantly." She decided to exclude Khefir's involvement.

"Did anyone at Kuldiga Academy learn of Njar?"

Kyra shook her head. "He wasn't found out by any of them, and I am certain none of them had anything to do with his disappearance."

"And you said you battled Severin alone, without Njar's help?"

Kyra nodded. "Njar wasn't there."

"Then perhaps Severin got to him first." Asteri took in a slow breath and turned her head to the side. "If Severin killed him, then we are lost."

Kyra tried to think. Where could Njar be? If he was dead, then what could be done for Nonac? "Is there some remedy we can search for?"

Asteri shrugged. "Nonac is very sick. I am the restorer, but I am not as experienced as my predecessors. It would be a difficult task even with Njar to guide and help me, but without him I fear it is impossible."

"What can I do?" Kyra asked. "There must be something."

Asteri shook her head. "If Njar left you for Viverandon, then there are no clues to follow out here anymore."

"What about the Pools of Fate?" Kyra asked.

"No, I cannot use them. Njar can summon them, but I do not have that power, otherwise I would have done so."

"What about me?" Kyra asked. A smile stretched her lips then. "When Njar showed me the Pools of Fate, I was able to interact with them in a way he had never seen before. Perhaps I can do so again."

"I don't think so." Asteri shook her head and sighed.

"What's the harm in letting me try?" Kyra pressed.

"Harm?" Asteri echoed. "There could be a lot of harm done by such things. The Pools of Fate are not to be taken lightly."

"I know that, but I am a friend to your people, and I want to find Njar as much as you do. Please, let me try."

Asteri sat there for a few moments, her eyes locked with Kyra's. After a while, she stretched her hands out over the grass and called up a glowing mist from the ground itself. "If you will allow me, I would use my powers to better understand you."

Kyra snorted. "The priests at Valtuu Temple didn't like what they saw," she warned her.

Asteri nodded. "I am not a priest, nor do I make the judgment myself. Terramyr is alive, coursing with energy and intelligence in much the same way that our bodies are filled with blood and spirit. I would use part of this essence to understand you. It is part of my powers as restorer. I promise it will not hurt."

"Well, if it's the only way to let me use the Pools of Fate, then do as you will."

"Stand up, and hold your arms out to your sides," Asteri instructed. "Then just remain still until I am finished.

Kyra rose to her feet and held her arms out while the green energy swirled around her ankles. It felt cold at first, similar to a mountain brook, but then it warmed and stretched over her legs. Within moments it covered her entire body. Flashes of yellow light sparked within the green energy, and then the sparks dashed through her. She nearly jumped away reflexively, but after the first spark passed through without causing pain she held firm in place, waiting as the energy flowed through and around her for several minutes. Then, once the energy had completed its scan, it withdrew from Kyra and formed itself into a ball that fit into Asteri's waiting palm. The energy then melted into the satyr's hand.

Asteri closed her eyes as if in deep meditation. Two minutes later, she opened her eyes and exhaled. "You are quite beautiful, Kyra Dimwater," Asteri said. "I can see why Njar cared for you so much."

Kyra drew her brow into a knot. She accepted the compliment easily enough, but expected the insult to follow. *Sure, but tell me now how you can't trust me because of the darkness inside me.*

"I see in you a great combination of powers, some light and some dark," Asteri began.

Here it comes. Kyra thought, bracing herself for the rejection.

"We satyrs often strive to maintain balance, for that is the best environment for Terramyr to thrive. With life comes death, with light, there is dark, and with joy there must be grief. If not so, then the balance is thrown off and the energies cannot flow. You, Kyra, embody this very principle. It's wondrous to see and marvelous to feel. You have both light and darkness within you, each power bringing you its strengths and weaknesses in perfect harmony and balance. Never before have I seen such beauty in a human."

Kyra opened her mouth, her argument ready to issue forth before she had fully comprehended Asteri's words. As the satyr's comments finally reached Kyra's mind, she stood there open mouthed and staring.

"Wait… what?"

Asteri giggled. "I will take you to the Pools of Fate. Come, hold my hand."

Chapter 11

Kathair, Wendin, and Magnus stopped at the edge of a dark forest northwest of Valtuu Temple.

"This should be the way," Wendin said, pointing to a thin trail running between a tall pair of pines.

The trio entered the forest, making good time along the trail. Kathair hadn't seen any Blacktongues since Alva's death, but he still couldn't shake the feeling that something wasn't right. Every rustle through the leaves made the small hairs of his neck stand on end. It was as if he could feel eyes watching his every move.

Magnus seemed to be thinking the same thing. He kept looking to either side of the trail, scanning the forest with his left hand on his weapon and occasionally reaching up to his wife's wedding ring, which he wore around his neck with a necklace made of a leather strip.

The last day and a half of travel had eased Kathair's guilt just enough that he didn't feel like shrinking away whenever Magnus looked at him or spoke to him, but it was still difficult. He couldn't imagine what Magnus was feeling. Having lost his wife and then left Brenna in the temple's care so he could hunt the Blacktongues. Kathair shook his head just before his thoughts could fully capture him in grief, forcing himself to think instead about Herion and the letter the old wizard had burned.

His mind ran through several scenarios, puzzling out why the old wizard had done such a thing, but he knew he would have the true answers soon enough. The group traveled for nearly half a day before they came to a small iron gate set in a six foot tall fence made of stone and mortar.

Wendin pushed on the gate, easily swinging it open. "No lock," the elf warrior said.

"He's a wizard," Magnus commented. "I imagine he has other barriers at his disposal should he feel the need."

Wendin nodded and went through. Magnus followed, then Kathair. The three of them stopped and stared. From outside the wall, it had appeared as though the forest continued on the other side, with tall trees and scattered brush, but once they stepped through the gate they were met with an entirely different sight. There were no pines or oaks inside the fence. Instead, there were exquisitely manicured flower beds, hedges in neat rows, and ferns dotting the gardens stretching several hundred feet until they reached a yellow manor house that stood three stories tall, with a glass roof and several balconies along the third floor.

An old man emerged from the double doors and waved toward them. "I have been expecting you," Herion said.

Kathair shook his head, trying to orient himself to the paradisiacal gardens. After a moment, the other two moved forward toward the house, but Kathair stepped out through the gate once more and looked over the fence as best he could, jumping up and down to clear the barrier. Again, he could see only trees like the rest of the forest. A most clever disguise.

He passed through the gate again and closed the iron behind himself.

"It keeps the riff-raff out," Herion said. The old man was now only a few feet away. "I found many years ago that if one wishes to avoid thieves and burglars, it is best to make it look like there is nothing worth taking." Herion turned and gestured toward his manor. "Of course, if anyone comes through the gate and should be tempted by this sight, I have other means of dealing with them."

Wendin nodded. "Master Herion, we have come for—"

Herion patted the air. "I know. Come, let's not waste time with idle chatter. I'll tell you what I can, and then give you the name of a contact who will take you across the sea to the northern territory." He eyed Kathair from head to toe. "You certain you want to make the journey? It won't be an easy one."

Kathair glanced at Magnus and then nodded. "We've come too far to turn back now."

Herion followed Kathair's glance and looked to Magnus. "Magnus, has something happened?"

The large man nodded. "Blacktongues killed Alva."

Herion put a hand to his mouth and gasped. "And what of Brenna? Where is your daughter?"

"She is safe," Magnus said. "I'd rather not discuss it further."

Herion gave a single nod. "You have my sympathies. Come, let's go inside."

Kathair followed the group in silence as they entered the large double doors of the manor house. The inside reminded the young swordsman quite a bit of Kuldiga Academy. There were paintings and statuettes lining the walls. Relics and placards were hung up as well. The antechamber opened to a large staircase of dark wood with a red carpet running along the middle. Off to the sides were grand parlors, each replete with books and desks.

"My studies," Herion said when he noted Kathair's staring. "I may not be at Kuldiga Academy anymore, but a man cannot let his brain sit idly too long lest it waste away." He pointed to the parlor on the left. "Potions and alchemical research." He then turned and pointed to his right. "Spells and enchantments."

"You mentioned a contact?" Magnus interrupted.

"So I did," Herion replied. "Come, the second floor." He led them up the stairs and into a grand sitting room upon the second floor. Several high-backed armchairs sat around a small table, upon which was a map and three books. Kathair moved to the table and turned his head to the side so he could read the book titles.

"Wards and Traps, The Nebekar's Sea, Highlander's Plight," Kathair said. His eyes then caught sight of something that looked like a small, transparent dragon scale. It was just about the size of

164

his hand, and sat on the table next to the books. "What's this?" he asked, reaching out for it.

"Light reading for when I can't sleep," Herion said with a wink, patting Kathair on the shoulder and then stooping in front of him to rearrange the books so that each of them was stacked neatly. Herion then picked up the strange lens and placed it into his pocket. "This helps me see the words. My eyes aren't as good as they used to be, and sometimes I need something stronger than my spectacles."

Kathair smiled and gave an understanding nod. "Wards and Traps," Kathair said again after he reexamined the title. "Would that also tell you how to get through wards?" Wendin and Magnus took their seats and removed their backpacks while Herion circled around the table and picked up the book. "You see, Kyra has the deed to her family manor, but she can't get in. Some sort of magical spell is keeping it closed."

Herion nodded and flipped through the pages. "Yes, this will have what she needs. Though, I suspect I know what it is."

"What?" Kathair asked.

"I imagine it is a familial cypher ward. All she needs to do is prick her finger and place a drop of blood upon the key when she inserts it for the first time. Then, once the magic senses her genealogy, she will be allowed to open the lock. Simple as that."

"Would you mind if I shared the book with her?" Kathair asked

Herion frowned and glanced around. "Is she with you?"

Kathair shook his head. "No, but I have a summoning stone. I can call her with it and she can open up a portal. I could give her the book then and she could try to unlock the door."

Herion wagged a finger in the air. "No portals, not here! I have a lot of wards in place, why else would I be reading up on the subject?" Herion narrowed his eyes on Kathair for a moment and then his expression softened. "Tell you what, if you promise not to stay out too late, I can take down some of my wards in the garden and make it safe for you to see her. You can take the book, and I'll give you a needle as well. Just make sure to bring my things back, okay?"

Kathair nodded and smiled.

Herion nodded. "Let's talk, then we can eat, and then you can go and see if the door is locked with a familial cypher."

Kathair grinned wider. "Great, thank you."

Herion shrugged and placed his hands on the table for leverage as he slowly lowered himself down into his chair. "Now, I suspect you want to know the contents of Telstian's letter, but I am sorry to say I never read it. I only know that it spoke of your parents, Kathair."

"If you never read it, why burn it?" Kathair asked.

Herion snorted. "Because Telstian told me you weren't to have it until you graduated, under any circumstances. He said if you tried to take it before then, I should burn it. So I did. Though, I should say that even if he hadn't I would have likely done so anyway just because you were snooping around in my things."

Magnus smirked. "A chip off the old block then eh?"

Wendin shot the northman a look.

Magnus folded his arms. "It's true, his old man certainly got into some mischief."

"Be that as it may, it doesn't excuse Kathair's actions," Herion groused. "In any case, I knew Telstian could easily send a new letter at the appropriate time, so no harm was done. Besides that, I suppose that Magnus has told you everything that Telstian would be able to anyway."

"True," Magnus said.

"So, what else do you need from me?"

"Help moving north," Wendin said. "We have already been attacked once."

Herion nodded. "I already told you, I have a contact who can sail you across the waters."

"We need to move faster," Wendin said. "There is a traitor working against us."

"A traitor?" Herion said. "And who is this traitor?"

Wendin shook his head. "Telstian doesn't know for certain, but we have already seen the destruction he can cause. Only a select few knew the village where Magnus and Alva lived, and we were attacked shortly after leaving that village."

"An elf then," Herion guessed. "I wouldn't ever have thought such a thing likely… but then I suppose it was an elf who created Nagar's Blight."

"Not an elf of Tualdern," Wendin said, his tone cold and his eyes narrowing.

Herion patted the air. "No, no, of course not. Still…" It seemed to Kathair that Herion wanted to say more, but the old man stopped himself and sat back in his chair. "My contact will get you across the water safely. I can't help his ship move faster though, that is beyond my powers."

"No, but you can open a portal to get us across the rest of the Middle Kingdom," Wendin said.

"That would help us bypass a lot of dangerous country," Magnus put in. "And it wouldn't be hardly any effort at all for someone like you."

Herion arched his snow-white brow and tapped a finger against his chin. "My contact wasn't expecting you for a few more days, but… I suppose we could move things up a bit. In light of recent events, it would be prudent." Herion nodded. "Very well. I will help you. We'll rest here for tonight, and then I will send you out in the morning."

"Wait," Kathair interjected. "If you can create a portal, why not send us all the way into the northern territory?"

Herion smiled. "I would if I could," he said. "The northern territory is beyond the bounds of the Middle Kingdom. Here, I enjoy great powers. However, across the sea is a different matter altogether."

Wendin cut in. "The farther away from the heart of the world one goes, the weaker magical forces become."

Herion nodded. "The Middle Kingdom is still connected to the continent through which the heart of the world pumps the most magic. Here, I can do many great things. However, the northern territory is separated by waters so great that my magic would not be reliable enough to travel from here to there."

"Not to mention the curse," Magnus put in.

"Curse?" Kathair asked, turning to Magnus.

"The northern territories were cursed long ago by a sorcerer named Malifacs. Malifacs had a twin brother, Argus, who used charm spells to steal away his wife. The two fought bitterly for years until the land was nearly burned clean of all life. Then, when Malifacs' wife killed herself to put an end to the war, things only got worse. Eventually, Malifacs placed trees and towers that sap magical energy in an effort to destroy all sorcerers. The towers drained the life from both twins, and ever since then the only magic strong enough to survive the curse have been of the darkest kinds. Vampires, shades, warlocks, and the like. Even then, only the very strongest can use their powers in the northern territory with any degree of efficacy."

Herion nodded. "Precisely. It is a dark and rugged place. That is why you must be sure you are ready to face it."

Kathair sighed. "That's why Telstian wanted me to read the letter after I graduated. He wanted me to be stronger."

"If you wish to wait, we can still put this off," Herion said. "There would be no shame in—"

"No," Magnus said. "We have sworn to hunt down those responsible for the murders in our families. We will not turn back now until we have either succeeded in avenging our families or our spirits have been separated from our bodies and laid to rest alongside our loved ones."

A quiet filled the room. No one dared to move, not even Wendin. Only when Magnus looked to Kathair did the young swordsman speak.

"He is right," Kathair said. "We will not turn away now, not until we have done all we can."

Herion whistled through his teeth. "I thought Kyra was headstrong," he said with a shake of his head. He reached out and took Kathair by the hand. "Dine with me tonight. Then we will get you to the coast in the morning."

Magnus nodded and slapped the table. "Then it is agreed."

"It is," Herion said. "I will go into the kitchen and prepare the meal."

"Shall I help?" Wendin asked.

Herion stood and shook his head. "No, I can manage. I may be old, but I still have my magic. I will prepare venison along with roasted potatoes, carrots, celery, and bread enough to fill an army. And Kathair, I will put a needle on top of the book for you to get after supper. Remind me then to show you the spot in the garden where you can safely open a portal."

"We aren't putting you out?" Magnus asked, nearly smacking his lips together as he licked his lips.

Herion shook his head and smiled. "Relax here, I will take care of all the arrangements. After all, this will be your final meal in the Middle Kingdom, it is the least I can do."

Kathair smiled for a moment, and then frowned as the old wizard turned to walk down the stairs. Something about the words he used, or maybe it was the way Herion had said them, didn't sit quite right with the young swordsman.

*****

Kyra stepped through the portal, still holding Asteri's furry hand. A cool breeze tugged at her hair, carrying with it the scent of smoke. She turned to look upwind and found several satyrs dancing around a large bonfire.

"They are performing a ritual dance, praying for Njar's safe return, and for Terramyr to heal Nonac," Asteri said. "Best we don't stare."

Kyra couldn't help herself. She watched as the graceful satyrs leapt and twirled through the air. Beyond their circle two more satyrs played panpipes while a third beat upon a leather drum. It was a thing of beauty to behold, but there was no mirth in the dance. Even from a distance she could feel the weight resting upon the satyrs. The young sorceress took in a breath and nodded.

"Let's see if we can help find Njar," she said.

The two hurried to the Pools of Fate, rushing by serene cottages bedecked with ivy and morning glory. Within minutes they arrive at the pond. Asteri remained several yards back, but gestured for Kyra to approach the water's edge.

"Please, be careful," Asteri said.

Kyra nodded. "I will." She approached the water and studied the clam, mirror-like surface. She had seen Njar call upon the waters here before, but she did not have his powers. He was a creature of magic born of the very world itself. She was a human –half human anyway, though she doubted the vampire lineage would count for anything here. She stretched out her hand and called a clarity spell up in her mind. Thoughts cleared and her focus sharpened, then her eyesight penetrated the depths before her. There, at the bottom of the pool's center was some sort of golden light. She couldn't quite tell what it was, but she could sense a power coming from it. She took a single step into the water, letting the warm liquid wash over her feet and ankles.

"Kyra," Asteri called out.

The young sorceress ignored the satyr. There was something out there, deep in the water. Feeling it might hold a clue for Njar's whereabouts, she had no choice but to get closer. She bent down and touched the waters with her hands. She knew only limited telekinesis spells, and doubted anything she could do would reach through the water's weight to pull up whatever was making the golden light, but she had another idea that might prove useful. She sent her energy out to toward the light. She called to it with her mind, hoping that a minor summoning spell might make the object respond with magic of its own.

A flash of purple rippled through the depths as her magic contacted the golden light. The sky around her grew dark red and heavy, black clouds flowed in from every direction.

"You!" a voice called out as loud as thunder.

Kyra turned around, but Asteri was nowhere to be seen. In fact, neither was the village. A darkness settled upon the land like a domed ceiling, cutting Kyra off from everything but the Pools of Fate.

"How did you come to be here?" the voice asked.

Kyra looked up to the heavy clouds and saw a face she recognized. The sharp, angular features and the long silvery hair were hard to forget. "Severin?" Kyra asked.

The face grinned and laughed at her, then Severin stepped out from the cloud and floated down toward her. "So, you have come to challenge me?"

"I already challenged you," Kyra said. "And I won."

Severin shook his head. "Yet here I am."

Kyra felt the waters around her ankles constrict and pull her a step deeper into the lake. She resisted, trying to step back toward the shore while Severin laughed.

"If you defeated me, then how could I stand before you?"

She knew he couldn't be real. Severin had been vanquished, there was no doubt about it. This had to be some sort of trick. Kyra narrowed her eyes on the creature. "I know you are dead," she said. She called upon her powers, focusing her energy into a spell that would dispel false images and reveal the truth.

"I am very much alive," Severin said. "But you have met your end, Kyra." Severin lunged toward her, closing the last several feet in an instant and producing a curved sword, aiming at her chest. Kyra cast her spell. The magic exploded from her hand like a torrent of invisible fire, blasting Severin backward through the air. The false illusion stared at her in horror as it melted from existence. The waters released their grip on her legs, and Kyra was able to walk back toward the shore, but the clouds remained in the red sky. She cast her spell four more times, each one resounding with the force of thunder and shaking the ground around her. Finally, the dome around her cracked and split, allowing her to glimpse the blue sky beyond. A fifth time brought the whole illusion crashing down around her, each cloud vanishing like vapor in the wind.

"Kyra!" Asteri cried out. Kyra turned and saw the satyr standing just beside her now. "Where did you go?"

Kyra pointed to the middle of the pool. A golden orb floated out from the waters now, its light dim and pulsing as if about to fail. "Someone placed a dark curse upon the Pools of Fate," Kyra said.

"Who?"

"The shade I was hunting." Kyra took two more steps into the water and used her magic to summon a wind from the other side of the pond. The wind created a series of swells that turned to waves which carried the orb to her. Kyra then chanted a pair of spells to break Severin's final hold on the Pools of Fate. The orb went dark and then shattered in place, dropping shards of metal into the water at Kyra's feet.

"Njar!" Asteri called out.

Kyra turned around and saw Njar lying supine a few feet away. The two ran to him and checked him for signs of life.

"I can feel his pulse," Asteri cried. She smiled wide and looked to Kyra. "You found him!"

Kyra returned the smile. "I am afraid he has been put through a lot," she said. "When the spell assaulted me, I saw Severin, and he tried to kill me. I think that Njar has been similarly fighting off the illusion, but he would have been doing it since he was first trapped inside."

"That was… weeks ago," Asteri whispered. "If this is where he disappeared to, then…" Asteri didn't need to finish her thought. Kyra was thinking it too. Njar would be injured and weak."

Njar opened his golden eyes and blinked up at Kyra. "Kyra… no… not again…" his breathing was shallow and quick. His eyes closed and his neck went limp.

"I must take him to the village," Asteri said. "The others can help heal him."

Kyra nodded. "I'll help you." The two grabbed hold of Njar and then bolstered their efforts with magic that made him feel lighter and kept him from dragging on the ground as they carried him to the village.

"Roshi!" Asteri shouted as they came nearer to the bonfire. "Roshi, Mior, come and help, we found Njar!"

The satyrs around the fire stopped dancing and rushed over to them. A few of them cast wary glances at Kyra, but Asteri assured everyone that she was a friend of Njar's, and of satyrs as a people. A couple of them appeared not to believe it fully, but they focused on Njar rather than push the point. Within seconds, several satyrs whisked Njar off into a nearby cottage and closed the door.

"They will heal him," a tall satyr said.

Kyra turned and nodded. "I hope so. He was taken by Severin's magic. I think he poisoned the Pools of Fate somehow, with a giant orb of some kind."

The satyr smiled and reached out for Kyra's hand. "And you brought him back to us," she said as she took Kyra's hand and held it. "Thank you."

How did you know where to look?" asked a male satyr holding a leather drum.

"I didn't," Kyra said. "But Njar once showed me the Pools of Fate and I thought I could use them to find him."

"No human can summon the Pools of Fate," the male satyr said.

"Yet this one obviously succeeded where all of us have failed," the female replied. "We owe them thanks. Asteri, Restorer, you have done well."

Asteri bowed her head. "Kyra is the one we should thank."

"And I intend to," the female said. She reached up and pulled a necklace of wooden beads from her neck. "This was given to me by my mother," she said. "The beads are made from the ironwood tree. My mother said they would be a protection to me, and now I want you to have them."

"No, I couldn't," Kyra said.

"I have no children to pass it to," she said. "Njar is my brother, and you have not only served our people, but you have brought back my brother. It is the least I can do."

"I didn't know he had a sister," Kyra said.

"I am Erea, and I would call you my new sister, Kyra." Erea placed the necklace over Kyra's head and adjusted it so that it hung just right. "Thank you."

Kyra bowed her head. "Thank you," she said.

Erea then turned to Asteri. "Njar will need rest, but when he wakes, he can help you restore Nonac. Until then, we should send our guest home for now." Erea smiled at Kyra. "When Njar is ready, we will send for you once more. He will want to thank you as well."

They said their farewells and then Asteri created a portal back to the aspen grove.

"Shall we go?"

Kyra nodded. They stepped through the portal and then embraced once more before Asteri went back to Viverandon, leaving Kyra in the grove.

The young sorceress couldn't help but smile. She had found her friend, and he was alive. It would be something worth telling Kathair, if she knew where he was. She sat in the grass and sighed, all of her previous worries for Njar melting away in the evening air. He was hurt, but he would be all right. She could feel it. Then, just as she was about to lie down in the grass and watch the sky, she felt something pull at her mind.

"Kyra, can you hear me?"

It was Kathair's voice. Kyra closed her eyes and let the power of the summoning stone come to her in full, showing her a yellow manor house and part of a row of hedges. Kathair stood there, holding the stone in his hands and whispering to it.

"Can you hear me?"

Kyra jumped up and created a portal. Under normal circumstances it would be impossible to create a portal to a place she had never been, but the stone acted as an anchor to her magic, pulling it to the right place and holding it secure. She stepped through and tapped him on the shoulder.

Kathair opened his eyes. "It worked!" he exclaimed.

"Of course it worked," she said.

"I have something to tell you!" they both said in unison. They shared a laugh.

"You go first," Kyra said.

"No, you go," Kathair replied.

"No, you summoned me, so you can go first."

Kathair nodded and held up a book. "Herion told me how to get into your house!"

Kyra cocked her head and looked at the book. "Wards and Traps."

"Yeah, the book is just in case his first idea fails, but he said it's probably a family cypher ward. If we put a drop of your blood on the key, the ward should allow you in."

Kyra smiled. "You always have my back, don't you?" Kyra said.

175

Kathair shrugged. "Of course."

"I have something really great to share. I found Njar, and he's alive!"

"That's wonderful!" Kathair shouted. "Where was he?"

"Trapped by a spell, actually," Kyra said. "The other satyrs are helping him recover now, but I think he'll be okay."

"That's fantastic!" Kathair said.

Kyra nodded. "So... are we at Herion's house?"

"Yeah, we stopped here for some help. He's going to teleport us northward tomorrow, which is why I used the stone today."

Kyra arched a brow.

"Herion said his magic can't reach the north country, so I figured yours wouldn't either. So tonight is the only chance I might have for a while to help you get inside your house."

Kyra smiled. "Alright." She turned and conjured a portal to her manor. The two held hands and stepped through. They walked up to the front door and stopped as Kyra pulled out the key. "I'm a bit nervous," she said.

"Here, I brought a needle," Kathair said. "Herion let me take it after dinner so I could help."

Kyra took the needle quickly jabbed her left pinky finger on the side. A tiny crimson dot appeared, then grew to a sizeable drop. Kathair held the key in his hand while Kyra used her other hand to squeeze her finger, making the drop grow until it fell onto the key. "Here goes..." Kyra took the key back and slid it into the lock. She turned the key and then reached for the knob, but before she could grab it the door unlocked and glided inward, opening up for the first time.

"You did it!" Kathair exclaimed.

"*We* did it," Kyra corrected. She stepped in first and held the door open for Kathair. "Smells like..."

"Like roses," Kathair said quickly. "I thought it would smell of dust and mold."

Kyra smiled as candles burst to life around her, casting light upon every corner of the front room. There were several chairs, a couch, and a small table in the main room, with bookshelves lining the walls. She walked into the room and let her fingers brush the upholstery. "This is my family home," she said.

Kathair stood in the entrance, closing the door and sliding the lock into place while Kyra explored the front room. In the corner stood a bronze bust upon a white pedestal. She moved to it and read the name Alister Dimwater. "This is one of my ancestors," Kyra told Kathair.

"Not just any ancestor," the bust said as it shook its head to life.

Kyra jumped back and let out a squeal.

"Oh come now, no granddaughter of mine is as skittish as all that," Alister said.

"I'm a little farther down the line than granddaughter," Kyra said.

"Yes, yes, but I don't really like saying all those greats that come with each new generation. I tried it, but after great-great-great-grandpa, I started to feel a bit old. So, you will simply call me grandpa, understood?"

Kyra glanced to Kathair, who was holding a hand to his mouth and doing his best not to show his boyish grin. "Very well, grandpa."

"Good, now, come here and put your hand on my head."

"What?" Kyra asked.

"Oh don't tell me you're deaf *and* skittish!" Alister frowned and wrinkled his nose. "I SAID COME HERE AND PUT YOUR HAND ON MY HEAD!"

Kyra winced. For a statue, his voice was quite loud, nearly piercing her eardrums. "I'm not deaf, grandpa, I just don't know why you would want me to do it, that's all."

"So I can see your life, dearie, why else would I do it?"

Kyra shrugged and stepped forward. Without even thinking about the ramifications, she placed her hand on Alister's bronze head. Her skin felt as though it melded with the metal, tugging her toward the pedestal and pulling her memories from her. Everything flowed out, even memories she had long ago forgotten. Flashes and images appeared and then disappeared in a matter of moments. There was a final flash of white light, and then Kyra's hand was released.

"My, my, dearie, you have had an interesting start to life now, haven't you?"

Kyra rubbed her hand and took a step back. "Maybe I should have warned you about—"

Alister shook his bronze head. "Kyra, you are a Dimwater, through and through. I don't care if your father is Lord Caspin or the vampire. Makes no never mind to me. You are the mistress of this house now, and everything in it will serve you, including me."

"You aren't… disappointed?"

"HA!" Alister snorted. "I'm your grandpa. You're my grandgirl, and that's that. Besides, you think you're the only one in the family with a dark secret? Families watch after each other, secrets and all. Why, I remember when one of your great-great-aunts started running around the forest with a werewolf. The two were inseparable, the best of friends. Believe you me, they got into more than their fair share of trouble."

Kyra giggled. "That isn't true, is it?" Kyra asked.

Alister arched his metal brow and narrowed his left eye. "Not polite to call your grandpa a liar." He turned his eyes to Kathair. "Now then, this must be Kathair Lepkin, the great and loyal champion who has stood by your side through the last little while. Come closer boy, let me see you clearly. My old eyes were dimmed with age in life, and their current bronzed form isn't much better."

Kathair approached and offered a bow of his head. "A pleasure to meet your, Lord Dimwater."

"Lord?" Alister echoed. "Call me Alister, I wasn't much for titles in life, and I am not about to start now."

Kathair smiled and nodded his head. "Alright, Alister, sir."

"Knock off the 'sir' business as well. Just Alister." He turned his eyes to Kyra. "He's of good stock," he said. "Of course, he'd have to be to win your—"

"Grandpa!" Kyra cut him off, but it was too late. Kathair was blushing and looking at the floor. "We're just friends," she added.

Alister kept his mouth closed, but even as a bronze bust his expression clearly conveyed that he didn't believe her. "Give me your hand," Alister told Kathair. "Any friend who fights beside a Dimwater is welcome in the manor."

"You're going to read my memories too?" Kathair asked, taking a half step back.

"No, I can only do that with direct descendants. Doesn't work with anyone else."

"Oh," Kathair said.

"I'm going to put a mark on you so the house recognizes you as a friend." Kathair looked to Kyra, and then slowly reached out and placed his hand on top of the bronze bust. A blue light flashed in the room, and then Alister gave a nod. "All done," he said. "You can take your hand off now."

"I don't see anything," Kathair said as he turned his palm over.

"No, of course not. It isn't that kind of mark," Alister said. "Loyal, but not very smart about magic is he?"

"Grandpa!" Kyra protested.

"Just saying," Alister said with a roll of his eyes. "Now, go ahead and explore the rest of the house. You'll find the laboratory downstairs, a special herb garden in the third floor, and various bedrooms and studies scattered about the second floor. The kitchen is down the hall and to your left, and the parlor is opposite that. I had thought to build a dining room, but after my nephew

Quillon started that fight with my niece Brikka, there were parts of the family that could never be in the same room again."

"What happened to family always being there for each other?" Kathair said.

Alister arched a brow and gave him a steely glare. "Sometimes pride is stronger than blood, and some fools don't know when to apologize and take responsibility. I still love them all, each and every one, but Quillon got more than a few tongue lashings from me. Never did change and do the honorable thing though. Remained bitter to the end, pretending it was all her fault." Alister made a noise that might have sounded like clearing his throat had he been made of flesh, but as a bronze bust it sounded more like a knife scraping against granite. "Run along now, let your grandpa sleep. Wake me later on and we can discuss a great many things. The house has many secrets, as is proper for a family of wizards, and I have the combined wisdom of generations of Dimwaters. I'll help you in any way I can," Alister said.

"Thank you, grandpa," Kyra replied.

The two started down the hall toward the kitchen when Alister called out once more.

"And Kyra?"

Kyra turned around. "Yes, grandpa?"

"Welcome home child. Welcome home." Kyra smiled as Grandpa Alister closed his eyes. "Feels good to have family around once more."

Kyra nodded. "Yes, it does."

Chapter 12

"So, where is Mindaugas?" Kathair asked as they entered a large library on the second floor. "Is he back at the temple?"

Kyra huffed. "The priests kicked me out of the temple."

Kathair stopped and turned around. "They what?"

Kyra shrugged and continued browsing a nearby bookshelf. "Let's just say they didn't think I belonged there anymore on account of who I was."

"Then they are blind in more ways than one," Kathair said. "Stupid fools, the lot of them."

Kyra cast a quick smile his way. "It's all right. Now that I have my new home, I can study without interruption, and Grandpa Alister can help guide my research."

"What about Mindaugas? Surely he didn't agree with them, did he?"

Kyra's smile vanished and she turned back to the books. "I think he agrees with them more than he will admit. We had a sort of… falling out."

"Then he is a fool too," Kathair declared. "I'll be a horned-toad before I ever work with any of them."

Kyra giggled. "It's all right, really."

Kathair moved to a table and found a map sitting on it. "Where is Leatherback?" he asked. "I mean, is there a place on the map that would lead to where he is now?"

Kyra turned and looked at him with eyes sadder than he had seen in a long time. "Not really," she said. "Most other dimensions that I have learned about so far seem to be accessible from anywhere, so long as you know the right spell."

Kathair frowned. "If that is true, then why not go there, and then open a portal to somewhere else?"

Kyra shrugged. "I would have to know where I am going for that to work. Besides, I don't think other dimensions function that way. I think you have to exit the same way you entered, but I am not certain."

"How is he?" Kathair asked. "Is he doing well?"

Kyra sighed. "He is in trouble," she said flatly. "He's safe for now, but I don't know how much longer he can keep the curse at bay."

"So, you can't use the other dimensions to travel through to other places in Terramyr, and you can't teleport with him to the north, because of what Herion said right? Magic is weaker farther away from this land. But, can you teleport a short way and then rest before doing another teleport jump?"

Kyra shook her head. "Even if a plan like that could work, I would have to have more power than I do now. Sustaining portals large enough for myself is one thing, but to create a gateway large enough for Leatherback is quite another."

"How far away do you have to go to beat the curse?" Kathair asked.

Kyra shrugged and moved to sit in a nearby chair. "I haven't found any answers to that. Some say the curse will reach him no matter how far I travel. Others say just beyond the impassable mountains that separate the northern territory from the larger oceans would be enough."

"Would your magic work that far away?" Kathair asked. "Herion said his stopped roughly at the edge of the sea, but it's nothing compared to the ocean beyond the northern territory that separates it from the next continent." Kathair looked down and pointed at the map on the table. "It looks like it would be nearly impossible for a dragon to fly across the waters too." Upon the table, the map displayed all of Terramyr, with the Middle Kingdom situated on the northwestern point of a central continent. The northern territory, which would take days of sailing to reach across the sea, was only an inch or so away from the Middle Kingdom on the map, yet the next continent north was several inches away, and others were even farther. "The world is a very large place," he said.

Kyra rose from her chair and came to examine the map. "Yes, it is." She tapped a finger on a far away continent in the north western part of the world. "This is where I want to go."

Kathair whistled. "That's about as far away as you can get from here," he said. Suddenly, he felt a stab of panic hit him. If she attained her goal, he would never see her again.

"It's far away from the curse, and out of Feberik Orres' reach as well," she said.

Kathair nodded. "Can't you change it? The marriage I mean?"

Kyra shook her head and shrugged. "I have told him I will not marry, but he refuses to let me go. The law says he must be the one to dissolve the arrangement, since the agreed upon bargain has been met by him and Lord Caspin."

"But if Lord Caspin isn't your real father, then what right does he have to—"

"No one outside of Kuldiga Academy and the priests at Valtuu Temple know the truth. Legally speaking, I am still Kyra Caspin, daughter of Lord Caspin, and subject to his will."

Kathair growled and thumped a knuckle on the table. "Then I must help you escape," he said. "We have to find a way to get you and Leatherback to a new home, one where both of you will be free."

Kyra stopped and looked up, her dark eyes meeting his. She tilted her head to the side ever so slightly and the softest of smiles graced her face. "You are always there for me, why is that?"

Kathair's heart slammed against his ribs and his throat went dry. He lost himself in her eyes for just a moment, but quickly recovered and put on his own wide grin, waving the notion away. "That's what friends are for… right?" *Friends…* Kyra nodded and then turned back to a bookshelf. Kathair puffed air and closed his eyes. *Friends!* That most certainly was not why he was always ready to support her. He opened his eyes, letting them linger upon her for a second or two before he turned away and forced himself to search through a bookshelf on the opposite side of the room. "What kind of books did your family keep? Anything on other dimensions?"

"Not sure," Kyra said.

The conversation died out then as the two searched through the room. There were a lot of interesting books on magic, but Kathair didn't see anything that hinted at other dimensions. He did, find a journal belonging to Alister, and pulled it from the shelf. "Hey, look what I found. Grandpa's journal."

He opened the cover as Kyra walked toward him and peered over his shoulder.

"Huh? The pages are blank," Kathair said.

Kyra took the journal and flipped through a few more pages. "I bet it has a spell on it, to hide the words. We'll need a password to break the spell."

"Think Alister would give it to us?" Kathair asked, grinning mischievously from ear to ear.

"He said he would help with anything I wanted to know, and he has the family's collective memory, so I doubt we need to pry into his personal journal."

Kathair shrugged and let out an involuntary yawn.

"I should get you back to Herion," Kyra said.

"No, no, I'm fine," Kathair protested.

"You have a long journey ahead of you," Kyra replied. "You'll need some sleep."

"Meh, I can sleep on the ship. I'd rather stay and help you here."

Kyra shook her head. "I should go and talk with Mindaugas. At the very least, I left my other books with him."

"So, I can help you do that," Kathair put in, but even as he offered he knew she would not accept it.

"I can work with Grandpa Alister in the morning, and the research will go quickly then, I'm sure of it. Besides, Njar will be better soon, and he can lend a hand as well."

Kathair nodded. "All right. I'll go, but just make sure to come and get me if you change your mind."

Kyra smiled. "If Herion can't reach you once you are upon the sea, then I doubt my summoning stone will work."

Grunting, Kathair said, "I'll keep it with me just in case."

Kyra opened a portal and the two stepped through to the gardens in front of Herion's manor house. Immediately, they were met by Herion himself.

"Ah, good, you made it," Herion said. "I wasn't sure if you might have trouble anchoring the portal to my gardens. I disabled all the wards I could remember, but was worried I might have forgotten one or two."

Kyra and Kathair both laughed.

"No, we're all right," Kyra said.

"Wonderful. Now, if you don't mind, I'll be taking my things back now." Herion held out his hand. "I assume the book was helpful."

Kathair nodded and gave the book on wards back to the wizard. "It was like you said, she just needed a drop of her blood on the key."

"Ah, yes, the needle. I'll need to wash that off before putting it away." He held out his other hand.

Kyra giggle and handed him the needle.

"Now, don't be long, I want to lock the place down and get some sleep." With that, the old wizard turned and started walking toward the house. "Good to see you, Miss Dimwater," he called out over his shoulder without breaking pace.

"You too," Kyra said.

"I think he's getting stranger," Kathair said.

"I think you might be right," Kyra replied.

"Well…" Kathair turned back to her and slapped his arms to his sides in a sort of shrugging motion. "I suppose this is where we say goodbye."

"Take good care of yourself," Kyra said.

"You too," Kathair replied. The two embraced, holding the hug for just a second longer than was proper, and then she turned and walked back through the portal. Kathair watched until the magical doorway closed, cutting him off from her entirely. He fingered the stone in his pocket. He would almost abandon his mission to stay with her, but he knew that even that would do no good. For now, their roads would have to part, and he could only hope they would cross again soon.

"You like her," a voice called out.

Kathair turned to see Magnus sitting on a bench in front of a well-manicured hedge. "How long have you been sitting there?"

"Since you left," Magnus replied. "The gardens are quiet, gave me time to think."

Kathair moved to sit on what little bench remained unoccupied by Magnus. "I like her quite a lot," he said in a voice barely above a whisper.

"It was the same with me and Alva," Magnus said. "It was something I could feel since we were very young. She was the only one I ever had eyes for." Magnus nudged Kathair with an elbow. "It took Alva a few years longer to realize it though, so don't give up hope."

Kathair snorted. "She's betrothed," he said.

"Hmm." Magnus crossed his arms and stretched his legs out in front of the bench. "I suppose that might complicate things a bit."

The young swordsman shook his head. "A bit."

Magnus slapped Kathair on the back of the shoulder. "Well, first things first, let's go deal with Malech."

The large northman rose from the bench and reached down to Kathair. He yanked the young swordsman from his seat and the two walked back to the manor. Kathair was shown to a bedroom the three shared for the night. Wendin fell asleep quickly, but Kathair and Magnus had trouble. Every now and again, one of them would exhale heavily and roll over on their bed. Kathair figured Magnus was thinking of his wife, and of little Brenna. As for Kathair, he was still thinking of Kyra, finding it impossible to banish her image from his mind. Only when the late night turned to the early morning did he finally find relief and drift off to the land of dreams.

He woke just after the sun had broken through the window, slapping his face with the full force of its brightness. Wendin stretched and dressed, seemingly refreshed and ready for the journey ahead. Magnus, on the other hand, looked as bad as Kathair felt. The man's hair was standing up on the right side of his head, while the left was matted flat against his skin. A dark red line creased his left cheek, and he was shaking his left arm and grumbling about the needles in his fingers.

Kathair stretched and followed the other two downstairs to breakfast, which Herion had already provided in the form of fresh fruits and bread.

"A good breakfast leads to a productive day," he said. "At least, that's what my father used to say when I was younger."

Wendin nodded his thanks and sat down to eat. Magnus tried to smooth out his hair, but failed miserably, making it wilder with each stroke of his hand. Kathair sat at the table and stared at the fruit. His legs had managed to bring him here, but his stomach was still struggling to catch up.

"Go on, tuck in," Herion said. "You'll need your strength."

Kathair obediently ripped off a hunk of bread and plopped it into his mouth. The warm, moist texture helped awaken his taste buds, which in turn helped his stomach come alive. Before he managed to ask for a drink, Herion summoned a glass of orange juice for him.

"I appreciate your hospitality," Magnus said between bites.

Herion nodded in response and smiled while raising his own glass.

None of them said anything else during the meal. They ate, then finished their preparations and went to the garden where Herion summoned a portal for them. Like portals Kyra had created, this one started as a small point of light that ripped through the air, growing and crackling with little streaks of lightning until it was large enough to pass through. Then it hollowed out and displayed their destination.

"May the gods smile favorably upon you," Herion said.

Wendin bowed his head. "May the road always rise to meet you, and may your way ever be clear before you."

Then they walked through the portal.

Kathair felt a chill as he stepped out onto the docks. A few longshoremen stopped to look at him, but they didn't say much other than whispering to each other and pointing at Wendin and Magnus.

"Best keep moving," Magnus said.

Kathair followed them as Wendin led the way to a large ship near the end of the docks. Crewmen were busy loading crates and barrels, presumably food and fresh water for drinking, and the captain was standing at the top of the ramp barking out orders. The captain was a tall, skinny man with wiry hair that did its best to resist the southerly breeze. He wore a long coat over a beige tunic and black trousers, sporting a cutlass on each side of his waist. When the captain spotted them, he held up a hand and started down the ramp.

"This isn't a passenger ferry," he grunted. "You'll want to charter passage with another ship."

Wendin stopped and gave a short nod of his head. "Master Herion sends his greetings," he said.

The captain stopped short and glanced down the dock. "So you're the ones he wants me to take on, eh?"

"Didn't he mention who we were?" Magnus asked.

The captain shook his head. "Just asked me to do him a favor. Didn't specify how many would be coming, or who you were. I had also expected you a little later, but no matter. I can adjust our timetables." He turned to one of his crewmen and whistled to get his attention. A bald, wide-shouldered man with tattoos along his shoulder looked up while holding a crate large enough that two or three men should have been carrying it.

"Yessir?"

"Are the guest quarters ready?"

"Yessir."

The captain nodded and then gestured for the crewman to continue his work. "Very well," he said, turning back to Wendin. "Come with me and I will show you to your quarters."

They followed him up the ramp and then to a wooden door near the rear of the ship that opened to a stairway leading downward. At the bottom of the stairs they turned right and went along a short, narrow hallway to another room. The captain used a key to open the door and then gestured for them to follow.

"It isn't the palace at Drakei' Glazei, but it is the best we have to offer."

The room had two bunkbeds, each with a footlocker at the end, a single table in the middle of the room with two chairs, and a small bucket near the back for a chamber pot.

"It'll do," Magnus said.

"I won't bother asking your names," the captain said. "If Herion had wanted me to know, he would have told me himself. Whatever it is you're doing, I know better than to stick my nose into it. Same goes for my crew. This isn't the first time we have rendered services, if you catch my meaning."

Wendin nodded. "Your discretion is appreciated."

"Breakfast is served an hour after sunrise. Supper is at dusk. If you're used to having lunch, then you'll have to scrounge that up whenever you can; our cook doesn't normally do that. My men are accustomed to working on two meals a day, but there is water

189

to be had whenever thirst strikes." He pointed to Magnus then and added, "Ale is rationed out, but maybe you can grab some at dinner if you ask one of the other sailors."

Kathair thought it odd that the captain would only offer the ale to Magnus, but he wasn't about to voice his opinion.

"As for me," the captain continued, "I figure you can just call me Captain. Everyone else does." He put a finger to his nose. "That way nobody knows any names, see?"

Magnus nodded. "We understand."

The captain then handed the key to Magnus. "Close and lock the door as you like. If you catch anyone snooping, let me know and I will handle it, but I doubt you will be bothered. As I said, we're accustomed to these sorts of tasks." With a final glance around the room, the captain nodded and started for the door. "I'll leave you to it, then. We'll put out to sea shortly. Hope you had breakfast already, my cook doesn't start work until suppertime after we set out." He didn't wait long enough for an answer, just walked out and closed the door behind himself.

"Seems decent enough," Magnus said.

Wendin nodded and moved to set his backpack down on a lower bunk.

"Looks like you're taking a top bunk," Magnus said as he moved to the other lower bunk and claimed it by flopping down atop the mattress and shifting his weight around a bit. The bed creaked and groaned under him, but held sturdily enough.

Kathair put his things on the bunk above Magnus and then turned for the door. "I'm going to get some fresh air."

"Wait until we are at sea," Wendin said. "Best keep as low a profile as possible."

"I agree," Magnus said. "Try to relax for a bit."

Kathair went to the table and pulled out his summoning stone. He was careful not to concentrate hard enough to call Kyra's attention to him, but he thought of her all the same. He placed the stone in the center of the table and stared at it, letting his attention wander through the jumbled emotions and thoughts clouding his mind. After a while, his thoughts centered on Malech, and whether they would be able to find him. If they did find him, would he have any information worth the trouble, or would the only compensation for this trip be his death at Magnus' hands? Kathair figured that might be enough for Magnus, but it wouldn't be for him. He had to know who the other traitors were. Who would work with Malech to murder northmen traveling through the Middle Kingdom? Who would care so much about the Keeper of Secrets that they would attack whole families just in case they might become connected with Valtuu Temple? Had Kathair's father really been so important?

He thought of Valtuu Temple then, and tried to comprehend how any group so foolish as to expel Kyra would ever be considered wise and threatening by anyone else. The priests had apparently been unable to help Leatherback, or even help Kyra figure out how to do so, and yet there was a secret group out there somewhere that feared the temple. More than that, they feared anyone who held the title Keeper of Secrets. Kathair could see how people might fear Mindaugas as a warrior, but enough to hire groups of Blacktongue assassins to prevent someone from becoming a Keeper? No, that didn't make any sense. If the group wanted power, why not just go after the king? Assassinate Mathias and take over the kingdom, simple as that. Why try to pull strings from the shadows?

He spent a couple hours trying to puzzle it all out, but answers eluded him. In the end, he concluded that he was either too inexperienced, or perhaps was missing some piece of vital information that connected it all together. Whatever it was, his only hope for solving the mystery was to find Malech and make the man talk.

The first day at sea was spent mostly getting accustomed to the way the crew moved about the ship. Kathair did his best to stay out of their way while Magnus chatted a few of the sailors up about the northern territory and whether they had seen many pirates out at sea. Wendin, on the other hand, hardly left the cabin, preferring instead to meditate. By early evening on the second day, they had all fallen into a bit of a lull. The ship rocked gently from side to side as it navigated the waves, which seemed much larger far away from land. Magnus had spent most of the day lying about in the bunkbed, and his snoring had gone from annoyingly loud to unbearably horrendous as the day gave way to evening. Kathair could hardly think, and even Wendin couldn't concentrate. Kathair and the elf warrior left and went above deck. They walked to the side and watched the seemingly endless blue all around them. A few clouds stretched across the sky, turning orange, red, and purple as the sun lowered off in the distance.

"I have never seen the sea," Wendin said.

Kathair nodded. "I suppose I did when I came this way with my father as a child, but I don't remember it. It's beautiful."

Wendin gripped the side rail. "I prefer the feel of land beneath my feet."

"Seasick?" Kathair asked.

Wendin arched a brow and turned to regard him. "Elves don't get seasick."

Kathair shrugged. At least Wendin was talking more now that they had been traveling together. "I think the sea is pretty, and the air smells fresh, but I wouldn't want to sail as a career," he said. "I like the forests and mountains better."

Wendin nodded. "The trees," he added.

"Still, I suppose it is nice to be away from danger for a while, so we can rest. No blacktongues out here, unless they can run on water and track us." Kathair laughed and slapped the side rail. "Feels good to put them behind us."

The two spent the next hour in silence, watching the sea and occasionally glancing back toward the crew as they rushed about, carrying out the captain's shouted orders or seeing to loose rigging. The ship cut through the water easily, gliding northward and cresting over the larger swells without causing too much spray onto the deck. As the sun dropped below the horizon, the dinner bell rang out and the crew rushed down for supper.

Wendin and Kathair arrived to find that Magnus had not only roused himself, but was already seated, playing dice with a pair of men and apparently winning as he had collected two flasks, a leather arm band, and an iron bracelet with several charms dangling from it.

"Salted pork," Magnus called out to Kathair.

"And beans," one of the other players added.

Magnus made a point of looking up at Kathair. "No beans for you," he said. "Just eat the pork and some bread. You're sleeping above me after all and I do not want a repeat of last night."

A few of the men laughed. Kathair blushed just a bit, but didn't bother to respond. He was happy to see Magnus acting more normal and having a bit of fun. After supper was over, the crew filtered out of the mess and back to their regular stations. Some went to bed while others went above deck. Kathair decided to take one last stroll to see the night sky. Magnus went with him.

"Good group," Magnus said after they reached the front of the ship.

"You did well," Kathair said, noting the baubles Magnus had won.

"The flasks were full when I won them too," Magnus said. He tapped one, making a metallic sound. "I'll have to play again and win some more. Good ale."

Kathair laughed. He looked up to the sky and suddenly felt so very small that a chill ran up his spine. They were on the sea, alone, with a group of sailors they didn't know, and trusting their lives to them. Just as Kathair tried to banish the thought by reminding himself that Herion had arranged it, he recalled the way Herion had said that dinner would be their last meal in the Middle Kingdom. For a reason he couldn't explain, it still bothered him deep down in his stomach, nagging at the back of his mind. He turned around and leaned his back against the side railing. "Magnus?"

"Yeah?" Magnus said.

Kathair had thought to ask about Herion, but then thought better of it. What would he say? Magnus would laugh at his worries. "Nothing, never mind," Kathair said.

Magnus pushed back from the railing. "You know, it was easy to beat those guys down below. I think luck is shining on us now. Our ancestors, Kathair, our ancestors are blessing this journey." Magnus held up a finger to drive the point home. "They're watching over us."

Kathair looked up to Magnus and realized that the large man's eyes were starting to droop. "Magnus, how much ale did you drink?"

"Just two flasks," Magnus said. "That's nothing for a guy like me," he added. "We northmen can drink anyone else under the table. Why, I once had…" Magnus reeled back, nearly losing his grip on the side rail as a large wave tilted the ship. He turned and locked eyes with Kathair. "Kathair, I don't feel right."

His right leg collapsed, and Magnus fell to the deck.

"Magnus!" Kathair reached out to steady the large man, barely succeeding in catching him just before his head hit the deck. He lowered Magnus the last couple inches to the ground and looked up to a nearby sailor. "I need help!"

The door leading below the deck burst open and Wendin came rushing out. "Kathair!"

Kathair looked up and saw Wendin holding his sword. The blade dripped crimson and the elf's eyes darted around the deck. "It's a trap!"

A sailor leapt over the railing from the helm, but Wendin sidestepped and countered the attack with a deft swing of his sword that separated the sailor's head from his body. Wendin then slammed the door shut and jammed the body in front as someone collided with it.

The sailor in front of Kathair pulled a short wooden club and a hand ax from his belt, grinning wildly as he approached.

Kathair didn't have his sword, but Magnus had a long knife tucked into his own belt that he could take. The young swordsman retrieved the blade and launched into a quick attack. The sailor must not have expected Kathair to challenge him, for his eyes shot open wide and he hesitated just long enough for Kathair to slice across the man's stomach. It was a shallow wound, but painful enough that the sailor took a step backward. Kathair pressed the attack, landing a straight kick to the wound and driving the man down to the deck. Wendin was there an instant later, thrusting his sword into the sailor's chest.

"We need to escape," Wendin said. "There's a longboat on the side. Can you get Magnus to it while I disable the helm?"

"I'll try." Kathair tucked the knife away and grabbed Magnus by the wrist, dragging him a few feet toward the aft section where the longboat was secured. Wendin cut his way through two more sailors and then vaulted up to the helm with a graceful leap, slicing a third sailor across the chest and dumping him over the side.

Two sailors from the forward section raced toward Kathair now, each brandishing a hand ax. Kathair released Magnus' arm and rushed back to the first sailor that had attacked him, taking the man's club and ax. He threw the club first, catching one of the attackers in the left shoulder. Then he came up with the ax and rushed the second attacker. The sailor swung diagonally, but Kathair twirled to the side and caught the man at the wrist, cutting his hand off and sending it, still clenching the ax, to the deck in a splatter of dark red blood. The first attacker then kicked Kathair in the gut before chopping downward, but Kathair somersaulted to the man's left, clear of the attack. Kathair then got to his knees and twisted sharply, swinging his own ax behind him and catching the first sailor in the back of the leg. The blade bit in deep, catching the bone. Kathair released it and came up with the long knife, driving it up through the man's back ribs and into his lungs. The sailor collapsed to the deck.

The other sailor with the cut-off hand was busy trying to stem the spurting blood, grunting and screaming frantically as his life continued to shoot out from his open wrist.

"I've got it," Wendin cried from the helm.

Kathair looked up. Two more sailors' bodies were draped over the railing, and the wheel had been removed from the helm. Wendin ran to the side and threw the steering wheel overboard just as the door to the lower sections was forced open and the sailor's dead body that had wedged it closed was thrown aside.

Kathair's mouth fell open. He had expected more sailors, but instead he saw seven blacktongues emerge, weapons ready and eyes crazily scouring the decks. One of them leveled a mini crossbow at Kathair. The young swordsman barely managed to duck behind the mast before the bolt slammed into it.

Wendin shouted something in elvish, and then Kathair could hear the sound of swords clashing. He lunged out, taking back a hand ax from his defeated foes just as a blacktongue closed on him. The assassin thrusted a narrow blade at Kathair, but the young swordsman managed to jump back just out of reach. He countered with a swing of his ax, but the blacktongue sidestepped and then launched another attack of his own. Kathair parried with the long knife, just able to drive the enemy's blade away from his neck. He then came in hard and fast with the ax, but the blacktongue jumped back, easily escaping the blow. The ship rose sharply and then dropped down, crashing into the sea and spraying the deck with water at that moment, throwing both of them several feet toward the prow.

The blacktongue collided with the railing while Kathair was able to roll through the stumble, allowing him to regain his footing just a second faster than the assassin. Kathair threw his ax on an impulse, only realizing after the weapon was airborne that he had just discarded his best defensive equipment.

Please! Time seemed to freeze as his eyes trailed after the spinning blade. The ship rose again, but slowly. The blacktongue turned to look up, his head moving at a pace a snail could beat, and then the blade connected with the tattooed assassin's forehead, driving in and jerking the man's head backward.

Time regained its normal speed, and the ship came crashing down between waves once more.

Kathair retrieved his ax and then turned to go to Magnus. The large man was just starting to stir, groaning and mumbling something about salt water as he swiped at the liquid splashed onto his face. He hadn't even opened his eyes when a blacktongue reached him and drove his sword through Magnus' neck.

"NO!" Kathair shouted.

The blacktongue, a tall, lean man with a dark tattoo covering the whole of his face, grinned wickedly, displaying his perfectly white teeth.

Kathair rushed forward, swinging his ax time and time again, lashing out with his knife as the blacktongue danced around his onslaught. Suddenly, Kathair's left hand shot open as a pain erupted through his shoulder. Kathair stumbled backward and looked to a gushing wound that poured blood over his upper arm. He looked back at the blacktongue and drew his brow into a knot. He hadn't seen the attack. Even now, the only confirmation that the assassin had struck him was the blood dripping from the curved blade of a thick dagger.

The young swordsman glanced beyond the blacktongue and saw that Wendin was also having trouble. Four blacktongues had him pressed into a corner at the rear of the ship. He couldn't see in the darkness whether Wendin was wounded, but even if the elf somehow managed to live, he would never reach Kathair in time.

The blacktongue squared up against Kathair and motioned for Kathair to attack.

A million thoughts ran through Kathair's mind. His parents, Alva, Wendin, Magnus. So much death, and for what? What was so special about him – or his family? He wished he could have spent more time with Kyra, though even with her magic he was glad that the summoning stone was back in the cabin below deck. He would never want her summoned here. Then it hit him. How did the blacktongues get here? Herion had used a portal to help Kathair and the others get ahead of the blacktongues, and the assassins couldn't have known which ship they would take. Unless…

"At least I know one thing," Kathair said.

The blacktongue tilted his head and arched a dark brow.

"Herion is the other traitor," Kathair said.

The blacktongue's grin widened.

Kathair nodded and took in a breath. He tried to push the pain in his left shoulder out of his mind and prepared to fight once more. The blacktongue twirled his bloodied blade and stepped forward. Kathair parried the first strike with his ax, then sidestepped the follow-up. The young swordsman countered with a chop that caught just enough of the blacktongue's hip to force the man to step off to the side. A small rivulet of blood oozed from the cut, but the assassin pressed the offense a moment later.

A red, stinging line appeared on Kathair's chest, and then part of his tunic curled outward. The assassin was too fast. Kathair focused, parrying the next attack and blocking the third as well, but a moment later there was a heavy blow to his gut that lifted him from the deck. He seemed to stick in the air as the ship lurched down between massive swells. The blacktongue stepped back and braced himself, then as spray covered the deck, Kathair slammed into the hardwood and lost his footing. A savage kick to the face snapped Kathair's head back and dimmed his vision. A slicing burn on his right shoulder told him that the blacktongue had scored another hit.

Searing, hot pain caused his vision to flash white, then spin around him as if he was tumbling down a steep hill. Warm blood spilled out of his upper back. Kathair coughed and tried to push himself up from the deck, but another kick sent him tumbling across the deck.

Kathair could hardly breathe. His lungs fought to draw air in, but the deep wound in his back fought against him, burning every second and forcing his muscles to spasm. The blacktongue stepped toward him. Kathair struggled to crane his head up to look at his murderer.

The blacktongue raised his sword high above his head, but before he could bring it down, an explosion of blood sprayed out from his chest and he was thrown to the side. Wendin stood where the blacktongue had just been.

"Come on, young northman," Wendin whispered. The elf bent down, grunting as he pulled Kathair to his feet. "Time to go."

"Magnus," Kathair whispered, wincing in pain.

"I know," Wendin replied. The two hobbled to the rear of the ship. Wendin helped Kathair over the side and into the longboat.

Kathair felt fire ripple through him as he stumbled into the boat and crashed into the seat. He looked up to see Wendin untying the ropes that secured the longboat in place. In the moonlight, Kathair could see several dark lines on the elf's face and arms. He knew at once that Wendin was grievously wounded.

Wendin reached for the final tie when there was a loud *k-click!* The elf went rigid for a moment, and then slowly turned around to face the deck. Kathair saw the end of a crossbow bolt protruding from Wendin's back.

"Can't let you leave," someone said from somewhere on deck that Kathair couldn't see. He assumed it was the captain. Another *k-click* was heard and a second crossbow bolt thumped into Wendin's chest. Wendin turned his head just enough to send Kathair a wink. For the briefest moment, Kathair thought perhaps the elf warrior had a plan to beat the captain, but those hopes were shattered when Wendin spun back to the rail, raised his sword, and cut the remaining ropes. The longboat fell from the ship and crashed into the sea below.

"Kill the boy!" the captain shouted.

A pair of men appeared at the side rails above and took aim with bows. Kathair scrambled under the seat as arrows began to pelt the boat and plink into the water around him.

The tall waves helped Kathair avoid the enemy arrows as the larger ship continued to sail full speed northward, while the longboat merely rode the swells up and down.

"Where is the ship's wheel?" the captain shouted.

"I can't turn the ship!" someone else shouted.

"He'll be out of range soon," a third called out.

Their protests and shouts soon faded as the ship continued its course.

"Wendin…" If only they had been faster, or if Magnus hadn't been poisoned during the game of dice, they might have survived. If only they had all reached the longboat in time. Kathair coughed and positioned himself so that his left shoulder wasn't pressed into the boat's hull. He tried to survey the boat for supplies, but found it hard to concentrate. Kathair could hardly keep his eyes open. The loss of blood mixed with the agonizing pain took what little resolve the young man had left. He slipped from consciousness, drifting on the sea wherever the swells decided to carry him.

Chapter 13

Kyra woke the next morning feeling more refreshed than she had been in a long time. The last day and a half had felt so free. No priests, no school masters, no rules other than her own. Of course, Grandpa tended to be a bit chatty, but he was far more pleasant than most people she had met anywhere else.

She stretched and slid off the soft mattress, slipping her feet into a pair of warm house slippers and made her way down to the kitchen. She found tomatoes, an orange, and several cuts of meat waiting for her on a plate – grandpa's doing, she knew. Since her arrival the house had come to life in many areas, catering to her needs and freeing most of her time for study and research. The only trouble was, she still wanted the books in her bag, and those were with Mindaugas. She wasn't even sure the man would be waiting where she had left him, but she figured she would have to take a look for herself.

Kyra ate her food and then went into the front room where grandpa was just coming to life again.

"Do me a favor, granddaughter, open up the shutters, will you? *You* may be half vampire, but I have long missed the feel of sunlight on my face."

Kyra took the playful jab in stride, firing back with her own. "I should think you would miss your actual face."

"Oh!" Grandpa called out with a playful frown. "How rude!" He then glanced toward the window, using his eyes to indicate the nearest one. "Now seriously, go and open the window."

Kyra smiled and went to the window, throwing open the drapes and then pushing the shutters out to let both light and fresh air into the room.

"Much better," Grandpa said. "Although, it looks like the garden could do with a bit of weeding. Any good with plants, granddaughter?"

Kyra laughed and shook her head. "I have other things to tend to today."

"Bah, they can wait. After all, you have legs and can move around. Me, what do I have? A pedestal and a window, is all. You could at least help me improve the view of the garden."

"Another time," Kyra replied. Grandpa puffed a bit of air and shook his bronze head, but it was all in jest, she knew. The two got along quite well, as if they had known each other for their whole lives. She tossed a wave at him and then turned to go upstairs into one of the studies. She went to a bookshelf she had started to catalogue the night before and stood for a moment, trying to find where she had left off.

"Grandpa is one of the few men I actually like," a voice called from behind her.

Kyra turned around, a fireball dancing to life in her left hand and a ward spell ready in her right. A woman sat in a high-backed chair on the far side of the room. How Kyra had missed her when she came in was beyond her. She might have attacked the intruder, except for the fact that lying beside her was the same large, gray wolf that had helped her fight off Feistos.

"Who are you?" Kyra asked.

The dark haired woman smiled and crossed her right leg up over her left knee. "A friend," she said. "More than that, I am a friend with a mutual enemy."

"Enemy?" Kyra asked.

The woman nodded. "Hatmul will kill your dragon if he finds him, or worse," she said.

Kyra felt a flush of anger, but chose to hold back for now rather than unleash it. "What would you know about that?"

The woman waved away the question and leaned forward as her right leg slid off her left. "Kyra, I have been watching you for a long time, and you know what I have seen? I have seen a very talented, smart, fierce young woman fight for everything she believes in while time and time again she is betrayed by those who are supposed to take her in."

Kyra narrowed her eyes, but didn't say anything in response as the woman rose from her chair and took a step forward.

"Lord Caspin," the intruder said as she held up a finger. "Cyrus," she said, raising a second finger. "The priests at Valtuu Temple." She let several fingers go up this time. "Mindaugas." She paused, tilting her head to the side and studying Kyra's face. "I could go on, but I think we understand each other."

"And you are different?" Kyra asked.

The woman smiled. "Let's say that I have suffered similar betrayals, so I know what it's like." A moment later a glass vial filled with a dark red liquid appeared in her left hand. She raised it up to show Kyra. "I have some information that will help you find what you are looking for."

"And what is that?" Kyra asked.

The woman's smile widened. "You want to know how to save your dragon friend, and I have the answers for that. More importantly, I know someone else that would betray you, and sell your dragon to Hatmul."

Kyra wondered if the woman spoke of Khefir, but she couldn't be. Kyra and Khefir had a solid pact. Even the gods had to obey certain rules.

"There is a house, secluded away in the woods, that has a valuable book. I want you to retrieve this book for me, as it details some of Hatmul's associates."

"You seem skilled enough to appear wherever you would like," Kyra said. "Why not go and get it yourself?"

The woman laughed and shook her head. "Hatmul is cunning, and if he had any idea how close I have come to breaking his grip on Terramyr, he would move against me."

"So you want me to do the sneaking for you, and keep suspicion off, is that it?"

The woman arched a brow. "As I said, you are a smart one."

"Why should I help you?"

"Because, I am Kyra, daughter to Icadion, and I want to help you."

Kyra's mouth fell open. "*You're* Kyra?"

The goddess nodded. "I am."

"My mother named me after you," Kyra said.

The goddess smiled. "I know. Truth be told, I have been involved with your family from time to time. Dimwater men are among the few I have found to be honorable on the whole, with few exceptions."

"Why would you help me?"

"We want the same thing. You want Leatherback to be free, and so do I. However, I cannot walk into Hammenfein and save him for you. You must figure a way to do that on your own. I can render assistance, help you find the answers you are looking for, and I know I can trust you to help me."

"How?"

The goddess let out a short laugh. "As I said, I have been watching you."

Kyra shook her head. It was all a bit much to take in. "How do I know you are who you say?"

The goddess shrugged and then gestured back to the wolf. "I thought he might help convince you."

"Was it you that sent him to me?"

"I have a way with wolves," the goddess said. "He is a faithful companion."

"What's his name?"

The goddess turned around and looked at the wolf. Without any spoken words or visible signal from the goddess, the wolf got up and walked to her side. She reached out and stroked the wolf's head. "His name is Silverfang."

"Silverfang," Kyra repeated.

"He has taken quite a shine to you, so I thought you might appreciate his company."

Kyra nodded. "I would, but that doesn't prove you are who you say you are."

The goddess gave a single nod. "Very well. Let's have Grandpa sort it out."

Kyra followed the goddess and Silverfang down to the front room where Grandpa sat gazing out the window.

"Oh bloody ghosts!" Grandpa shouted. "Kyra, is that you?" The bronze eyes narrowed, then the bust shook its head. "After reading my granddaughter's memories, I thought you might show up sooner or later, but I hadn't expected you *this* soon. You didn't even give me time to prep her."

The goddess laughed. "It's all right. I think we have made a good start of things."

"Grandpa?" Kyra started. "You know her?"

Grandpa nodded. "I do. I won't go into the details of how we first met—"

"He tried to buy me dinner," the goddess cut in.

"I said we *weren't* going to discuss that!" Grandpa shouted. Kyra giggled, sure that Grandpa would be blushing if he wasn't made of bronze. "Besides, how was I supposed to know? I was seventeen, fresh out of the academy, and I saw a beautiful young woman and thought I would give it a whirl."

The goddess turned back to Kyra and put a hand to her cheek to shield her whisper. "Little did Alister know, I had just come from another sorcery academy where I had rooted out a whole group of dishonorable wizards. He couldn't have picked a worse time to try an impress me by stating *he* was the youngest wizard to graduate from Kuldiga Academy."

Kyra laughed aloud now. "So what happened next?"

"I don't want to talk about it," Grandpa insisted. "You asked if I know her, I said I do. Let's move on now." Alister turned to look at the goddess. "What do you want with my granddaughter?"

The goddess' smile faded and she held up the vial of liquid. "I need her to get something for me. A mutual enemy has something that will help me in my pursuit against Hatmul. It should also help her with her pursuit of finding Leatherback a new home."

"You know of another plane?" Alister asked pointedly.

"In this same house are two books. They discuss several dimensions that I believe would keep Leatherback safe from Hatmul *and* the curse. She gets me my item, and she gets her answers. Fair transaction, no ongoing commitments."

Alister nodded, seemingly satisfied. "Kyra, it's up to you, but given our family's history with her, you can trust her. So long as we are honest, she won't play any tricks."

"That isn't what my mother said," Kyra replied. "My mother told me of all sorts of people caught in traps by you," she said, turning to the goddess.

The goddess shrugged. "The people I entrap are dishonorable to begin with. I don't play games, trying to seduce or entice otherwise good people to become evil as you may have heard. I only find those that are already on the path to destruction. Sometimes I help them along faster, but only so I can try to restore order by mitigating damage they would otherwise inflict, or by removing troublesome people and replacing them with honest ones."

"Usually women," Alister jumped in.

"On balance, that is likely true, but I do not judge by gender, only by integrity," the goddess said, her voice a bit colder than it had been previously.

"All right, what is it you need me to find?"

The goddess reached into her pocket and came up with a tightly rolled paper. "The list is here."

"List?" Alister said. "You said *item*. As in, one single item."

The goddess rolled her eyes and snapped her fingers. Alister's lips closed together and, despite his mumbling protests, kept him quiet. "The list has three items that I am looking for. I suspect the first one will be there, but if the other two are there as well, I would not want to waste an opportunity."

"I understand," the young sorceress replied.

"Now, I will tell you that while most of the people are gone, there may be some guards. You will need to be careful. These men are in league with Hatmul, and they will not hesitate to kill you."

Kyra nodded. "And the books for me?"

"Also written down on the list, so you can find them easily." The goddess then held out the vial. "You should be familiar with this concept, but there will be a magical ward on the door. Use this vial of blood, pour a couple drops on the key I will give you, and you will be able to get inside." Kyra took the vial and then the goddess produced a thick-handled key that had long since lost its original shine. "Now, you haven't been there before, so I will open up the portal for you. You're looking for a trapper's shack—I'll be able to get you within fifty feet or so."

A portal opened up instantaneously in the front room, casting dancing shadows along the wall as sparks of electricity jumped off the portal. The young sorceress took a last look at Grandpa, whose mouth was still sealed. The bronze head gave her a resolute nod that seemed to convey all the good wishes one would want for such a quest.

"Remember, don't get caught. I won't be able to help you. I can't have Hatmul know how close I am to unraveling his plans."

The young sorceress nodded. "I'll grab a bag," she said. She ran up to one of the bedrooms she had already searched and found a satchel she could use. She quickly enchanted it similar to her other book bags so it would hold more than its normal physical limitations would have allowed, and then she rushed back to the front room. Finally, she took the rolled paper from the goddess and stepped through the portal.

207

The air in the forest smelled of petrichor, and the sky remained gray, heavy with puffy clouds that had just finished dropped their water. She glanced around, ensuring no guards were outside the shack. When she set eyes upon the building, she could hardly believe anyone would have anything of interest inside. The roof was collapsing, and the side walls leaned as if a strong breeze would finish ruining the structure. Moss crawled up the front of the dark wooden front, and the stone chimney was little more than a jagged remnant of what it had once been.

She hurried toward the building, clutching the key in one hand and the vial of blood in the other. She almost tried to open the door without the items, but thought better of it, realizing that if a goddess had come to her with specific items, the ward on this door was likely far more powerful than the building's overall appearance would suggest. She opened the vial and dripped several drops on the key, and then slid it into the lock. As she turned it, a green glow covered the door, brightening for a couple of seconds and then dimming. After a moment, the green glow dissolved, starting at the lock and eating outward until the door opened, swinging inward.

Kyra stepped inside and instantly stopped. She turned around and leaned out the doorway, looking to each side and inspecting the building. She could hardly comprehend what she was seeing. From outside, the building was a dilapidated structure unfit for any living creature, but inside, there was an antechamber with marble floors that stretched farther in all directions than the trapper's shack was wide.

"Curious," Kyra said, realizing there was a lot of magic in this place. Suddenly, she was quite relieved that she had chosen to use the key instead of trying to force the door open by hand. If the illusion spell was any indication, then the ward surely would have been something catastrophic to trigger.

She capped the vial and slipped it into her pocket. She unrolled the paper and read the list quickly. Not only did it have the list, but as she read it, a small map of rooms appeared on the paper, guiding her through the hallway on the right, up a flight of stairs to the third floor, and then through a series of parlors and studies until she came to a long, narrow hallway that led to a room that was half observatory, and half library. Bookshelves lined the walls in the back half of the room. The front half had work benches and tables, some with beakers and stoves, others with herbs and powders. As she entered the room, she saw a short set of stairs that led into a wing of the chamber that had been specially designed to hold an orrery. Off to the right was an equally sized wing of the chamber, but it held a single desk and more bookshelves.

Figuring the desk was an appropriate place to start, she moved to the wing on the right and started searching atop the desk. The first item on the list was a crystal sphere, which she found set in a brass base atop the desk. Kyra grabbed the item, base and all, and stuffed it down into her bag. Next she pulled the drawers, looking for either a golden feather, or a dragon's scale. She didn't find either, but she did find a stack of papers tied into a bundle with a brown string. She noticed a smudged mark on the top paper that caught her interest.

"I know this mark," she said as she raised the bundle of papers closer to her eyes. She flipped the top paper's corner to inspect the next sheet. Her guess was confirmed when she saw an identical mark, this one in much better condition, neither smudged nor aged. It was the same mark that Master Fenn had shown her when discussing joining the secret group at Kuldiga Academy. "How did these end up here?" She almost untied the string to investigate, but then reminded herself that speed was of the essence. She could inspect the bundle at her leisure later. She set it inside her bag and moved on to the work tables near the center of the room.

She scanned each table for the golden feather, but couldn't find it. She did, however, find something that resembled a dragon scale. She had been around Leatherback enough to know what she was looking at, even though the scale itself was transparent. She rushed to it and placed it into the bag as well.

"Now for the books I need," she said.

The paper in her hand vibrated, catching her attention. A faint arrow appeared on the page, pointing to a bookshelf somewhere in the back of the room. As she followed, the arrow shifted its direction slightly, leading her to a shelf just off to the right in the very back of the chamber, near a large, stained glass window. The arrow then disappeared, replaced by two titles.

She memorized the titles and quickly started scanning the bookshelves. She found one on the top shelf, but the second eluded her. She searched each shelf twice, and was still unable to find it. She checked the paper, but no arrow appeared this time.

"Come on," Kyra huffed. "Where is it?" She set her finger to each title, touching every book she inspected. Then, on the third shelf she realized that there was a book with a binding nearly identical to its neighbor. She pulled the second one out, seeing only the most faded of letters on its spine, but the front of the book had the correct title stamped into it. "There you are." She put it into the bag and then started to turn away when her eyes caught a peculiar book resting on top of the others near the spot she had taken the second book from. Realizing she must have shifted it by removing the second book, she craned her head to the side to see better. Intrigued by the lack of title, she reached for it and picked it up. There was no title on the front either, but there was a mark on the front, a brand that had been stamped into the leather. The book felt warm to her touch, and she realized magic was at work. Kyra quickly tucked it into the bag and turned to leave.

She went to the center of the room and attempted to conjure a portal back to her home. She felt panic rise in her as the portal popped and hissed, dissolving into a wisp of smoke rather than opening up for her. She tried again, but the results were the same. Realizing the house must be shielded from portals, she started for the door, but she had only gone two steps before the door opened and in came two men. They were tall, lean and muscular, and had tattoos across their bare chests, arms, and faces.

One of them drew a pair of daggers and rushed forward while the second pulled a mini crossbow.

Kyra sent a fireball at the crossbowman. It consumed his crossbow and then continued onward to burn a hole through his chest. His lifeless, smoking body collapsed to the floor while the second guard came within striking range. Kyra conjured a ward powerful enough to stop each dagger as they sliced and thrusted at her. Then, focusing her energy on the protective shell, she expanded it outward with enough force to knock the blacktongue backward, sending him sprawling over a table and shattering several beakers.

The young sorceress seized the opportunity to summon a small bolt of lightning that drove through the guard's skull. She ran for the door, certain that anyone else nearby would have heard the scuffle.

She was right.

As she entered the hallway, another blacktongue was running toward her from the opposite side. She conjured a psionic blast that slammed the blacktongue into the wall on the left, and then a second that sent him crashing through the nearby window and out to the ground some thirty feet below. As fast as she could, she retraced her path through the house. She didn't encounter any further resistance until she exited the house itself and found three more blacktongues walking toward the house as if returning from a patrol of some sort. One of the blacktongues raised a bow, nocking an arrow and firing nearly faster than Kyra could conjure another ward to protect herself. Only a millisecond after the protective shell solidified around her, the missile struck it with such force that the arrowhead snapped off. The other two blacktongues sprinted toward her, one wielding a sword and the other a small pair of hand axes.

211

Kyra closed her eyes and conjured a flurry of lightning that struck all around her. Silver and purple bolts crashed into the ground and nearby trees. Dirt and grass exploded from the impact, a tree snapped in half and caught fire, and one of the bolts hit the disguised manor house and ricocheted off into the forest, blowing a thick oak to splinters.

The blacktongue armed with a sword was struck, his blade acting like a lightning rod and sending the shock coursing through him so violently that his skin smoked and hissed while he opened his mouth in a silent scream.

The blacktongue with the axes managed to avoid the lightning and reached Kyra a moment later, hacking and chopping away at her ward while the archer reloaded his bow.

Kyra took in a steadying breath and summoned all of her strength. It started as a tingle deep in her bones, and then grew to something that felt similar to fire, except the heat didn't cause pain. Then, as the energy gathered into her hands, amassing to the point she could hardly hold it back, she let out a yell and pointed a hand at each remaining blacktongue. A column of yellow energy flowed out from her hands, destroying her ward from the inside and smashing into her attackers. Their bodies were torn from the ground and thrown outward into the forest. The one on her right was thrown into a pine tree, his spine snapping as his body bent in half backwards and wrapped around the trunk. The blacktongue on her left was launched so far that she couldn't see where he landed, though she was certain he wouldn't pose a threat any longer.

Kyra, breathing hard from the exertion, struggled to summon her return portal, but managed to arrive home safely, closing the portal behind her as she entered the front room and saw grandpa and the goddess waiting for her.

"Well done," the goddess said.

Kyra caught her breath and sat on a nearby chair. "There were a few blacktongues there," she said.

The goddess nodded. "I thought there would be. Still, you should be thankful, the bulk of their forces were elsewhere."

"Are you hurt?" Grandpa asked.

Kyra shook her head. "No, just a bit tired."

The goddess reached out and gently took the bag from the sorceress. "You have the item, I presume."

The young sorceress nodded. "I found the crystal sphere and the dragon scale."

The goddess smiled. "Well done indeed." She reached into the bag and pulled the items out, inspecting each one for a moment before using her magic to send it somewhere else. "The key and vial of blood?" The young sorceress nodded and fished in her pocket for the items. "And the books I said would help you, did you manage to retrieve them?" The young sorceress was about to answer, but the goddess peered into the bag and nodded to herself after finding them. "Ah, I see you did. Excellent work, Kyra."

"Thank you," Kyra said.

The goddess then handed the bag back to the young sorceress. "I need to go now, but I will return soon. Also, I saw the bundle of papers you found, what do you intend to do with them?"

Kyra shrugged. "I need to figure out why they were there," she said. "They bear the mark of a secret group that works for the king out of Kuldiga Academy."

The goddess wrinkled her nose and held up a finger. "If I may, I would suggest that you give them to Mindaugas."

Kyra scrunched up her brow. "But he—"

The goddess held her palm out to quiet the young sorceress. "Trust me on this one. He needs to see the papers. I know you two aren't on the best of terms right now, but this is something he needs to work out."

Kyra huffed and shook her head. "I'm not sure he'll listen to me now."

"He will when you show him these. You did well, better than I had hoped in fact. Give these to Mindaugas and you will earn a valuable ally. He's more than a little hot-headed, but he has a good heart. He'll come around, especially with this."

"You know what these are?"

The goddess nodded. "I know what they will reveal to him, and it is something he needs to see for himself, without your help. When you go to him for your books, give him these."

"What do I say to him?"

The goddess winked. "Don't tell him about me, if that's what you're asking. Do tell him that you found them in possession of a Hatmul worshipping cult. That will be enough to pique his interest."

"He'll want to know why I was there," Kyra remarked.

"Because they are hunting Leatherback, and you wanted to stop them. It's the truth, after all."

The young sorceress nodded. "All right."

"He won't be where you left him, he is heading back to Kuldiga Academy. Find him there and give him the stack of papers. Now, I must go." The goddess started to turn but then stopped herself and held up a finger. "Oh, I promised to teach you how to summon Silverfang." She smiled and placed her index finger on Kyra's forehead. "This won't hurt, just relax."

Within a matter of seconds, Kyra felt a wave of information enter her brain. She understood not only how to summon Silverfang, but also learned the wolf's special powers, and how he could regenerate in his own plane of existence, as well as how to communicate with him by thought.

"Until we meet again," the goddess said. She turned and walked three steps away, disappearing into thin air without conjuring a portal to use.

The young sorceress looked to Grandpa and smiled. "I got the books to help Leatherback," she said.

Alister nodded. "I suppose you'll be too busy reading to tend the garden outside then?"

Kyra laughed. "Yes, Grandpa, I will be too busy for that."

Alister made a metallic sighing sound and frowned.

As Kyra turned to take her books upstairs, she heard Alister mutter something about how things might have turned out if the goddess had accepted his dinner invitation. The young sorceress clutched her bag to her chest and smiled.

Chapter 14

The midday sun beat down upon Kathair relentlessly. The longboat rose and fell with the swells as he drifted along with the current. There were no landmarks to navigate by, nor did he know the stars well enough to hope to read them if he survived until the night.

The intense stinging had died down to dull aches across his body. He was still unsure how he had lasted through the night, but he wasn't sure it mattered. He had no food, and no fresh water to drink. He took in a short breath, filling his lungs as much as he could without reigniting the burning pain in his back. He hadn't dared to look at the hole in his left shoulder either, knowing there was likely little he could do about it. His mind worked through thoughts and regrets, not settling on any one of them for too long.

He could only barely see over the side of the longboat as the craft shifted and bobbed in the water. His eyes scanned the endless blue as his thoughts turned to acceptance of his fate. He had failed. No one would be avenged. Magnus and Alva died for nothing, Wendin too. Kathair shifted his head to look upward.

"I failed you too," he said to his father. "I wasn't strong enough. I couldn't stop them." He coughed, his body straining with the effort of talking and starting to spasm. He closed his eyes, a single tear escaping from his left eye. If only he could understand why this had happened. Maybe then he could try to think of something that would make everyone's sacrifices seem worthwhile.

"And if you were stronger, what would you do then?"

Kathair opened his eyes and looked to the seat of the longboat. He saw a pretty woman with long, dark hair sitting there, looking at him with curious, blue eyes. Figuring he was seeing a mirage brought on by heat exhaustion, he closed his eyes once more.

"Kathair, I am not some image conjured by your mind, I am real."

Kathair opened his eyes and looked at her. "No," he said.

The woman reached down and put a hand along the cut on his right arm. The stinging sensation burned hot and fierce, snapping his mind to attention. "Believe me now?" she asked.

Kathair struggled, but try as he might he couldn't force his body to sit up. "Who…"

"I am a friend of Kyra's," she said.

"Kyra, is she all right?" Kathair asked.

The woman smiled. "You love her," she said.

Kathair offered a half-nod.

"Would you swear an oath to never betray her in any way, nor dishonor her?"

Kathair frowned. What was this woman talking about? He coughed again, pain shooting from his back through his hips and down his leg. He grimaced and shifted further onto his side, almost whimpering as another tear formed and then fell down his cheek.

"Very well," the woman said. "Answer me this one question then." She leaned down close and put her hand on Kathair's chest. At her touch, his pain subsided and some semblance of strength returned to him. "If you were big, strong, and had enough skill to hunt all of your enemies, what would you do with such power?"

Kathair, strengthened by the woman's magic, gave her his best answer. "I would avenge my family, and Alva, Magnus, and Wendin. I would keep Brenna safe, and I would figure out what Herion is up to, and then I would stop him."

The woman smiled. "I wonder, is your heart strong enough to remain honest? Men are easily corrupted by power."

Kathair shook his head. "I don't want power, I just want justice."

The woman stared into his eyes for several moments, and then offered a single nod. "Most men I would disregard as liars, simply plying me with words to attain reprieve from their pain, and an escape from death. But you, you have fire behind your words." She pressed her hand just a bit harder to his chest and more healing energy flowed into him. "I can offer you a chance, but you must be warned, the path ahead of you will not be easy. If you choose to accept my help, you will be tried and challenged more than you can imagine. But, if you triumph through the next challenges, you will emerge strong enough to exact the justice you seek. Do you have the courage to walk through the fires of fate?"

Kathair took in the first painless breath since before the fight on the ship and nodded. "I am a northman; I will face any challenge."

"And would you honor a pledge to me?"

Kathair paused and tilted his head to the side, trying to decipher the woman's face for any hint of her intentions. "What do you demand in return?"

"My help comes at a price, but it is not something you can pay with gold or trinkets of this world. There are only two ways by which you can settle your debt to me. The first is by living an honorable life, free of deception and vice. You must be kind to those who are weaker than you, and your sword must protect them from those who would abuse them."

"I can do that," Kathair said.

The woman held up a finger with her free hand. "If you fail to live uprightly, then the only other way you can repay me will be with your soul." She paused and let the words sink in. "Can you make such an oath?"

Kathair thought it over for a few seconds, trying to consider the woman's motivations. "Why?" he asked. "Why pick me? Why not Wendin? Why not Magnus, or my father or mother?"

The woman smiled. "I am starting to see in you what Kyra does," she said. "You are far more important to the Middle

Kingdom than you can imagine, young Kathair. If raising the dead were within my power, I would consider resurrecting your friends and family, but the best I can do is give you another chance at life. The question still remains though, can you commit to the oath of living a life worthy of my help, and the sacrifices made by so many others in your behalf?"

Kathair nodded. "I will live worthy of their sacrifices, and do pledge my soul should I ever fail so to do."

The woman closed her eyes and a great pulse of bright light enveloped Kathair as warmth coursed through his body. His tissues healed and fused back together as though he had never been wounded, and his strength returned in full, and then grew beyond what he had previously known. Within seconds, he was able to stand, no longer in pain or suffering from hunger or thirst. He watched as the woman opened her eyes and the two of them stood inside a great sphere of light.

"Remember, the way ahead is perilous. Even with my boon, you will have to use all of your skills if you want to survive. Not many in the history of Terramyr would be able to do what you are about to attempt. If I could simply send you back to the Middle Kingdom, I would, but this is the only way to prepare you for what is to come. Good luck, Kathair Lepkin, and remember your oath, for I will collect your soul should you ever fail to live up to your commitment."

The light faded, and the woman was gone.

A wind picked up, turning the longboat and pushing it through the waters at a speed that forced Kathair to kneel and grab onto the side for fear of falling overboard. By dusk, a large mountain rose from the depths in the distance, shrouded by a veil of silvery mist. Chills ran down Kathair's spine as the longboat approached the island. He had little experience with magic, but even he could tell that this place was saturated with it, and if he had to guess, the powers in this place were purely evil.

Epilogue

Herion sat in a soft-backed armchair, brandy in his left hand and a smoking pipe in his right. He lazily sipped from the brandy while letting the aroma of his cherry-tobacco fill the room around him. His eyes remained focused on the chair opposite him. Currently, it was empty, but he had already sent his message, and his visitor would be arriving any moment now.

Several minutes, and half a brandy later, Hatmul appeared in the other chair.

"You said you had some information for me that couldn't be delivered except in person," Hatmul said.

Herion nodded and then gestured to a brandy that had been poured and set on the table next to Hatmul's chair. "I think you will find it quite interesting indeed," he said as the god of Hammenfein picked up his drink and took a sip. Herion held up the needle with Kyra's blood on it.

"Still using blood to spy on people?" Hatmul said.

"Is there a better way?"

"Not for mortals," Hatmul admitted, taking another drink and draining his glass.

"This belongs to a young sorceress that I am hoping to convince to join your followers," Herion began. "However, in her blood I found memories that point to betrayal in your house."

"Betrayal in my house?" Hatmul said. "Speak plainly."

"The young sorceress has made a deal with your brother to hide a dragon in one of your special planes attached to Hammenfein."

Hatmul squeezed his glass until it shattered. Bits of glass cut through his flesh, but his hand healed a moment later without the god so much as wincing from pain. "If you are lying—"

"We have had our differences, but I know better than to lie to you, especially about this," Herion said.

Hatmul raised his hand and called the needle to him. As soon as his fingers touched it, he closed his eyes for a couple of seconds. "This is the dragon you helped her hide in the forest," Hatmul said. "I told you not to."

Herion shrugged. "I thought there might be another way."

"The curse is the only way," Hatmul snarled. "And now this filthy creature is in *my* domain! My own brother hiding him there like a rat lurking in the shadows of a ship!"

"As I said, I knew you would want to know."

Hatmul nodded. "I will deal with my brother in my own time. Until then, it appears I have a dragon to capture."

Herion emptied his glass and then set it on the table next to his chair. "The girl can still be useful, perhaps even more so if you can curse the dragon. She loves it more than family."

Hatmul sneered. "I will let you know what your next assignment is. Until then, stay the course I have already given you."

Herion nodded. "Of course," he said.

Hatmul vanished from the room without another word. Herion sighed and then set his pipe to his mouth and puffed the cherry-tobacco. "What interesting games we all play," he said as he tilted his head back and blew smoke rings toward his ceiling. "What interesting games indeed."

About the Author

Sam Ferguson is the proud author of more than twenty fantasy novels. He launched his writing career with The Dragon's Champion series, cracking the Top 100 for epic fantasy books. He has also written Son of the Dragon, The Sorceress of Aspenwood series, and The Haymaker Adventures to name just a few. He has had several #1 best-sellers in the U.K. and Australia, as well as a couple of top 20 hits in the U.S.

Nearly all of his novels take place on Terramyr, a single world rife with varying races, religions, and conflicts that propel the world itself along through its timeline toward a final climax. So, while each novel or series can be savored on its own, the more a person reads, the more immersed they become with Terramyr, its gods, and the grand events that will ultimately prove the worth and decide the fate of its inhabitants. (Sam has also hidden a few Easter Eggs such as crossover characters and other fun tid-bits for the eager reader!)

In his free time, Sam Ferguson is a competitive powerlifter. While he spent his first career as a U.S. diplomat, living in Latvia, Hungary, and Armenia, he is now quite content to travel the far reaches of Terramyr instead, and hopes to bring many of you fun-loving adventure seekers along for the ride!